"Here's my idea,"

"Let's simply get to know
You can't deny that there's
happening with us, with your sister, my son, the
donkeys..."

Maura's laugh raised a few heads in the busy diner.

"So, let's go along with it. Have some fun. Enjoy
each other's company. When it's time to leave,
you and I can talk. Maybe work something out."

She wanted to believe all that he said, but as she
nodded, part of her mind centered on the one
word *maybe*. Still, he had a point. Some fun in her
life—and a little romance—sounded like a good
antidote to stress. "You're right. One day at a time
kind of thing, then?"

"One day at a time and no analyzing or predicting
as we go along."

"I see you already know things about me," she
quipped.

"Some things, but my goal is *everything*..."

Dear Reader,

I'm thrilled to introduce you to my new Harlequin Heartwarming series, Home to Maple Glen, a little community tucked in a deep valley near the Appalachian Long Trail of Vermont.

Maura and Maddie Stuart operate a donkey-riding therapy business on the farm they inherited in the Glen. Their father's death and a promise to take care of his beloved donkeys, Jake and Matilda, have led to a tentative peace between the two previously estranged sisters. That peace is threatened when Maura's adolescent crush, Theo Danby, returns to the Glen.

Recently divorced, Theo has taken a six-week leave from his work as an ER doctor in Maine to reconnect with his preteen son, Luke. The task of selling the farm he inherited from his aunt and uncle is the perfect opportunity for Theo to show his son Maple Glen, the place where Theo spent idyllic summers every year with Maddie and Maura.

The two are aided and abetted in their reunion by a team of unruly donkeys, a reclusive beekeeper and an eccentric fortune teller to finally understand what they really want—each other and a life together in Maple Glen.

I hope you enjoy this book as much as I enjoyed writing it! Stay tuned for book two in the series and more heartwarming characters in Maple Glen.

Janice Carter

HEARTWARMING

A Small Town Fourth of July

———

Janice Carter

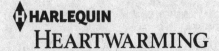

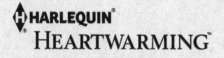

HARLEQUIN®
HEARTWARMING™

Recycling programs
for this product may
not exist in your area.

ISBN-13: 978-1-335-47585-5

A Small Town Fourth of July

Copyright © 2024 by Janice Hess

For questions and comments about the quality of this book,
please contact us at CustomerService@Harlequin.com.

TM and ® are trademarks of Harlequin Enterprises ULC.

Harlequin Enterprises ULC
22 Adelaide St. West, 41st Floor
Toronto, Ontario M5H 4E3, Canada
www.Harlequin.com

Printed in U.S.A.

DEDICATION

For my feisty family-loving aunt,
Sylvia Marie Dimmel—knitter supreme,
bird watcher and avid romance reader
—with much love.

ACKNOWLEDGMENT

A big thank-you to my cousin, Nancy Dimmel Row,
for sharing her expertise and experience as a
riding therapist along with anecdotes of her
donkey, Dory, who disliked rain.

CHAPTER ONE

WHERE'S JAKE?

Maura Stuart dropped the pitchfork of hay into the stall trough, muttering at the same time. Stomping down the length of the barn to its opened doors, she stood for a moment, shading her eyes from the early-morning sun. No sign of him anywhere. *Great. Just what I needed today.* And no sign of Maddie, either. Too much to hope that she'd gone looking for Jake—the enticing aroma of coffee was probably just now luring her out of bed. She took a deep breath. Giving in to this constant frustration would gain her nothing, especially if they continued to be business partners. But there were moments—plenty of them—when Maura silently questioned her decision to bring her twin sister on board. Yet there'd be no business at all if she'd had to manage on her own.

She scanned the property, from the two-story farmhouse straight ahead and its adjacent garage, to the shed on the far side of the garage. It was closed up, so no Jake there. She knew the chicken coop behind the barn and the small, fenced riding ring next to it wouldn't be a draw for Jake. Thankfully, he wasn't trotting down the long gravel drive out to the road. Then her gaze drifted east, to their neighbor's fields, overgrown with weeds. No sign of Jake, but she suddenly caught a glimmer of red through the thicket of vegetation separating the two farms.

Maura walked across the drive to the row of cedars along the property line and pushed through them into the adjacent land. She and Maddie used to come this way when they were kids, but the cedars had been newly planted then and only waist-high. Now they were taller than her shoulders.

Stepping onto what was once the Danby homestead felt strange. The elderly owners, Stan and Vera, had passed away several months ago, but the farm had been left derelict since their admission to a nursing home in Rutland two years before. When Maura and Maddie took over their own family farm a year ago, the Danby place was already run-down. The neighboring families had been close when the girls were growing up, but that gradually changed after the sisters left for college.

It was only natural, Maura knew. People aged, withdrew from community and old friends due to health or mobility issues, and lost touch with one another. She and Maddie had experienced a similar loss of contact after being away from Maple

Glen for so long. But thankfully, they'd been able to reconnect with former schoolmates and other neighbors since their return.

Maura waded through the field toward the Danby farmhouse, realizing as she got closer that the flash of red was a car—a fancy sports car. When she reached the drive, she could hear the low rumble of a male voice. She paused for a second, debating whether to retreat or continue looking for Jake. The voice pitched nervously as she was rounding the back end of the car to see Jake standing between it and the closed barn door, his stocky frame blocking the object of his interest from Maura's view.

"He won't bite," she said, stifling a laugh as she drew near. "He's just curious."

The man splayed against the barn door grimaced. "Maybe call him off?"

She closed in on Jake, wrapping an arm around his neck and gently pulling him away from his attempt to nuzzle the man. She recognized him then, despite the passage of years and his transformation from teenager to adult.

"Welcome back, Theo." She kept her eyes on him, fighting to ignore the sudden throbbing at her temples, then turned Jake around, slapped him on the rump and ordered, "Home, Jake."

Theo Danby watched the donkey amble off. "Thanks…uh…Maura?"

The fact that he was slow to identify her irked. "Yes," she snapped.

He moved away from the barn door and unzipped his windbreaker. "Warmer than I remember," he mumbled.

So he's going for small talk. "Yeah, climate change and all that. Plus, it's the middle of June." She shifted her attention away from the well-toned chest muscles emerging through his short-sleeved shirt—muscles that the Theo she remembered hadn't had. She felt her cheeks warm up as a trace of a smile crossed his face.

"Are you visiting your folks or…?" he asked.

"No, Mom died about three years ago and my father, last June."

"I'm sorry." His face softened, and she peered down at the ground, hiding unexpected tears.

"We moved back here more than a year ago," she went on.

"We?"

She raised her head, meeting his dark brown eyes again. "Maddie and I."

"Ah."

"So…you're here to…" she continued.

"Have a look at this place before I sell it."

Of course. She'd been expecting that from the day she and Maddie first returned home and had seen that the Danby homestead had been left to ruin. Though she couldn't figure out why it had taken Theo so long to return after his aunt and uncle passed away. She was about to ask him more about his plans when a slamming door and a young voice got her attention.

"Dad?" A boy who looked to be a preteen was standing on the farmhouse veranda, his face wrinkled in disgust. "This place is a dump!" He caught sight of Maura and hesitated before descending the porch steps and walking their way.

Maura shot a glance at Theo. He flushed slightly as he said, "My son."

Maura scolded herself for automatically assuming that Theo might still be single, too. The boy heading their way was a near replica of a young Theo—same thick dark hair and eyes. He sidled up to his father but kept his eyes on Maura.

"Uh, Luke, this is Maura—" The last part of his introduction dropped off, as if he were unsure of her current surname. "Her family owns the place over there." He gestured to his right, though the boy kept his attention on her.

"It's Maura Stuart. Nice to meet you, Luke." She held out her right hand, and after an elbow nudge from Theo, the boy shook it. "My sister and I knew your father years ago, when he used to spend his summer vacations here, with his aunt and uncle."

"Dad told me about that, but he made it sound more interesting than—"

"What you see here?" Maura smiled. She resisted glancing at Theo, but thought she heard a faint sigh.

"Yeah." He looked at Theo and asked, "So now what?"

"Well, uh, I thought after we looked around, we could go into Maple Glen for some lunch and then talk about our plans."

"*Our* plans? It wasn't *my* idea to come here."

Maura took in the disgruntled face and voice. Time to head back to the farm, she decided. "Okay, well, nice to see you again, Theo and Luke… The bakery in the village sells sandwiches and pizzas, but if you want anything substantial, you'll have to drive to Wallingford."

Theo's smile was strained. "Thanks, Maura. I think a bite to eat will help us both. And…uh… is there a place to stay? It's been a while since I was last here."

"Maybe you remember the Watsons? Bernie used to manage the gas station at the junction to Route 7, but he bought the old Harrison place about ten years ago and turned it into a B and B. The Shady Nook. I hear it's quite nice. If you're planning to stay in the area for a few days, of course." When Theo failed to respond, she added, "Unless you'd rather stay somewhere with more to offer, like Rutland or Bennington." Theo was staring, and she realized she'd been babbling. "Okay, well, I better go."

She was about to turn around when he finally spoke. "Thanks, Maura. Um, my plan is to stick around until I can make a decision about my aunt and uncle's place. A few days, anyway—maybe more." He shot Luke a quick look. "Nothing definite yet. But maybe we'll see you around. And Maddie, too, of course. Say hi for me."

"Sure." She managed a smile and headed off, taking the same route across the weed-filled field and through the cedars, feeling two sets of eyes tracking her. Her mind buzzed with random thoughts and questions. *Theo Danby is back. He has a son. Presumably he's married. Or was.*

But the important question was, how long would he be around?

The very thought of Theo spending any amount of time in Maple Glen made Maura's stomach churn. Was it too much to hope that Theo Danby would just drop out of their lives again, as he had twenty years ago, and never discover her secret?

By the time she reached the barn, Jake had instinctively headed for his stall and was munching the hay she'd deposited. She took a moment to inspect the stall door and noticed the hasp was loose enough to give way with a solid push. A small thing to fix, but one more item on the long list of jobs. The other two donkeys, Matilda and Lizzie, were too busy eating to give her more than a half glance, their long ears twitching as she walked by their stalls.

Maura decided that after the encounter with Theo—and his son!—a second cup of coffee was definitely on the day's agenda and headed for the side door of the farmhouse that led through a tiny mudroom into the kitchen. Maddie was sitting at the table eating cereal and skimming through yesterday's Rutland newspaper. She looked up when Maura entered the room.

"What's up?" she immediately asked.

They'd always been good at reading one another, Maura knew. Even though they were nonidentical twins, there was still that inexplicable twin connection. At least, until the summer they'd turned eighteen, when they'd withdrawn from one another and begun new, separate lives.

Maura sighed. There was no point postponing the inevitable. "Jake got out of his stall—it's okay," she quickly put in, seeing Maddie was about to ask how. "I've figured it out. We have to fix the stall gate. Anyway, he'd wandered over to the Danbys', and I followed him." She paused. "Someone was at the house."

Maddie put her spoon down. "Who?"

"Theo."

Their eyes locked for what seemed ages. "He's come to get the place ready to sell," Maura added. "And he has a son who looks to be about eleven or twelve."

Maddie's impassive face revealed nothing. "Okay," she said and resumed eating.

That went well, Maura thought. Clearly her sister was still unhappy with her after last night's disagreement over the ongoing plans for the business, as well as finances. She poured herself a coffee and sat across from Maddie, whose head was still bent over the newspaper. The kitchen filled with the silence that had fallen between the sisters seventeen years ago, and Maura hoped it wouldn't last five years this time around, too. *Not if you do something about it right now*, she told herself.

"Look, Mads, Theo is ancient history. We were all teenagers the last time we were together, and presumably—" she attempted a half laugh "—we're a whole lot smarter now. I got the impression he and his son are here only long enough to sell the farm. Then he'll be gone."

Maddie finally looked at her. "I'm not worried about any of that, Maura. Like you said, that last summer is ancient history. I've moved on, and I hope you have, too."

Maura felt her face heat up under her sister's penetrating gaze. She bit down on her lower lip, quelling an instant rise of hurt. She wasn't going to be drawn into a debate they'd both sworn to put behind them. "Okay," she mumbled. "You're right." She got up from her chair and rinsed her coffee mug, letting the tension seep out. "So, who have we got riding today?"

IT *HAD* TO HAPPEN. Theo parked the car in front of the Shady Nook B and B and sat, unmoving. He'd known from the start that meeting up with the Stuart sisters—or at least one of them—was a possibility, but he wished fervently that it hadn't happened under such humiliating circumstances. Trapped by a donkey, for heaven's sake! Only to be rescued by one of the sisters. Worst of all, for a second he couldn't recall which was the redhead and which the raven-haired. They weren't identical twins, so it shouldn't have been so difficult. When he was a boy and then a teen, he'd never have made such a mistake.

"Are we going in or what?"

Luke's grumble finally registered. Theo blinked. He was back in Maple Glen. Thirty-six years old, divorced and on leave from his job. With a twelve-year-old son he barely knew who didn't want to be there any more than he did. He sighed. Those few minutes back at the farm with Maura had been a cold-water-shock reminder that time didn't change everything. Her stony expression and clipped voice took him immediately back to his last summer in Maple Glen countless years ago.

"Dad? Jeez!"

"Yeah, yeah. C'mon. We'll leave our stuff here until we know if we can get a room."

"Why don't we go back to the highway? I saw some motels there. Maybe we could get one with a pool, like we did yesterday."

Theo ignored Luke's plaintive tone, which had been incessant since he'd made the decision to take a road trip to Maple Glen and finally deal with his inheritance. Reconnecting with his son was meant to be part of a new, postdivorce direction in Theo's life, but he had a sinking feeling he'd already taken a wrong turn somewhere and now was lost. Like the rookie hikers on the nearby Appalachian Long Trail that the locals used to complain about.

At least the B and B looked like a welcoming place, with its smoky-blue clapboard siding, white gingerbread-trimmed veranda and wicker chairs and tables. Theo vaguely recalled the original Colonial-style home had been painted white, but any memory of the people who'd lived there—the Harrisons, Maura had said—escaped him. Though come to think of it, had there been a boy roughly his own age?

"Well?" Luke was staring up at him from the bottom porch step.

His expression was a mix of frustration and concern, which made Theo feel a tad guilty. He hadn't been paying full attention to him since leaving Maine. Perhaps their road trip's destination should have been somewhere more exciting than a small place like Maple Glen, Vermont. He reached down and tousled Luke's hair. "C'mon," he said and opened the screen door.

Theo's eyes were adjusting to the cool darkness inside the entryway when a voice called out from somewhere farther inside. "Give me a sec!"

The interior gradually took shape, from the hall table with a vase of flowers and a small display of tourist pamphlets, to the staircase straight ahead. There were rooms to the left and right off the entry, and Theo spotted tables and chairs in one of them. A good sign, he thought. Even if there wasn't a room available, maybe they could get a bite to eat. Breakfast had been early, at a fast-food place on the highway.

Luke was fidgeting beside him, but at least he wasn't complaining. Not yet. Theo was about to reassure him that the next town, Wallingford, was only minutes away and they could always get some lunch there when a large, gray-haired man wearing an apron over baggy pants and a T-shirt emerged from a room at the end of the hall and lumbered toward them.

"Had to pop my bread rolls into the oven," he explained, his big, welcoming smile shooting from Theo to Luke. "What can I do for you folks?"

"We'd like a room, if you have one."

"Aha! That I do. You came at the right time— it's Sunday and I've just had two checkouts, plus the Fourth of July holiday is a couple of weeks away. How many nights are you thinking?" Before Theo could reply, the man headed for one of the rooms leading off the hall and, after a second's hesitation, Theo and Luke followed.

The room still exhibited its early days as a parlor, with a cluster of seating arrangements and an impressive bowlegged table with a Tiffany-style, stained glass lamp in the center of the bay window that looked onto the veranda. The man—Bernie Watson, Theo assumed—was rifling through a drawer in the table. Pulling out a small ledger book and pen, he swung around to say, "Here we go. Have a seat there—" he gestured to a chintz-upholstered wing chair "—and fill in the information I need while I go check on my dinner rolls."

Theo grasped the book and pen that were thrust at him and, casting a quick grin at Luke, sat where he was told. He wrote his name and address on the page headed with the day's date, hesitated over the "length of stay" column before jotting *2-3 nights* and hoped Luke, now standing at his elbow, hadn't noticed. He had yet to tell the boy that his plan was to fix up a couple of rooms in the farmhouse for them until the meeting with the Realtor.

Despite Luke's disparagement of the house as a "dump," the place had been dusted and aired only the week before their arrival by a company from Rutland that Theo had hired. The Stuart sisters obviously hadn't noticed the recent activity there, though the weeds in the fields between the two places could have hidden the cleaning agency's vehicle. Maura's search for her donkey had likely been the only reason for her to discover he was back. A donkey! Theo was pretty certain the Stuarts had never had animals larger than goats.

"Dad? I'm hungry." Luke was pulling on his arm.

Theo roused himself from thoughts that were leading nowhere. He was hungry, too, and the heavy footfalls along the hallway were reassuring. They'd be getting a room and, hopefully, lunch as well.

"Excuse my bad manners," the man was saying as he reentered the room. "I'm Bernie Watson, the owner, general manager as well as cook here."

Theo shook his hand and passed the sign-in book to Bernie, who peered down at it.

"Good heavens," he exclaimed. "Theo Danby!" His beaming grin faltered immediately. "I was sorry to hear about Stan and Vera."

"Thank you," Theo murmured. Luke shuffled impatiently, and he added, "Is it possible to get some lunch?"

"Definitely. Go get your things from your car. It'll be okay parked out front for now. I've got a small lot behind where you can move it later. As for lunch, I don't have any other patrons at the moment, but I can rustle something up for you two." He turned to Luke. "How about a grilled cheese sandwich with fries? I can even manage a chocolate milkshake, if you're up to it."

The smile on Luke's face was the first Theo had seen since the motel with pool they'd stayed at. "I think he's up to it," he said.

CHAPTER TWO

THEO SETTLED HIS sunglasses onto the bridge of his nose and sneaked a peek at Luke, standing a few feet away on the sidewalk outside Shady Nook B and B. The blissful expression on his son's face as he'd wolfed down waffles and strawberries for breakfast moments ago had morphed to petulance. Theo clenched his jaw, but he wasn't going to give up.

"So, we have a couple of options for this morning, Luke. At some point while we're here, I'm hoping we can do some hiking. There's an easy access route from the village into the Long Trail section of the Appalachian Trail. Remember I told you about my hiking a few times when I used to spend my summers here? Or we can explore the village a bit more before heading back to the farm."

His son looked up and down the street. "Except this is it, isn't it? The whole place?"

Theo could relate to the resignation in his son's voice. He'd had similar feelings his last summer in Maple Glen, when the village boundaries had pressed in. When even the magic of the Stuart sisters—one in particular—failed to raise any enthusiasm for the weeks ahead. But when he'd been Luke's age, the place had still held a promise of adventure and exploration.

Perhaps he ought to have brought Luke here years ago, connected him to Uncle Stan and Aunt Vera, who'd provided the stability his own divorced parents could not. That thought instantly raised the specter of his divorce months ago. Theo sighed. This was his chance to start anew with his son. He couldn't blow it.

"I know it seems like there's not a lot to do here, but once we've settled into the farmhouse and I've organized its sale, we'll have time to explore the parts of this area that are special—the Trail, the parks. *Nature*. That's really what this place is all about. And the people, too. Though we might not be here long enough to meet too many of the residents." He heard Luke mumble something and added, "Pardon?"

"I said, what's the point?" Luke turned to face him. "Why bother meeting anyone when we won't be staying?"

Theo swore silently. He knew he ought to have been more transparent about the trip with Luke than he had been. His ex had asked him to take full custody of their son during his six weeks' leave from his job as head of the hospital emergency department in Augusta so she could finalize plans for a move from Maine with the man she'd left Theo for a year ago. Luke was aware of some of the details, but not all. A decision about where he would eventually end up living—and with whom—was still up in the air.

The timing was perfect, but the reality of having Luke all to himself for more than a month was both gratifying and frightening. Still, the opportunity to bond with his only child was one he couldn't miss, though he probably ought to have told the boy that organizing the farm's sale could take longer than the week he'd mentioned. Plus, he'd have to clear the place out—go through all the possessions, papers and general stuff his aunt and uncle had accumulated over the years. As a teen, Theo had realized the couple were pack rats, and a quick glance inside yesterday had confirmed nothing had been removed from the house, even after their move into the nursing home. Having plenty of time to complete the job was a bonus, but he'd known he'd never get Luke onside with the trip unless he implied a week would be sufficient.

"I could have gone to camp," Luke muttered.

Theo sighed. Camp had been the fallback plan. "I suppose that's always an option for later in the summer."

"Not really. You have to register early if you want a place. Mom told you that." Luke shifted his gaze to his feet.

So camp wasn't a likely possibility now. Maybe he should reassess his plans, but Theo hated to give in too quickly. Luke needed to learn to compromise, or at the very least, to be more open to new experiences. "Maybe later this afternoon we could take a drive into Rutland and watch a movie."

There was a barely audible sigh and then, "Sure."

Theo took a deep breath. "Okay, so let's wander in that direction—" he pointed east toward the distant wooded slopes "—and check out the access to the Trail. If we decide to hike a bit, we could buy you some appropriate footwear when we go into Rutland." He took the lead and after a few seconds heard Luke follow. "I noticed from the sign when we turned off Route 7 that the Glen has a current population of 550. I think that's only an increase of about twenty people since I was here last."

"When was that?" Luke asked.

"My last summer here was when I was sixteen. Twenty years ago." He glanced down at his son, now walking beside him.

"And how old were you when you first came here?"

"Turning nine."

"So for seven years you came every summer."

"Yep."

There was a brief silence, followed by, "I can't imagine spending seven summers in this place."

Theo hid a quick grin. The kid was a real city boy, as Theo himself had been until those summers transformed him. A fragrant aroma distracted him from rambling on, and he stopped in front of a white-framed cottage. A hand-painted sign decorated with gingerbread trim hung above the cottage door—Tasty Delights. An extension attached to the right of the cottage bore a United States Postal Service sign that Theo didn't recall from his summer visits. He was certain that in those days a van delivered mail to the box fronting his uncle's farm.

"This bakery was here then, but not the post office. My aunt gave me a weekly allowance, and I always spent some of it on a doughnut, hot out of the oven." He didn't remember the names of the people who ran the bakery, only that they'd always been friendly, especially to the kids. "Want anything?"

"Dad! I just ate three waffles!"

"Yeah, right." He grinned at Luke's expression.

When his son added, "I bet *you'd* like something, though," Theo laughed.

"Caught me!"

Luke's smile warmed him. Maybe today was going to be all right. They continued walking, then paused in front of the church. "They had fantastic community potluck suppers here every Friday," Theo said. He pointed to the legion hall on the opposite side of the street. "That was a one-room schoolhouse in the 1800s. I think it was turned into a legion after the Second World War, and when I used to come to the Glen, it was often used as a community center."

They stared silently at the A-framed building with its bright coat of blue paint and yellow trim. The sign above the front door lintel read Legion but a smaller sign below, next to the door, added Maple Glen Community Center and Town Hall. "Guess it's multipurpose now," Theo murmured.

"Where do kids go to school?" Luke asked, adding, "If there even *are* any kids here."

"I'm sure there are kids here," Theo said. He hadn't seen any yet, but he hoped so. If they were going to be in the village longer than a week, it'd be nice for Luke to meet some kids his age. The group of kids he recalled from his visits had made those summers extra special. "When I arrived here in late June, it was always fun to meet up with everyone I hadn't seen since the year before. We had a lot of catching up to do, but we quickly got back into the summer vibe."

"*Vibe*, Dad?"

Theo shrugged. "Whatever."

Luke rolled his eyes. "So where did they go to school?"

"Wallingford, by bus, I think. At least, they did back then."

Luke nodded. He could relate to the bus, which was his mode of transport to the pricey private school his mother had insisted on. That was another point of contention to be negotiated. Theo stifled a sigh. This week was meant to be a stress-free adventure. He and his ex, Trish, had even agreed to not text or email unless there was an emergency. Theo welcomed the break.

"Remember when we were driving here yesterday, and I pointed out that range in front of us—the Green Mountains?" Theo asked as they approached the trees at the end of the street and the mountains looming beyond.

Luke nodded.

"Well, that summit is White Rocks Mountain. You can get to it from the part of the Long Trail that exits into Maple Glen."

"The same mountain we saw at the recreation area in Wallingford?"

"The same. I'm hoping we can have a bit of a wander there before we leave."

"Sure." But Luke's voice sounded uncertain.

"It's not a difficult hike, even for newbies like us," Theo hastened to reassure him.

After a minute, Luke added, "Yeah, but I was thinking we might not be here long enough for that."

Okay, Theo thought. Back to square one. "Let's walk up to the bridge anyway and have a closer look." He resumed walking, listening to Luke shuffling behind. A movie later today for sure, he was thinking. As they drew nearer, memories flooded his mind. The bridge was newer, its former wood planks and handrails replaced by metal, though its height and span looked the same.

Stopping in front of it, Theo said, "That's Otter Creek. We used to swim in it."

Luke stepped forward on the crest of the gentle slope leading down to the water. "Is it deep?"

"Not really. Maybe in early spring after the winter snowmelt, but not in the summer, especially when the days were hot and dry. And we didn't go in here, but over there." He pointed left to what he remembered was the McAllister homestead. The place looked exactly the same.

Luke's attention shifted to the imposing house. "It's big. Are the owners rich or something?"

"No, but their ancestors were some of the first people to settle here." He thought about the boy who'd lived there. A bit older, with an unusual name. Started with an *F*, he recalled. He strolled over to the sign by the front gate, but there was only the surname McAllister, painted in faded black letters. Theo wondered if anyone was even still living there until he noticed the main front door on the wraparound veranda was open, revealing an ornately carved screen door.

Just then the screen door flew open and a little girl with blond ponytails, one on either side of her face, stepped onto the porch. She looked at them, and Theo was about to wave when he heard a voice calling out from somewhere among the trees speckling the expansive front lawn. "Kaya? I'm over here."

The child didn't move but continued her silent stare. When she failed to reply, a woman suddenly appeared from the area closest to the creek. She carried a basket and held what looked like a gardening tool. Stopping at the foot of the porch steps, the woman turned around and noticed Theo and Luke.

Theo waved, and she walked toward them. As she got closer, Theo could see wisps of gray hair beneath the straw sun hat she was wearing, and despite her large dark sunglasses, Theo thought he recognized her. "Mrs. McAllister?"

"Yes." She stepped right up to the gate. "Um…"

"Theo Danby," he quickly said, extending his right hand.

"Oh my goodness!" She lowered the basket to the ground and, rising up, shook his hand. "I never would have recognized you." She glanced at Luke. "And this must be…"

"My son, Luke." Theo gave Luke a slight nudge and was proud to see the boy quickly extend his own hand.

"Granny?"

They all looked to the porch, where the little girl was descending the steps. "Come here, sweetie, and meet an old friend of your uncle's."

"Your granddaughter, Mrs. McAllister?"

She smiled. "Indeed! And please, call me Marion. You're clearly not a teenager anymore. Are you here for a while or...?"

"I came back to take care of the farm."

"By 'take care,' do you mean you plan to stay and take it over?"

Theo ignored the audible snort from Luke. "Oh, no. I'm just here to clear everything out before putting it up for sale. You may have heard I inherited it from my aunt and uncle."

"Yes, and I was sorry to hear about Vera and Stan. They were strong community supporters for many years."

Theo nodded and waited a second before asking, "And...uh...Mr. McAllister? How's he?"

Her smile shifted. "Lewis is in a nursing home in Bennington. He has Alzheimer's."

"Oh, I'm so sorry to hear that."

The little girl had reached her grandmother's side. "Kaya, this is Mr. Danby and his son, Luke. Mr. Danby—"

"Theo!" he interjected.

"Theo used to spend his summers here when he was a boy and a teenager," she explained.

The information didn't impress the girl, who continued to stare solemnly at them. Theo smiled at her. "And are you spending your summer holiday here with your grandmother, Kaya?"

"No!"

"Kaya and her mother, Roxanne—maybe you remember her? She was in a younger group than you and Finn. Anyway, they're living with us now…for a bit." She sighed as Kaya ran back to the veranda. "They've just moved in a week ago, so she's still adjusting."

Theo could relate to the child's obvious unhappy mood. "And Finn?" he asked, grateful for the name reminder.

"Finn lives with me now, too. He moved back three and a half years ago to help out when Lewis had to go into care. I had health issues and needed the support." Her face brightened suddenly. "He's on his shift right now, at the Wallingford Fire Department, but I'm sure he'd love to meet up with you before you leave."

Maybe, Theo thought, knowing from personal experience how awkward old friends' reunions could be. The image of Maura Stuart's stunned face yesterday flashed across his mind. "Sure," he said. He felt Luke tug on his shirtsleeve. "Um, guess we ought to be going. It was great to see you again, and please pass on my best to Finn."

"I'll let him know you're back. Are you staying at the farm?"

"We spent last night at the B and B but will be moving into the farm tomorrow or the next day." He heard a loud sigh from Luke and noticed from her quick smile that Marion had, too.

"Wonderful! Maybe we can arrange for you both to come for a meal while you're here."

"That would be great," Theo said, hoping she hadn't noticed the frown on Luke's face.

A quick wave and she was heading toward the veranda, where Kaya was waiting.

"Let's ask Mr. Watson to make us some lunch before heading for Rutland," Theo suggested as Luke stomped ahead. The boy barely slowed down. A movie might just save the day after all, Theo thought.

MAURA HEAVED THE last bag of chicken feed into the back of the pickup truck and leaned against the driver side, panting from the exertion. She wiped off the droplets of sweat trickling down her cheek and was about to climb into the truck when a shout stopped her. The cashier at the farm co-op was running her way, waving a sheet of paper.

"A customer has a question about the Fourth of July festival," the woman said between gasping breaths as she drew near. "He wants to know if people will be able to ride the donkeys that day or will they just be looking at them."

Good question and Maura wished she had an answer. She and Maddie were still debating the idea, and since Maddie was the person in charge of the therapy riding, her opinion would decide. Maura had argued that they needed to advertise the program when people from outside the Glen would be attending the fair.

"Um, not sure yet, but we'll definitely have someone on hand to answer any questions."

"Okay, that's fine. He has a young son who might benefit from it. And thanks for the flyers—" she held up the paper "—I'll post them around and pass the rest to some other businesses here."

"Thank you…uh…Wendy," Maura replied, reading the woman's ID tag. "I meant to do that myself but got behind in my chores today."

"How many donkeys do you have now?"

"Three."

Wendy smiled. "I remember when your father got the first one. What was his name again?"

"Jake?" Maura paused her climb into the truck.

"That was it! Your father was so excited. Like a little boy."

Maura smiled. "You knew my dad?"

"Oh, yes, we had lots of chats when he came to the co-op. I was so sorry when he passed last year. I was on maternity leave and couldn't make it to his funeral, but I know others from the co-op went. Everyone here loved Charlie Stuart."

The unexpected lump in Maura's throat made a reply impossible. The two women smiled at one another until Wendy said, "Better get back to my customer. Maybe I'll see you at the fair— I'm bringing my baby, too." She gave a small wave and bustled toward the co-op entrance.

Maura got behind the wheel and turned on the ignition. The encounter was another reminder why she liked living in the Glen. So many people knew one another or had heard of one another, even here in Wallingford. She hadn't appreciated that chain of familiarity when she was a teenager and, like her twin, could hardly wait to escape.

The moment fifteen months ago was so fresh she could still envision the scene—her father slumped in a wheelchair, holding her hand. "Find a way, Maura, to keep the farm and the donkeys," he'd begged. "You won't regret it." And she hadn't, really. Several anxious and sleepless nights didn't add up to regret. The image of a red sports car suddenly flashed across her mind. Not yet, anyway, she thought.

She drove out of the co-op parking lot and turned onto Route 7 toward Maple Glen. It was a beautiful, sunny day and promising to heat up. She ought to have picked up the feed earlier but had spent most of the morning fixing the lock on Jake's stall. The run into Wallingford couldn't be put off, either, as supplies were running low. When the woman—Wendy—had come running out of the store, Maura's first thought was that her credit card had been refused.

The possibility of that happening was frightening, and Maura knew she and Maddie had to have the money talk soon. Maybe after the festival, she thought. She and Maddie were involved with the planning and organization, along with several Glen residents and even a few from Wallingford.

Maura turned off Route 7 onto the county road

that changed into Church Street at the village lim-
its and, spotting the Quick Stop gas and convenience store up ahead, glanced at her dashboard.
Might as well fill up now, she thought, and made
a hard right into the lot, parking at the nearest
pump. Minutes later she handed cash to the clerk
inside, thinking she shouldn't press her luck by
using her card again. Her stomach rumbled, and
the clerk—in his late teens, she guessed—looked
up and grinned. He nodded to the display of potato chips on a nearby rack. "Lunch?"

Maura shrugged. "Why not?"

After paying, she tore into the bag of chips,
shoving a small handful into her mouth. The young
man was busy on his cell phone and Maura was
noisily crunching, so she didn't register the tinkle
of the store's door until she turned to leave. Theo
Danby and his son were standing in front of her.

He was grinning as he pushed his sunglasses
up onto his brow. "Hi again," he said, his quiet
baritone voice distracting the store clerk for a second. Then he noticed the bag in her hand and his
grin widened. "Late lunch…or afternoon snack?"

Maura felt all the eyes on her. Her face heated
up, its typical giveaway at embarrassment. She
was certain there were chip crumbs on her lips,
as well as a sprinkle of salt, but opted for silence
rather than explanation.

He let her off the hook then, swiftly saying,

"Luke and I are on our way to a movie in Rutland and thought we'd pick up some snacks, too."

Maura kept her eyes on Theo but nodded at Luke, who had slipped past her on his way to the junk-food aisle. "Should be cool in the cinema, anyway."

He stood aside as she made for the door. "I thought we might drop by later, after the movie. Or maybe in the morning. Luke wants to see the donkeys." When she hesitated, he added, "If that's okay."

The uncertainty in his voice touched her. Why was she being so prickly? "Sure, though the morning would be better. If you come about nine, you might see a couple of them in action. Giving rides," she explained at his puzzled face.

"Great! Luke will be thrilled."

Would he? She hadn't seen much enthusiasm in the boy so far, though there was a bit of satisfaction on his face as he went up to the cash counter with bags of snacks and a can of soda.

"Okay, tomorrow, then."

"For sure," he said as she opened the door. "And…uh…I see you still like salt and vinegar."

She swung around, frowning.

He nodded at the crumpled chip bag.

She was saved from replying by Luke.

"Dad? Money?"

Back in the truck, Maura shook her head at the

pathetic scene. At least Theo's face had reddened, too, after his inane comment about the chips.

Driving off the lot, she glanced at the rearview mirror to see Theo and Luke getting into their car. She blew out a mouthful of vinegar breath. *With any luck, Theo Danby will be on his way back to wherever he's living now, and there'll be no more embarrassing encounters like that one. And so what if I still like salt and vinegar? I can't believe he ever noticed back then...*

CHAPTER THREE

"Seriously?"

The disbelief in Maddie's voice caught Maura off guard. "What's the problem? You give lots of tours to people. Just because it's Theo—"

"He has nothing to do with this. Bernie's niece, Ashley, is coming to help. I told you she'd be volunteering this summer, and I have two clients riding while she's here. We still haven't decided on a plan for the festival—organizing the vendor tables and so on—plus the stables need mucking out."

Maura almost smiled. The stables always needed cleaning. "They're only going to be watching, Mads. It's not a big deal."

Maddie dropped the tea towel she was holding onto the kitchen counter. "Fine, then you can answer any questions they have, because I can't be interrupted." As she headed for the door leading into the mudroom, she tossed back one last comment. "And remember, there's only two weeks left and a lot more to organize."

"I delivered all the flyers yesterday," Maura

called as the outside door slammed shut. She couldn't figure out why Maddie was so worked up, unless the stress of hosting the Glen's annual Fourth of July festival this year was a factor. Usually, it was Maura's anxiety about commitments and deadlines that prevailed while Maddie was blissfully unaware of such mundane matters. But lately it seemed as if the two had switched personalities. She and Mads would definitely have to have a talk. But right then, she had work to do.

She finished stacking the breakfast dishes into the dishwasher and was about to pour the rest of the coffee down the sink when she thought she could offer a cup to Theo. Or even Ashley. She *had* forgotten about her returning this summer to help, along with their two adult volunteers— Nancy and Cathy—who'd been with them almost from the beginning.

The summer holidays would potentially be a busy time for the riding program. At least, Maura prayed the summer would be busy, because they needed the money. She and Maddie had put plans to buy another donkey on hold until they had a clear picture of the summer. Still, Maura was all set to start looking, but Maddie was resisting. "Let's wait and see how the summer pans out revenue wise," she'd said.

Revenue wise? That was a comment right out of *Maura's* playbook. She was the practical, nononsense, "let's wait and see" one, not Maddie.

The remark had been picking away at her ever since. Maddie had committed to one year with the farm and the business, and the end to that period was looming. In September, she'd know if her sister was going to stay on and become a real partner. Lately, she'd been unusually silent when decisions about the farm and the business arose. The change from her active participation in decision-making to taking a back seat had been gradual, but Maura guessed it may have begun six weeks ago, after their disagreement about applying for a bank loan.

Maura had resisted applying for a loan, but Maddie had argued that they could use the money on property and barn upgrades, along with more advertisement. She'd also suggested the funds might permit hiring an instructor, which disturbed Maura. Did that mean her sister was contemplating leaving? She didn't want to think about that possibility. Besides, a loan application might lead to something worse than a higher interest payment—something like a review of the farm accounts. There was no going back, she told herself. She'd made a decision two months ago not to tell Maddie what she'd found and would stick with it. *For now.*

She headed for the riding ring, where Maddie was prepping Matilda. Maura watched her sister saddle the gentle donkey, whose amiable nature was perfect for training potential volunteers, as well as providing therapy. To her far right, Jake and Lizzie were grazing contentedly in the pasture abutting the Danby farm.

Theo and Luke could arrive any minute, and playing tour guide was the last thing Maura felt like doing after the tiff with her sister. She needed to calm down and put on her business-friendly face, let her frustrations vanish. And what better way to accomplish that than mucking out stables? Half an hour later, she was finishing up when she heard the zoom of an engine.

As she exited the barn, she saw Theo's sports car emerging from a cloud of dust and gravel. The red car came to a stop yards away from the house, and the smile on Theo's face as he spotted her tugged at her heart. For an instant it was that same boyish face, aglow with the promise of a whole summer, when he would greet her and Maddie his first day back in the Glen. But the warmth that flowed through her now as he walked her way felt different.

"I hope this is a good time," Theo began the instant he drew near. "We just checked out of the B and B and were on our way to the farm when we saw the donkeys in the field, and I wondered if we could have our tour now."

That grin is the same, too. A tad sheepish, but confident he could get away with anything—and he always had. She cleared her throat, focusing on the present. "No problem. Um…Maddie's exercising Matilda and is expecting a trainee volunteer later this morning, so—"

"She's busy. Sure. I can catch up with her later." He paused. "Are *you* free now?"

"I can take you to the donkeys out in the pasture, but uh…are you okay with walking through a field? It might be a bit damp or even muddy." She peered down at their city footwear, noting Luke's white sneakers.

Theo turned to Luke, who shrugged. "I think we'll be fine," he said.

"Great. Well, follow me." She heard some whispering behind her as she started toward the pasture.

"Luke was wondering if he'd have a chance to ride one," Theo explained, catching up to her.

"Sure. Let's see how he responds to them close-up. They're small, but they can be a little intimidating. As you know." She couldn't resist adding the slight dig.

"Ah, well, you don't know the whole story," he protested in a light voice. "There's me, on my own land, about to open my garage door when a loud snuffling and hot breath caught me at the back of my neck."

"And?" Maura hid a smile as she unlatched the gate into the pasture.

"I think you know the rest."

She pushed open the gate and looked up at him. "Do I?"

"I think so, but if not, perhaps we can get back

to it later on. Tomorrow or the next day." His eyes bored into hers.

"Dad?" Luke had caught up to them.

Maura dropped her gaze and continued walking in the direction of the donkeys, relieved at the chance to hide her face. How did small talk get so loaded with meaning, or was she imagining his tone? Surely there was a wife somewhere! She was pondering this last point when Jake and Lizzie noticed them and began to trot their way.

"It's okay," she quickly assured Luke and Theo at the sound of scuffling. "They think we've got treats." She turned around to see Luke hiding behind his father.

"Do we have treats?"

Maura smiled at the nervousness in Theo's voice. "Not the apple or carrot they're hoping for, but I do have some turnip in my pocket." She dug into her jeans pockets and pulled out a small plastic bag. "They don't get treats on a daily basis, but I knew you were coming and thought you'd like to feed them."

Luke came out from behind Theo. "Will they bite?"

"Only when feeling threatened or frightened."

"So, uh, is this one of those times?" he asked.

Both Theo and Maura laughed. "No, 'cause I'm here," she said. "And even if you were here with your dad without me, they'd only be curious, not aggressive."

"They're smaller than I thought they'd be," Luke said.

"Jake is five feet tall. Lizzie's a bit shorter."

"They're bigger up close." Luke edged toward Theo as the donkeys were now standing in front of them.

"Hold out your hand and keep it flat." Maura placed four chunks of raw turnip on Luke's palm. Jake wouldn't bite, but she wasn't so certain about Lizzie, whose enthusiasm for treats could result in a nip. "Like this," she demonstrated, offering Lizzie some turnip, which was immediately lapped up.

Jake nudged Maura's arm. "Okay, okay, mister," she said, laughing. "Now your turn, Luke." She saw Theo gently tap Luke's forearm and stand aside as Luke extended his hand. Jake quickly got the message, and his long tongue flicked across Luke's palm, licking up the turnip in one sweep.

"Oooh!" Luke exclaimed. "Wet!"

"Yep!" Maura said.

Theo caught her eye and smiled a thank-you, which sent a rush of warmth through her, and for a moment, Maura couldn't think what to say until Luke asked, "Can I pat him?"

"Of course. The idea is not to startle him. He knows me and my sister well enough, so we can basically touch him anywhere, but he's still a bit wary of you, even after the treat. Start here on his side and work up to his head, then his cheek and then down his nose. Like this."

Luke cautiously followed her movements, lingering slightly on the bridge of Jake's nose. "It's so soft here on his nose, but his fur is thick and rougher than I thought it would be."

"Their coats are different than a horse's. He gets groomed regularly because he'll pick up thistles or seeds from the barley he eats when we move them into the other pasture."

"What do they do all day?"

Maura tried not to smile at a question prompted by his city upbringing. "Eat, mostly. We exercise them, and they also take part in our riding program."

"Riding program? You mean people pay to come and ride them, like horses?"

"Kind of. But some of the people who ride them are doing it for therapy." She noted his frown. "Say you had a lot of stress in your life and needed to chill. You could come here and ride one of them for an hour or so. When you sit on an animal, like a horse or pony or donkey, you get into the rhythm of their movement. You concentrate on the animal itself, how it's moving and where it's going. All of your attention is devoted to what's happening right at that moment, so you might be able to forget about the problems in your mind or in your body for at least that one hour."

Luke nodded. "Yeah, I can see that. My mom

told me that's what she liked about going to a spa and getting a massage."

Maura heard Theo's restless shuffle behind her. So, there was a mother and a wife, but not here with them. She was tempted to say something that would lead to an explanation for the mom's absence but sensed that would change the mood, and right now, she liked the easy dynamic between them. "Want to ride one?" she impulsively asked.

"Can I?"

The excitement in his voice made her smile. She looked across at Theo, who now was grinning. "Sure. We'll lead them back to the yard." She gave a low whistle, slapped her thigh and started walking while Jake and Lizzie followed.

"Just like that!" Luke's eyes widened.

Maura and Theo laughed. "Just like that," Maura said.

"Come on, son. I want to see you riding."

She led them toward the yard near the barn, slowing down as she spotted Maddie talking to a woman and a teenage girl—Ashley, she guessed. Maura's mood shifted slightly when she saw the resignation in her sister's face.

THERE WAS A time when Theo's arrival at the Stuart farm guaranteed pleasure and excitement for all of them. But yesterday's encounter with Maura at the convenience store had taken him immediately back to his last summer, when the friendship between them changed. Today, he'd seen glimpses of the younger Maura before all the teen melodrama back then and had thought perhaps the next several days would be easier than he'd anticipated—that returning as an adult meant they'd all be able to put the past behind them. But now, catching the frown on Maddie's face, he wasn't so certain.

Surely Maddie—the one Stuart twin with whom he'd had more of a friendship with—would be happy to see him? Maura hadn't been exactly welcoming the day before yesterday, and despite the lurch in his stomach when she'd smiled—even if the smile was at his expense over Jake cornering him—he'd hoped she might have changed enough to be a bit warmer, like Maddie. Yet now it seemed Maddie, too, was aloof. But why?

"Dad? You okay?"

The solicitous tone of his son's voice touched him. He couldn't recall the last time Luke had expressed any concern at all for him, but then, how could he blame the kid? The past year of arguments, tears and recriminations between him and Trish had alienated them all, especially Luke.

"Yes," he replied, "but I just remembered that the company I've hired to pick up stuff from the farmhouse is coming soon and maybe you should take that ride tomorrow." Or maybe never, he silently added. Then he winced at the disappointment in Luke's face.

"Tomorrow could work, too," Maura said, turning his way. "Maddie's busy training someone right now, so we could set a specific time in the morning for Luke."

She'd clearly overheard him. Theo realized there was no way to get out of a second trip to the Stuart farm. "Okay by me. Luke?"

Another maddening shrug, but this time without a scowl. "What time tomorrow?"

Before Maura replied, Theo noticed Maddie walking toward them. Her face lit up as she approached, and for the first time, Theo wondered if the look he'd witnessed earlier had been meant for Maura, not him.

"Maura told me you were coming over, but I had commitments this morning. So nice to see you again, Theo! I'm glad you stuck around. And this must be your son?" Her dazzling smile beamed down at Luke, who responded with one as well.

Theo was relieved to see that Maddie was as warm as she'd always been, though a quick glance at Maura's stony face hinted at some issue between them. *Not your problem*, he reminded himself. *Not anymore.* When he shook hands with her, she held on to his a few seconds longer, her dark brown eyes gleaming. The moment took him back to his confused sixteen-year-old self— a friendship with raven-haired Maddie but a secret crush on Maura, with her flaming red hair. He'd gravitated to Maddie, whose openness drew in everyone. She was easy to talk to. When Theo realized she had a crush on Shawn Harrison, he hadn't really minded. They became buddies, plotting ways to attract Shawn's attention to Maddie.

"Can Luke come back in the morning to ride Jake?" Maura's sharp voice broke the spell.

Theo thought he saw Maddie roll her eyes. "Of course! Does nine work for you?"

She turned her attention back to Theo, who noted the slight twitch at the corner of her mouth. *So it's not me she's angry with, but Maura.* He looked at Luke. "Okay with you?"

"Yes!" The pleasure in Luke's voice cleared the air.

They were all smiling now, and Theo felt his pent-up breath dissipate. As he and Luke headed for the car, he noticed Maura go up to Maddie, touching her arm while speaking to her. They were already deep in conversation by the time Theo was making a U-turn. He glanced into the rearview mirror and watched them move apart. One headed for the house and the other, the barn.

A memory suddenly struck—his uncle, shaking his head one day that last summer and saying, "Those Stuart girls! Something's up with them. Best not get too involved, Theo." At the time, all Theo could think was, *Too late for that, Uncle Stan.*

"Dad?"

Theo shifted his gaze from the windshield to Luke. "Hmm?"

"I asked you if you used to play with Maura and her sister when you came for the summer."

Theo smiled at the word *play*, a reminder that at twelve Luke was still sometimes a kid. "I did, but there were other kids our age here, too. We all played together, and later, when we were about your age, we…uh…kind of just hung out."

"What was there to do *here*?"

Theo smiled again at the disbelief in Luke's voice. "As a city boy, everything in the Glen fascinated me. The woods and the hiking trail, the creek where we swam pretty much every day. My aunt and uncle had a few goats and chickens then, and I helped take care of them. There was always some kind of event happening—a picnic or a barbecue fundraiser at the church, bake sales for various community clubs, potluck suppers. Lots to do."

Luke was silent for a few minutes. "What's a potluck supper?"

"Everyone brings something to eat, and we all sit down and share it."

"Kinda like when we go have dinner with the McNaught family? And Mom always takes a dessert or something?"

Theo felt a twinge of regret for Luke, that those get-togethers would soon only be memories. The fact that Luke had used the present tense, as if the two-family dinners were still happening, made him feel even sadder. "Kind of, but the whole community takes part."

Luke thought a bit longer. "I know what the word *community* means, but I don't really know how it feels."

Distracted by his last image of the Stuart twins, Theo had to ask Luke to repeat what he'd said. He took a few minutes to answer, realizing that his son was articulating the same feeling he himself had his first summer there. "Hopefully someday you will, son. Coming from a big city to a small place like Maple Glen all those summers made me see how different communities could be."

Then he thought, *But could that possibly happen in a week or so? And will it even matter once we've returned home to Augusta and unlikely ever to return to the Glen?*

CHAPTER FOUR

THEO WATCHED LUKE take his empty cereal bowl to the sink and thought at least the boy's mood had picked up. Once he'd reassured him that, yes, they were going to the Stuart farm so he could ride a donkey, the scowl etched on the boy's face since yesterday disappeared. He knew Luke had been disappointed that the ride hadn't happened, and the afterglow from meeting Jake and Lizzie had completely vanished when Theo had asked for help bringing boxes up from the farmhouse basement that afternoon. "It's gross down there," Luke had protested. "All those spiderwebs, and I think I saw a rat, too."

Theo had wanted to laugh but restrained himself. "No one's been down there for years, hence the spiderwebs. And maybe you saw a mouse, not a rat." He mentally crossed his fingers.

By the time the truck from the disposal company in Bennington had driven away with most of the basement's contents, Luke was barely speaking to him. Even the pizza Theo had picked up from the diner in Wallingford had been wolfed down in silence.

"When are we going?" Luke asked, turning away from the sink.

Theo looked up from skimming over the trucking company's invoice. "Um, anytime, I guess."

"How about right now?"

"Sure—let me finish my coffee first. Why don't you make your bed while I tidy up here?"

"I already made it."

Theo hid his surprise. "Great. Okay, give me a sec." He downed the rest of his coffee and stood up. "I need to confirm my meeting with the real-estate person for tomorrow."

"I'll wait outside," Luke said and left the room.

Theo checked the time. Nine o'clock and Luke had been up for an hour, dressed and had been eating cereal by the time Theo had showered and brewed the coffee. It was an auspicious start to a day that was going to be a long one with yet more clearing out before the meeting with the real-estate agent.

He left a message for the agent, and by the time he closed the screen door behind him, Luke was pacing by the car. "We can walk," Theo said. "You can see the barn roof from here." He pointed right.

Luke shrugged and headed toward the cedars marking the boundary between the farms.

"No, not that way! We'll take the road and

avoid all those weeds. I have to organize someone to come and mow this." Another shrug, but
Luke turned down the driveway to the road. Yep,
Theo thought as he followed him. Definitely excited about riding a donkey.

"Did they have donkeys when you used to come
here?" Luke asked as Theo caught up to him.

"Nope. They had chickens and I think maybe
a couple of goats. Mostly the farm was used for
growing crops. Like this place."

"Why do you think they decided to get donkeys
and have that…you know…that riding thing?"

"I don't know how they came to have donkeys,
but I remember that Maura was always keen on
animals of all kinds." He'd known a lot about the
young Maura Stuart yet knew nothing at all about
the adult version. Part of him suddenly wanted
to fix that, but the thought wasn't rational. He
wouldn't be in the Glen long enough.

They paused at the foot of the driveway to read
the large sign posted there—Jake & Friends Riding Stables.

"I like that," Luke commented. "'Cause Jake has
two friends already but maybe he'll get more. Like
another male donkey for company, since Matilda
and Lizzie are obviously female."

"Yeah, that would be good, and he wouldn't feel
outnumbered." He was suddenly aware of Luke's
thoughtful gaze. "What?"

"I was just wondering if you minded hanging out most of the time with...you know...two *girls*."

There was an incredulity in his voice that made Theo want to get the right answer. "When we were young, like nine or so, I never really thought of them as just *girls*. We always liked doing the same things and didn't really need to be around the other kids in the village so much. Know what I mean?"

Luke nodded slowly. "Kinda, though I've never had a best friend who was a girl. What about when you were older? You said you came here until you were about sixteen. Was it the same even then?"

"By then we hung out with the other kids who lived here." He pushed aside a memory that popped up, a sudden flash of jealousy for one of the boys clearly interested in Maura. He elbowed Luke. "Okay, let's go donkey riding! Remember that song? We used to sing it with you when you were really small and fussing. I'd bounce you on my knee and—"

"I'll take your word for it," Luke mumbled and picked up his pace, reaching the end of the drive well before Theo.

Will it always be this way, he wondered, *as both of us grow older? I'll be the one remembering, and he'll be eager to forget?* The weight of parenting felt suddenly intolerable, and for a dark moment Theo wished he could travel back to those years when a simple nursery song brought so much joy. Then he saw Maura, sitting in a wicker chair on the veranda, and everything on his mind disappeared.

Luke, walking ahead, turned around to ask, "Are you coming?"

He'd have been irked by the impatience in Luke's voice but was too distracted by watching Maura slowly get to her feet and head down the steps toward them. He felt the air whoosh out of him. She was wearing white shorts and a pale yellow filmy top that swirled around her as she walked and highlighted the reddish-gold tones of her hair. Today she wore sandals rather than sneakers, and Theo's eyes drifted down to the scarlet nail polish on her toes, a match for the color of her lips. The transformation from yesterday's Maura in torn jeans and mud-splattered boots was breathtaking. He missed what she was saying, hearing only the pounding at his temples, and stared foolishly as she repeated herself.

"Maddie's waiting with Matilda in the north pasture behind the barn. We thought she'd be a better ride for you, Luke. Are you coming with us, Theo?"

"Of course!" he blurted.

"I meant, are you riding, too?" Her hazel eyes teased.

"Um…I think I'll be too big for a donkey."

"They're built to carry very heavy loads."

"Yes, but—"

"C'mon, Dad." Luke was grinning.

Theo knew his face was flushed. "I guess I'd better try, anyway."

Maura's smile widened. "Luke, you go ahead to Maddie and your father can come with me while I saddle up Jake."

Luke dashed ahead.

"That's the fastest I've seen him move since we set out on our road trip," Theo remarked.

"Well, I don't know much about teenagers, other than from my own experience as one, but I'm sure enthusiasm for something is always paired with interest."

"Doesn't that also apply to adults?"

"Of course, but there are more factors involved." She began walking to the barn.

"Like what?" he asked, though he knew what they might be—time, cost, responsibilities—and was curious to hear her reply.

"Way too early in the day for a serious discussion!"

She'd sidestepped that one, he thought, as he followed her into the barn. But she was right. The day was meant for some levity, which he seriously needed after the challenges of the last year. Even if that fun was aimed at him, perched on a donkey.

He watched her remove her sandals and change into a pair of tattered sneakers sitting on the barn floor just inside the entrance and thought the shoe exchange made no difference to the glamour version moments ago. A memory of the teenage Maura and her eccentric fashion sense compared to the other Glen girls back then surfaced. Had her outfit today been meant for him? The idea pleased him, though he couldn't say why.

As she deftly saddled Jake, Theo wondered how and why she came to this stage in her life and career. When they were young, he remembered her saying she wanted to be a veterinarian. Of course, he'd wanted to be an astronaut, so...

"Let's get going," she said as she led Jake toward him. "Maddie will be wondering if we're coming or not. She wasn't sure if you'd be up for a ride, too, but I told her you wouldn't want to be a spoilsport in front of your son."

Ouch. Theo went for a smile. "I hope I can live up to such high expectations," he joked.

"I'm sure you can," she said, her eyes lingering on his face long enough to make him wonder if the remark was a dare. "So do you want to ride him out to the field or wait till we get there?"

"Which will be least humiliating?"

The teasing glint in her eyes disappeared. "You'll be fine, Theo. But maybe get on here, where I can help you without—"

"The mocking face of my son?"

"I was going to say without everyone staring. Don't make too many assumptions about your son. He may live up to *your* expectations yet."

That was an opener he wanted to pursue but not right then. Still, she had a point. Today was supposed to be about Luke, not him. "Sure. Tell me what to do."

She held Jake by the bit in his mouth. "Just like getting on a horse."

"Been a long time for that."

"Okay, mount on this side and put your left foot there in that stirrup. Left hand there, on the horn—" she pointed to a protuberance at the front of the saddle "—and swing up in one smooth movement."

"This saddle, is it big enough for me? It looks small."

"It's a mule or donkey saddle, and it *is* smaller. Donkeys and mules have V-shaped shoulders, so you'll be sitting in a different position than you would on a horse."

He knew overthinking it could lead to trouble, so he took a deep breath and followed through. Jake shifted as Theo settled on his back. "He's moving a bit. Sure I'm not too heavy?"

"You're okay," Maura said. "He's adjusting to your weight. Don't worry—he can handle it. Donkeys have been carrying heavier burdens than you for thousands of years."

"I feel a bit lopsided," he said. She leaned across him to tug on the straps beneath Jake's belly, and his senses were saturated with the flowery warmth of her body, the loose strands from her ponytail brushing against his cheek and her own cheek. He took a deep breath, realizing his teen-age self would never have noticed these things.

"That better?" she asked, rising up and away from him in one swoop. He nodded.

"Ready?" She smiled encouragement.

HE WAS A GOOD SPORT, she had to admit. Donkeys were fun to ride, but their short, stocky frames paled next to the physique of a horse, and a large man perched atop a donkey wasn't exactly an iconic image. But Theo had gone along with it all, letting her lead Jake and him around the pasture while Maddie gave Luke a lesson farther away.

After a couple of short circuits, she began to hear muffled groaning sounds. Not from Jake but from Theo. He was shifting a bit, and she figured he'd had enough. "Want to take a break, get some iced tea up on the porch?"

"Please!"

She bit back a chuckle. "Here, give me your left hand and use your right to hold on to the saddle horn as you swing off."

He did, stumbling a bit as his right foot hit the ground and lurching into her. She grasped his arms to steady him. "You okay?"

His face was near enough to hers that the pocket of warm air coming off it, along with a minty scent of toothpaste, enveloped her, and his breath-less reply—"I am now!"—sent shivers down her spine. Did he mean okay to be off the donkey, or that he liked their closeness? There was a fraction of a second when she considered touching his cheek, feeling what the adult Theo's face was like compared to his sixteen-year-old one. That time in the Danbys' barn when she'd almost kissed him.

Thankfully, he broke the spell. "I hate to say it, but my—"

"Butt? A tad tender?"

He matched her grin with a wider one, his eyes locking on hers long enough that Maura, realizing she was holding her breath, exhaled loudly and said, "Help me get this saddle off and we can leave Jake in the pasture."

He easily hefted the saddle off and carried it, along with the bridle, as they headed toward the farmhouse. Maddie noticed them leaving and waved. Luke gave a thumbs-up, and by his beaming face, Maura knew he wouldn't be cutting short his own ride. Theo followed her into the barn, where he set the saddle onto its rail and, while Maura put things in order for the client coming in an hour's time, wandered over to Lizzie, still in her stall.

Maura saw him stroking the donkey's face, along its snout, and hoped Lizzie was in a good mood. She'd been a donation from a hobby farm north of Rutland, her penchant for occasionally nipping at irksome pests—like humans—proving too troublesome for the family who owned her at the time. "Um, careful. She's an unpredictable biter."

Theo's hand jerked away, as if he'd set it on a hot stove. "Is she safe to use for people, then? Your riding program?"

"We usually match her with experienced riders, but she does have a favorite—a young girl with cerebral palsy—and Lizzie is very calm around her. They've made a connection that's quite amazing, really."

"I've read that some animals sense emotions in humans," he commented as he walked over to where she was setting up the tack for their next rider.

"It's true. We're only beginning to understand how communication works between us and other mammals, as well as with some bird species."

"I remember you were always reading about animals when we were kids and even as teenagers."

The comment pleased her. When they were teens, he'd never seemed to notice anything at all about her. Or so she'd believed at the time. Maura took a deep breath. She had to stop reverting to the past. This Theo Danby wasn't the one she'd thought about far too many years after he'd left the Glen.

"Didn't you once say you wanted to be a veterinarian?"

"Iced tea?" she asked suddenly, moving away from him.

His quick frown appeared and vanished. "You bet!"

He'd realized she hadn't answered his question but didn't press her. Maura was grateful. If she told Theo Danby anything at all about the years since she'd last seen him in Maple Glen, she wanted to decide what and how much of her life she was willing to reveal. Yet for some reason, once they were sitting in the wicker chairs on the veranda and sipping the iced tea she'd made earlier in the morning, Maura felt she *did* want to talk about herself.

"My freshman year at college got off to a rocky start," she began when he asked her what she'd done after high school graduation. "Maddie and I had all these plans. We'd both go to the University of Vermont, where I hoped to get into veterinarian medicine after my science degree and she was interested in occupational therapy. We even talked about setting up some kind of clinic together— much later, of course. But…" She paused, sighing. "…things didn't work out as planned."

"What happened?" Theo leaned forward to set his empty glass on the small table between them.

"She fell in love."

"And…?"

"She wanted to go where *he* was going—Northern Vermont University—while I kept my admission acceptance at the University of Vermont. I could have transferred, too, but didn't want to be a third wheel, as the saying goes." She felt his eyes on her while she swallowed the last of her drink.

"I'm guessing you were disappointed at this change in plans."

Disappointed? *Heartbroken. Betrayed.* Those were better words for how she felt at eighteen, but now, almost seventeen years later, Maura knew her expectations back then hadn't really matched her sister's. Their dreams about college and independence had focused on them being together, not apart. They'd always done everything together, since birth. Until Maddie had found someone to love, whereas Maura had not.

"You could say that," she finally replied.

"Then what happened? With Maddie, I mean," he explained when she shot him a questioning look.

"They broke up partway through first year. The typical cliché of the high school romance and first year of college."

"Oh? Who was he? Someone from around here?"

"Shawn Harrison."

She watched the surprise sweep across his face. A name from the past and Theo's long-ago competition for her sister's attention? A familiar stir of jealousy crept in. *Seriously? Even now, after all these years? Get a grip, Stuart.*

"I often wondered what became of her crush on him." After a minute, he added, "And your veterinary dream?"

"I bombed out my first year—for lots of reasons, none of which had to do with Maddie." *Of course not, because by then we seldom saw each other. By then we'd already unconsciously decided to get on with our own independent lives.* "I transferred over to Vermont State, where I ended up taking their veterinarian technician course. After graduation, I worked in a number of veterinarian clinics, went back to university for some business courses and ended up doing research for a feed-supply company. Then I eased my way into the management side of things, which I found I really enjoyed."

"I get that. You were always the organized Stuart twin."

Maura laughed. "Recently I've been wondering if Maddie and I have changed selves."

"Why's that?"

She hesitated. Perhaps their current state of affairs wasn't a wise conversation topic. "I'm joking, really. But it's true, don't you think, that people change as they get older? Become more like their parents or whatever? Sometimes she seems to be the practical one and I'm verging on the impulsive."

"You? Impulsive?"

She saw that he was teasing and laughed with him. If he only knew!

"I'm curious," he went on, "how all that led to the donkeys and riding therapy."

"Unexpectedly, for sure. I volunteered in a horse-riding therapy program when I was in college and loved it. Very satisfying work. After Dad died, we were left the farm along with Jake and Matilda. I guess you could say I fell in love then, too…only with a couple of donkeys." They both laughed, and for the first time since Theo's arrival, she felt herself relaxing into those past summer days, when everything was still easy and uncomplicated between the three of them.

"How about you? What's your situation? Luke mentioned his mother, but—"

"We're divorced," he said quickly. "Have been for several months now, and when I took leave from the hospital, I decided this trip would be a chance to make up to Luke all he went through during that time. A chance for us to reconnect, in a way, because I don't know what the future will look like for him—or for me."

There was a sadness in his voice that touched Maura, and she wanted to pat his arm, show her sympathy, when a voice stopped her.

"Dad?"

They shifted their attention to the bottom of the veranda stairs, where Luke was standing. Relief washed over her. She'd already said more than she'd intended, but not as much as she might have if Luke hadn't appeared. There was something about Theo Danby's face when he'd talked about his divorce and his desire to spend time with his son that Maura suspected might have led to more revelations from her than the few she'd imparted that day. Like the feelings she'd had for him when she was a teenager—feelings that hadn't changed even after he'd left the Glen. What was the point in revealing so much of herself when his time here was limited?

CHAPTER FIVE

THEO WALKED THE agent to the door.

"I'll arrange a survey first," she said, "before listing it. I should warn you, though, that sales in this area have been in a decline over the past couple of years. You mentioned that your aunt and uncle rented out some of their fields to local farmers?"

"Yes, and they also sold some acreage as they grew older. I haven't found any papers yet about the existing property, but I'm gradually sorting through stuff, so I'll give you a call when I find them. I also have an appointment with their lawyer and bank manager on Monday."

"The county registry office should have up-to-date paperwork. Your best bet may be development interest, rather than farming. Satellite communities are cropping up everywhere. You probably noticed that driving here from Maine."

He had, and the sight had made him fearful of what he'd see in Maple Glen, but the housing spread seemed to have ended a bit north of Bennington. An unpleasant image of a large subdivision on the outskirts of the Glen popped into his mind, and for an awful second, he pictured the impact of that on the idyllic place of his childhood.

But he had to do something with the farm. Renting it out and managing it from Augusta wasn't feasible. "I did, and honestly, the thought isn't appealing. This place has managed to escape all that so far but—"

"Maybe not for long," she said, smiling. "There are few options for sellers these days. I'll let you know when the survey will happen." She headed down the porch steps to her car.

Theo closed the screen door and, standing at the bottom of the staircase, shouted, "Are you ready to go shopping, Luke?"

After a moment, he appeared on the top landing. "Maddie said I could go over and help clean out the stables."

Theo fought to keep his jaw from gaping. This from a kid who'd struggled to keep a bedroom tidy only weeks ago. But the invite pleased him. It would be good for his son to participate in some physical labor. Heck, after seeing Maura yesterday, he'd willingly muck out a stable, too. "Um, okay. When will that happen?"

Luke shrugged. "She said anytime before noon."

He hadn't left Luke alone yet, but knew the kid was sensible. "So why don't I drop you off there on my way to get groceries? I'll give you a key, and if I'm not back before you're finished, you can come in and make yourself some lunch. There's salami and cheese in the fridge and bread on the counter."

Luke's eyes lit up, and Theo guessed he'd scored a point. "Sure!"

He didn't need to hurry Luke along and recalled Maura's words yesterday about interest and enthusiasm. Had she been that wise as a teenager? He knew he definitely had not.

When they were buckling up in the car, Luke suddenly remarked, "Did you know that donkeys are known for their intelligence and good nature?"

Theo pressed the ignition button. "I assumed that, seeing how Maddie and Maura decided to use them for a therapy program."

"A female is called a 'jenny' and a male is called a 'jack,' so Jake's name is kind of appropriate. Maddie said to watch out for Lizzie, though, 'cause she can be—"

"Unpredictable?"

"Yeah. I liked riding Matilda, but my goal is to ride Jake, 'cause he's bigger. And I'm tall for my age, aren't I? That's what people tell me."

It was the longest bit of conversation Luke had spouted on their trip, and given the part about his height, personal. Theo wondered for a minute who the "people" were but thought maybe Trish or her parents. What really stood out was the mention of a "goal." It would be good for Luke to have something to focus his attention on while they were in the Glen. That would give Theo more time to sort things out.

He also thought he'd like to spend some time with Maddie. They'd been such good friends those last couple of summers he was in the Glen. Besides, it would be interesting to get her take on the falling-out between them when Maddie opted to go with Shawn Harrison, rather than with Maura.

"Dad? Are we going or what?"

Theo blinked. The engine was running but they were still sitting in the driveway. "Oh, sorry. I was thinking about what we needed in the way of food."

"Didn't you make a list? Mom always does."

"Yeah, but she usually forgets to take it with her."

Luke snorted. "True! Anyway, can you get some soda for me? The sugar-free kind is what Mom likes me to have. And maybe some chips?"

Luke's relaxed tone warmed Theo. They were actually referring to Luke's mother without any tension. He shifted into Drive and tapped the accelerator. "Maybe I'll drop into that ice cream store and pick up a tub of— What kind do you like?"

"Cookies 'n' Cream."

"Done." Theo's sense that the day was going

to be a good one picked up as he parked and saw
Maura standing in the open barn door. The torn
jeans, T-shirt and rubber boots were back again,
but today her hair was in a single braid that fell
between her shoulders. Except for one summer
when they'd had short hair, the twins usually had
ponytails, pigtails or braids—

Luke flung open the car door and leaped out
as Maura walked their way.

"Ready to do some hard work?" she asked him.

Luke must have spotted the twinkle in her eye.
He grinned and gave a mock salute. "Aye, aye,
Captain."

Theo shrugged as Maura's smile met his.

"Maddie's gone into Wallingford, so you and
I will be mucking out today. The donkeys are already out to pasture." Then she raised her eyes to
Theo. "We should finish up about noonish. Will
you pick him up or…?"

"Oops. Here, Luke." Theo dug into his jeans
pocket and handed over the spare key he'd found
before they'd left the farm. "Tuck this into your
pocket." He waited while Luke stowed it away.
"Okay, then. Considering your work this morning, I'm not sure if I should say 'have fun' or
'good luck,' but be sure to follow Maura's instructions, Luke." As soon as those words popped out,
Theo knew from the slight shift in Luke's face
that he'd goofed up.

"I *am* a tough taskmaster," Maura quickly put

in, "but I have complete confidence in him." She placed a hand on Luke's shoulder, steering him away to the barn.

Neither looked back as Theo left, and he spent the short drive into Wallingford mentally kicking himself for his last comment. By the time he reached the small town, he'd rationalized that he was simply being a typical parent. No harm in that, surely. Except that since he and Trish had split, Theo had consciously worked to be much more—a super parent, in fact. Maybe he should let go of some of the guilt he felt over not spending enough quality time with his son and just try to be himself.

He was exiting Wallingford's only supermarket when he met Maddie on her way in.

"Theo!"

"Hey," he said. "Maura said you were in town."

"Yup. I had a couple of things to organize for the upcoming Fourth of July festival, and now I'm picking up some milk and bread. I guess Luke is helping in the stalls?"

"With almost as much enthusiasm as he had riding Matilda. And thanks so much for that. He was talking about it all night."

"He was great. Listened carefully and followed my instructions. A nice kid, by the way. You and your wife have done a great job."

It was the perfect lead-in, but he chose not to get into the whole sad cliché of a marital breakup while standing on the sidewalk in front of the supermarket. "If you're not in a rush, would you like to go for a coffee when you finish up here?"

"Definitely! There's a coffee place down that way—" she pointed to her left "—called Real Beans and I'll meet you in about ten minutes."

"Great. What can I order for you?"

She grinned. "Large latte, please."

Theo had just placed the order and found a corner table for two when she arrived.

"I wasn't sure if you wanted a pastry or not, so I asked for two Danishes."

"My childhood sweet tooth is still with me. Thanks!"

Her comment suddenly brought back a time when the three of them had baked cookies and eaten them all one rainy afternoon, and he was about to mention it when the barista called out his name.

"It was a surprise to see you turn up in the Glen again after all these years, Theo," she said as he set their order on the table. "But a nice one. Maura said you're intending to sell the farm."

"Pretty difficult to run a farm from miles away. I understand that land sales especially are in a slump now, though, so it may take me longer than I thought."

"We heard you were practicing medicine in Augusta."

"Yes, but in a hospital, not private practice. I

guess my aunt and uncle told you at some point that I was a doctor?"

"Probably, but also…you know…the Glen grapevine." She grinned.

He shook his head. "Right. Now you know something about me, what about you? How did *you* end up back in Maple Glen?"

Her grin disappeared. "A long story best told over a glass of wine."

"Coffee works, too."

"I suppose." She shrugged, smiling again. "Where to begin, then?"

He remembered how much easier Maddie was to talk with than Maura. How she never seemed to have secrets like her sister. He broke off pieces of Danish while she spoke, following every word that more or less matched Maura's story. High school graduation, senior prom, where she and Shawn officially became a couple, and, finally, her decision to head to the university he was going to rather than where she and Maura had applied.

"I knew Maura was upset because we'd found a housing unit to share on campus, and she was stuck having to reorganize all that and find somewhere else to live. I also caused an uproar at home, with my parents. They wanted me to stick with the original plan for a year anyway, but…what can I say? I was in love." Her face clouded. "I *thought* I was in love, anyway."

"I remember how you were always trying to get

Shawn's attention back when all the gang hung out together."

"You offered a great shoulder to cry on." She frowned. "I sometimes think Maura mistook your intentions, but who knows? She was always so testy as a teenager and kept her feelings to herself."

Theo grinned, thinking of Luke's recent moodiness. That he could relate to! "So you broke up with Shawn?" he asked after a moment.

She nodded and, after a few seconds, said, "But I ended up staying at that university because I got into an occupational therapy program I wanted, and Maura was accepted into a veterinarian tech program at—"

"Vermont State University."

"You already know all this?" Her eyes narrowed.

The past came back in a rush—how the openness of childhood conversations had disappeared with adolescence, and how he'd had to be careful about what he said to which twin. "Maura simply filled me in on what she'd been doing since her graduation."

"Well, except for the standard big holidays at the farm, we didn't see much of each other once we started working on our separate careers. Then Mom got cancer and we spent more time at the farm, but we obviously didn't want to use those days rehashing our falling-out years ago. After Mom passed away, Maura stayed awhile with

Dad. She ended up quitting her job and moving back here permanently when he had a stroke, a few months before he died. That brought us together again." She suddenly teared up.

"I always liked your folks," Theo said after a moment. "They were a bit more flexible than my aunt and uncle. Hanging out at your place meant a lot to me."

"Thanks for that." Taking a breath, she asked, "Why did you stop coming back?"

Trust Maddie to ask, rather than Maura. "My folks had divorced around the time I first came to the Glen, and my father moved out of state when I was about to turn sixteen. I wanted to go with him." Not the whole truth, though. He still could have spent his summers in Maple Glen—except by then his teenage self had accepted the hard fact that Maura Stuart wasn't the least bit interested in him. "Everyone kind of drifted apart that summer, didn't they? Getting jobs and so on."

"True."

"What brought you back, then? Seems to me all the gang was eager to leave."

"We were." She gave a light snort. "Though I always suspected Maura had a plan to come back. She never seemed as excited as the rest of us when we were sharing our fantasies about a life beyond the Glen. After Dad died, I wasn't really surprised when she told me she wanted to keep the farm rather than sell. By then most of our acreage had been sold to a farmer in Wallingford who grows commercial crops, leaving the ten we still have." She finished the rest of her latte. "That was yummy. Thanks, Theo."

He was eager to hear more, especially about why Maura wanted to stay. "This was when you set up Jake & Friends?"

"That was her idea, not mine. She had it all planned before she even told me about it." Her tone told him she was still irked at that.

"Luke told me Jake came to the farm first, then Matilda a few months before your father passed away."

"Jake was a rescue donkey that an old friend of Dad's persuaded him to adopt. Then someone dropped off Matilda. Dad never knew who. He just found her tethered in front of the barn one day when he'd been out. Dad loved those donkeys, which was why Maura wanted to keep them. Otherwise…"

She didn't need to fill in the blanks. "I guess Maura's vet tech training led her to the business venture—the riding program?" he probed.

"It did, plus I think she'd had some kind of disappointment…you know…with a love interest and was at loose ends. She'd read about horse therapy and thought—"

"Why not with a donkey?" he interjected, grinning.

Maddie's laugh brought back more memories.

He'd always liked her and felt comfortable around her, but there'd never been the spark between them that he'd felt with her twin—the intense yearning for something more than friendship as he coped with adolescent hormones.

"Honestly, the decision to set up a riding therapy stable would have been more characteristic of me than my sister. She told me the other day she thinks we've switched personalities."

Theo still saw a lot of the old Maura—her tendency to keep feelings to herself and the unpredictable shifts in mood. "You haven't said yet what brought *you* back."

She pulled a face, and for a moment, Theo thought she'd dismiss the nudge. But the old Maddie was still there, too.

"What can I say, except that my story is another cliché. I was engaged and…well…it didn't work out. I was at loose ends like my sister, and when she asked me to stay on while she got the business up and running, I promised her a year."

"Then you're here temporarily?" Maura hadn't mentioned that, and Theo wondered how she'd manage running the place on her own.

"That's the idea." She peered down at her plate littered with pastry crumbs. When she raised her head to Theo, she exhaled a sigh. "Frankly, I don't have any long-term plans of my own. But I do know I don't want to be stuck on a farm with donkeys and my sister." She gave a light laugh and added, "I want something more."

Uh-oh. Does Maura know that?

He was about to pursue her comment when she said, "I should get going. It's getting close to lunch, and we've got a client coming at one o'clock." She stood up, reaching for her plastic bag of groceries on the floor.

"Right. Luke must be finished by now, too." He retrieved his own groceries, and they walked out to the sidewalk. "I enjoyed catching up with you, Maddie. A bit like old times."

She smiled. "It was. I probably told you way more than necessary about our lives. I hope I didn't bore you."

"As I said, nice to go back to the past."

Her shrug suggested otherwise. "Maybe. But we have to move on, right? Those days are gone."

Now she *was* sounding like her sister, he thought. "Thanks again for accommodating Luke. He'll have lots of tales for his friends back home."

"He's a nice kid, Theo. Say, we didn't get around to you and what you've been doing all these years! Don't leave the Glen without coming to see us."

Not a chance, he was thinking. He definitely wouldn't leave without seeing Maura at least one more time.

CHAPTER SIX

MAURA STEPPED OUT the kitchen door and, coffee mug in hand, strolled over to the riding ring, where Maddie was leading Lizzie through the gate. It wasn't quite nine o'clock, but they were expecting their first client of the day—Katie Robinson—in a few minutes. She leaned against the fence and thought how she and her sister had finally mastered a good routine, working together without too much disagreement most of the time. She prayed the arrangement would be permanent.

"Heard from Cathy yet?" she asked. One of their regular volunteers had reported a bad cold last week.

Maddie looked her way and shook her head. "If she can't come, she ought to let us know well in advance. It's only fair."

Maura agreed, but Cathy was a volunteer, not an employee. She and Nancy were invaluable when kids like Katie, who had special requirements, rode. The sound of a car engine got her attention and, shielding her eyes from the bright morning sun, she saw the dust wake of a vehicle coming up the drive. "That might be one of them now. Or maybe Katie and her mother."

She hoped it was one of the volunteers. When Katie was riding, they needed two helpers, but she could fill in if one of them didn't show. Usually, she or Maddie would lead Lizzie around the ring while the two volunteers walked on either side of the donkey, making sure Katie didn't slide off. Katie's cerebral palsy was pretty much in check, but anything could happen. Fortunately, Lizzie seemed to sense the twelve-year-old's situation, because she was always patient, walking slowly and never balking when Katie rode. And never ever nipping.

The car's engine stopped, and a few seconds later, Theo appeared from around the corner of the barn. Maura frowned. Had they arranged yesterday to get together again? She looked over at Maddie, who shrugged.

"Sorry for the interruption," Theo began as soon as he was close enough. "Luke and I are going into Rutland, but I wanted to let you know that someone's coming in an hour to cut the front section of my land, and I was worried about how the donkeys might react. He'll be using one of those big mowing machines." When she didn't answer right away, he added, "Well, Luke's waiting in the car."

Maddie came up to the fence before Maura had a chance to respond.

"If Luke's not keen on going with you, he can hang around here. We're waiting for our first client of the day, and since our regular volunteers haven't shown up yet, Luke might be a welcome distraction for our rider."

The unexpected invite startled Maura. The other day Maddie had objected to having visitors when clients were riding, and there was no guarantee Luke would be helpful when Katie was on Lizzie. She was about to squelch the idea when Theo said, "He'd love that. Thanks! I'll go get him."

As he headed for the car, Maura turned to her sister. "What're you thinking? We don't know if Luke will be a help."

"You told me yourself he was great working with you in the barn yesterday."

"That's not the same thing at all."

"Katie's mother told me she's been having some problems with a couple of the girls in her class. I'm sure I don't have to spell it out for you. Usually when we take her out, one of us chats with her while she's riding to ease her nervousness. If either Cathy or Nancy fails to turn up, you or I will have to walk alongside, and we won't be able to chitchat with her. That's too much distraction for us. We need to keep aware of how Katie's sitting on the saddle. I just had a thought that Luke might be willing to walk with us and tell Katie something about life in Maine."

It wasn't a bad idea, Maura silently decided, and worth a try. "Okay. I'm going to finish the breakfast dishes while you explain what we want him to do."

As she headed for the kitchen door, she heard Theo driving away. He was becoming almost a fixture at the farm. She had serious qualms about that. Not only because his presence brought back too many memories—good and not-so-good—but because it was better for all of them if he kept out of their lives. Yet every time she saw him, her feelings overruled her common sense.

Nancy had arrived by the time Maura returned and was conferring with Maddie and Luke in the riding ring. "All set?" she asked.

Before anyone could reply, the sound of a car alerted them that Katie and her mother had arrived. Maura reached the driveway as Katie's mother was unloading a wheelchair from the trunk. Katie could walk with the assistance of canes, but her movements were unpredictable, and the uneven ground necessitated a wheelchair.

"Hi, kiddo!" Maura ducked down to greet the twelve-year-old strapped into her special car seat.

"Hi, Maura. Is Lizzie waiting for me?"

"She is, and today we have a new helper. His name is Luke, and he's twelve, too. He's visiting the farm next to us and already loves our donkeys."

Katie laughed, drawing big smiles from her mother and Maura. Together they got the girl into her chair and wheeled her past the barn to the ring behind the farmhouse. Nancy and Maddie led Lizzie to the gate to greet them. Luke hung back, watching as they helped Katie onto Lizzie's back and adjusted her position. She was afraid he might be shy, but seconds later he was heading their way.

"Hi, Katie! I'm Luke."

The big smiles the two kids exchanged told Maura all would be well. He was already chatting as everyone took up their positions. Maddie took Lizzie by the reins while Maura and Nancy walked on either side of the donkey, close enough to intervene should Katie lose her balance.

Luke took up a position just ahead of Maura, even with Lizzie's head, and started talking almost at once. "I haven't ridden Lizzie yet, only Matilda. But my goal is to ride Jake, and if you tell Lizzie not to bite, I might try her sometime, too."

Katie's laugh told Maura the ride today was going to be a success. Luke kept up a steady patter as he walked next to Katie and Lizzie. Maura noticed that the donkey didn't seem to mind his proximity, either. At first, she'd turned her large head toward Luke, curious about him, and Maura worried she might try to nudge him away, but she hadn't.

After a few minutes, Maura moved farther back, closer to Lizzie's haunches. Katie was sitting straight, and her balance was good now, compared to the first sessions months ago. Her success was gratifying and reaffirmed Maura's desire to keep the program running as long as possible. The money situation would be resolved as they got more clients. That had been her reasoning when she'd offered the farm as the site of this year's festival.

She was thinking about the organization of the event when she heard Katie ask, "Will you be here next week when I come?"

For the first time since they'd begun leading Lizzie around, Luke was silent. It was only when Katie prompted him that he finally replied, "Um, maybe. If I am here, I'll definitely come and see you."

"Yay," said Katie.

As they turned for their last lap of the ring, Maura caught sight of a large red machine chugging onto the front expanse of the Danby property. The tractor mower Theo had mentioned. Although it was only partially visible from where they were, she knew once the machine revved up the noise could bother the donkeys. Especially Jake and Matilda, who were grazing in the pasture closest to it.

Sure enough, minutes later a loud roaring sound traveled across the fields. Maddie caught Maura's eye and held up two crossed fingers. But then Maura saw Jake and Matilda raise their heads, their ears twitching, and almost immediately, they began to bray.

There was no cacophony quite like a donkey's bray, as Maura had learned over the past year. By now Lizzie was alerted to the potential danger of a mowing machine and stopped in her tracks, joining her friends. Luke covered his ears, and when he turned to look at Maura, she saw the almost comical but pained expression on his face. When Katie covered her ears, too, letting go of the pommel, Maura knew the ride today should finish. She reached up to hold on to Katie's right leg while Nancy grasped the other one. Maddie stopped and slowly turned Lizzie around, heading for the gate.

Theo must have returned while they were riding and was standing next to Katie's mother at the fence. Maura noticed them both grimacing at the noise. The riding group stopped where Katie's wheelchair was parked, and Maura and Nancy helped Katie down into her chair. By now, everyone was laughing and holding their ears at the same time.

"We'll take Lizzie's saddle off later," Maddie shouted over the din, and as Katie was being wheeled out of the ring, Maddie gave Lizzie a push that sent her trotting toward her friends, still braying.

"Wow, does that happen often?" Theo asked as they moved away from the noise.

"Whenever there's a dangerous predator around," Maura said. "In this case, a big lawn mower."

"Or sometimes they're just annoyed at something. We often don't know," added Maddie.

"But one starts and sets off the others," put in Nancy. "At least we were finishing up, anyway."

"I wouldn't want to be in the barn with them, when that happens," Luke said.

"Yeah," Katie agreed. "Once that did happen, and we all left very quickly." That prompted more laughter and then she looked up at Luke to ask, "Want to walk with me to our car?"

"Sure. I forgot in all that racket to tell you about my favorite video game, and you were going to show me your new cell phone. I want to get one, but my parents say I should wait."

"I know. I had to beg for ages," Katie said.

The adults all smiled, and Katie's mother mouthed a "thank you" that included everyone as she wheeled Katie toward the front yard and the driveway.

"I'm guessing Luke was helpful," Theo said as they disappeared out of sight.

"He was great."

"He's welcome to help out anytime!" Maddie called out to Theo as she and Nancy headed into the barn.

"I was worried he might be shy or something. You know, moody."

"Not at all. In fact, he didn't stop talking the whole time. Katie hardly got a word in." His smile was so pleased she wanted to hug him, to reassure him that his son was a kid to be proud of. "Katie even asked if Luke could come back for her session next week."

"Oh? What did he say?"

"If he was still here, he would." She waited a beat, then asked, "Will you? Be here, I mean?"

"Not sure yet. My plans have altered a bit. The real-estate agent told me a sale might take longer than I thought. I have six weeks off, of course, so there's no hurry, but I'd like to have everything in place before leaving. Plus, there's still a lot more stuff to clear out of the house." At the sound of Katie and her mother driving away, he added, "Guess we should get going, too."

Maura closed the gate and walked with him toward the front yard. She wanted to hear more about his plans, not only because of their potential impact on her own, but also because she liked being with him. If she pushed aside her anxiety about Jake & Friends, she knew she could relax around him and forget about the decision she'd soon have to make—telling him something she'd kept to herself for two months. Something that was bound to affect the sale of his farm, not to mention their rekindled friendship.

Luke was waiting by the car. "She has the latest iPhone, Dad. It's so cool!"

Maura caught Theo's eye and grinned. "Your days are numbered there," she predicted, and his rueful smile made her laugh. The chance to know more about him hinged on how much longer he'd be in Maple Glen, and that realization unexpectedly saddened her.

"Hey, would you and Luke like to come for dinner tonight?" she blurted.

"Yes!" Luke put in before Theo could speak.

Maura and Theo laughed. "There's your answer," Theo murmured, his face close enough to hers that the warmth of his breath made her shiver. "Can I bring anything? Besides a bottle of wine?"

"Um…dessert?" she managed to say.

Maddie was in the kitchen when Maura told her about the impulsive invitation. She turned from the sandwich she was making and asked, "So who's cooking?"

"Uh, well, I haven't nailed down the details yet." Then she saw the grin. "Okay, I will, obviously. I'll drive into Wallingford and pick up a lasagna from the supermarket. We have stuff for a salad. It's no big deal."

Maddie set the knife down on her plate. "Not for me it isn't."

"What's that supposed to mean?"

"Just be careful, Mo. We haven't time-traveled back to those summers."

"What're you getting at?" Though Maura knew.

"I've seen you peeking at him when his attention was elsewhere. You can fool him, but not me. I know how you felt about him back then, and I don't want you to get hurt again. That's all I'm saying," she called out as Maura left the room.

She waited in the hall for Maddie's last words, which she knew would come any second.

"We know each other too well, Mo!"

Maura sighed. That was the one comment she knew for certain was true.

THEO COULD HAVE been eating anything. Taste took a back seat to his other senses. The vision of Maura wearing an emerald green blouse over white jeans, serving salad and second helpings of lasagna to Luke and then leaning over him, her flowery scent wafting above the food and her breath warm against his ear as she asked, "More salad, Theo?" filled every part of him.

He thought he heard teasing in her voice and wanted to utter a fitting quip, except the words were stuck in his throat. And besides, everyone was looking and listening. He could only shake his head and resume eating, automatically chewing and swallowing, oblivious to everything but Maura, now sitting opposite him at the Stuart kitchen table, where he'd enjoyed many meals long ago. But not a single one like this.

Luke was chattering about the donkeys and the braying while Theo's attention was still fixed on the woman across from him, so he missed part of what Luke was saying.

"Theo?" Maura was smiling at him.

"Um…yes?"

Her smile widened, and he saw the twinkle in her eyes. "Luke was telling us that you two might be staying in the Glen longer than a week after all."

He looked at Luke, who said, "This afternoon when I told you I'd like to walk with Katie at her next lesson if we were still here, you said we probably would be."

"Oh, right." He hoped his face didn't show the embarrassment he was feeling. Tongue-tied at thirty-six wasn't nearly as excusable as it was at sixteen. He cleared his throat. "Well, the real-estate agent has organized a survey of our property, but it won't happen until Monday, and my meeting at my uncle's bank is that same day, too. So yes, we'll be sticking around a bit longer." There was a quick glance between the sisters then that Theo couldn't interpret. He kept his gaze on Maura, but she ducked her head, continuing to eat.

It was Maddie who spoke first. "That's great! Maybe you'll be around for the Fourth of July, then. The festival's going to be here at our farm this year."

"That sounds cool," Luke said between mouthfuls of lasagna.

"It's a lot of fun. Everyone in the village takes part, and there'll be tables set up with vendors coming from all over the county and beyond."

"Carnival rides, too?"

"Just donkey rides, I'm afraid. But I'm sure some kids' and teens' activities will be organized by community groups here and from Wallingford."

"Dad? Can we stay for it?"

The excitement on his son's face urged him to say, "Of course," but then Maura raised her head. The peculiar expression that flitted across her face was hard to read, though it was definitely not encouragement. His mind searched for the right word. *Apprehension*, he finally decided.

He finished his meal quickly, sensing that the party atmosphere was coming to an end. Maddie began to serve dessert, so Theo resisted dampening Luke's enthusiasm by suggesting an early night. When Maura stood up to clear the table, he said, "I'll help with that."

He noticed Maura's downturned mouth at his offer of help, but decided to ignore it, determined to find out why her mood had changed so abruptly. They weren't teens anymore, and he refused to be put off by her. They stood side by side at the counter, rinsing and stacking dishes into the dish-washer as if they'd been doing that task together all their lives. Theo had an unexpected what-if thought, wondering for a split second how his life might have changed if he'd been more assertive as a teen. *No, don't go down that road, Danby.*

When Maura closed the dishwasher door and pressed the On button, Theo took a chance.

"Let's go outside for a minute, see if that full moon is happening as predicted."

He saw her look at Maddie and Luke, eating ice cream and talking about donkeys, and worried she was about to refuse. But she surprised him, nodding and opening the kitchen door. Theo followed her out into the backyard.

The promised full moon hung in all its splendor, high in the sky. "See? What did I tell you?" he quipped, moving next to her.

She gazed upward, wrapping her arms around herself.

"Are you cold?"

"No, I'm fine, thanks." There was a pause, and then she said, "I'm sorry if I seem a bit—"

"Standoffish?" he teased. He heard a faint snort.

"Yeah, guess that's what you'd call it. It's nothing to do with you, although it might have seemed like that. I just... It's just that I've been worried about the business lately, keeping it running, and the talk about staying in the Glen suddenly re-

minded me that if Jake & Friends does go under…
well…there won't be any reason for us to keep
the farm. We couldn't afford it, and we couldn't
stay here, either."

He impulsively put his arm across her shoulders, and he almost expected her to shrug it off,
as she'd once pulled her hand from his that last
summer. But she didn't, and he stood quietly, reveling in the warmth from her body close against
his. The urge to do more, to raise her head to
his and kiss her, was overwhelming. Instead, he
looked up at the perfect moon, its brightness and
her nearness lighting up his heart.

But deep inside, he wondered if there was something she wasn't telling him.

CHAPTER SEVEN

MAURA ROLLED OVER and stared up at the ceiling, its crackled plaster and yellowed patches a reminder that her bedroom, as well as her childhood home, was in serious need of repair. Much like her personal life.

Last night's dinner with Theo and Luke had been an impulse she was now questioning. At first it had been like old times. She, Maddie and Theo easily slipping into the teasing banter of their childhood and adolescence as if there'd been no gap at all from then till now. When she'd returned to Maple Glen to care for her father in his last days, she'd found that getting reacquainted with friends from the past had been like putting on a pair of shoes that hadn't been worn for years. The feet eased in, and walking was as smooth as ever. Granted, the shoes might be a tad out of fashion and frayed, but they could be worn, and comfortably.

She sighed. *Where am I going with this metaphor? I need to get my mind under control, not scattered in a hundred directions, all with dead ends.* Swinging her legs out of bed, she sat on the edge a minute longer, her fingers running through her tousled hair as she tried to focus on today—Saturday. Three riders and a break midafternoon when she and Maddie had a festival committee meeting.

Followed by tomorrow, Sunday, when she'd planned to visit Walter Ingram and make sure he knew about the festival, that he and his honey products from his beekeeping business were welcome. The man was a bit of a recluse, and she doubted he'd read the flyers or even heard any of the village talk about the event. Then the day after, Monday, she and Maddie had an appointment with their bank manager in Wallingford.

Maddie had finally persuaded her that a bank loan was necessary to upgrade the barn and stables, citing their hoped-for increase in riders after the Fourth of July festival. Maura had seen her sister's point and reluctantly agreed, mentally crossing her fingers that the inevitable assessment of their finances wouldn't reveal anything unexpected. If that happened, Monday could be a game changer for Jake & Friends.

Standing outside the kitchen door with Theo last night, his arm around her and his solid frame pressing against her with such assurance, she'd allowed herself a brief fantasy of how her life might have been different, if she'd been more receptive to the sixteen-year-old Theo so many years ago.

All water under the bridge, she told herself now. Time to get busy. She showered and dressed and was about to head downstairs when she paused in front of her chest of drawers. Then she grasped hold of the handle on the third drawer from the top and pulled it open. Beneath the socks and T-shirts lay the manila envelope she'd hidden there two months ago. The familiar stomach clench she'd felt back then struck. She stared at the envelope a moment longer, afraid to open it and see those ominous pieces of paper but, at the same time, almost hoping she'd misread them. *Stop kidding yourself, Maura Stuart.* Her fingers fumbled on the clasp as she withdrew the papers.

I, Charles Andrew Stuart, agree to cede to Stanley Danby of Maple Glen, Vermont, four acres of my land abutting the Danby property should I fail to recompense him for the loan of ten thousand dollars, given today...

Maura closed her eyes. She knew the rest, having already memorized the agreement. It was dated four years ago, when her mother was receiving cancer treatment. Those treatments had only delayed the disease, though, and her mother had died a year later. She and Maddie had frequently asked about their parents' medical insurance, but their father had reassured them all was just fine.

She read the second sheet of paper.

I, Stanley Danby of Maple Glen, Vermont, agree to loan Charles Andrew Stuart ten thousand dollars. Should he fail to recompense me, four acres of his land abutting my property will be ceded to me.

The agreement read as though the two men had written it themselves, but it was signed and stamped by a notary public in Rutland, so she assumed it was legally valid. What she'd also discovered subsequently was that a payment of ten thousand dollars had been made to a hospital in Burlington from a bank account in her mother's name—an account that was closed shortly after. There was no indication in her father's accounts that he'd paid back the loan.

She knew she was wrong to keep the document a secret from Maddie, but Jake & Friends had already received some attention and was slowly attracting clients. She and Maddie had worked out a good routine, sharing tasks and chores, the therapy sessions and the costs. But there was never enough money left over. Certainly not enough to cover a loan of ten thousand dollars.

The fact that Theo hadn't mentioned anything about the loan possibly meant that he hadn't found a copy of the agreement. *Yet.* She just needed a bit more time to figure out her next step, and then she'd tell him and her sister. She stowed the envelope back in its hiding place and went downstairs.

Maddie looked up from loading the dishwasher when Maura walked into the kitchen.

"What?" Maura asked, catching her sister's sly grin.

"Nothing. Just that you and Theo must have been enjoying the full moon, 'cause you were out there a long time."

"Give me a break," Maura muttered, pouring coffee into her mug. "We were chatting, like you and Luke."

"Very quietly."

"Maybe you couldn't hear us over your own conversation with Luke." Ignoring her sister's scoff, she popped two slices of bread into the toaster and finished making her peanut butter sandwich. "I see we've got Sammy coming this morning. Have we heard whether Cathy will be here?"

"She will be. Her daughter had a cold yesterday and couldn't go to school."

"Still, she could have let us know," Maura said.

"How it goes. Volunteers, right?"

"Right. Say, what about asking Luke again? He was great with Katie."

"Sammy isn't Katie."

"He doesn't have a meltdown every time he comes," Maura said.

"But we never know. That's why we have one of his parents walking with us, ready to help."

Maura sighed. The nine-year-old needed the riding time, and he enjoyed it once he readjusted to the weekly routine. Problems occurred when anything changed in that well-established pattern. "Worth a try," she said.

"Go for it, then. I'll round up Jake for Heather, who's coming first, and Matilda for Sammy, right after."

"And Janet Hamilton?"

"She wants Jake this time," Maddie said as she headed for the door.

"Okay, well, since she's last, Jake will have a bit of a break when Sammy's riding. I'll text Theo right now to see if Luke is interested." She pulled her phone out of her jeans pocket and sent the message before changing her mind.

Seeing Luke would probably also mean seeing Theo, unless he walked over by himself. He could easily do that now, since the Danby front field had been mowed. She smiled, recalling the braying incident yesterday. It was funny in retrospect, but she knew there was nothing worse than three donkeys going at it all at once.

Theo's reply came almost immediately. Luke would love to and would walk over.

Okay, she thought, just as well. *A bit of space between standing with his arm around me, his body against mine for what seemed like ages, and seeing him again this morning might be a good thing.* She'd lain awake for a long time once she sneaked off to bed, avoiding her sister's watchful gaze. The heat from Theo's embrace had lingered long after he and Luke had left.

"I DON'T KNOW YOU," Sammy mumbled when he was introduced to Luke.

"I don't know you, either—not yet, anyway. But we both know Matilda. She's a very friendly donkey, isn't she?"

"I like her better than Lizzie."

"Does *anyone* like Lizzie?" Luke quipped.

Sammy laughed. "Maybe not." After a slight pause, he added, "I feel sorry for her, though. It's not nice when people don't like you."

Maura saw Sammy's mother wince. She was about to change the subject, to steer them toward the ring, where Maddie and Cathy were waiting with Matilda, when Luke said, "Yeah, I know what you mean. But when you get to be my age, which is twelve, you'll realize it doesn't matter if everyone doesn't like you, 'cause by then, you'll have best friends who will always like you. My dad told me that and he was right."

Sammy thought that over. "Are you going to walk beside me today?" he finally asked.

"If you want me to."

"Sure." He started toward the ring, with Luke behind.

Maura let out a whoosh of relief, causing Sammy's mother to say, "I don't know Luke's situation, but can you convince him to come back the next time?"

The ride was as successful as yesterday's, with Katie. As Maura waved goodbye to Sammy and his mother, she looked at Luke standing next to her. "If you're going to be in Maple Glen for a while, would you be interested in doing a bit more volunteering? And anytime you're free to muck out the stables…well…you're pretty good at that, too."

His smile reminded her of Theo's at the same age, and for a second, Maura wondered what it was like to have a child who resembled you in some way. She'd come to terms long ago with the reality that she might not have children. For that, you needed a partner—someone to love and to love you back. There'd been a couple of times in the past when she'd thought that was a possibility, but a reason to end the relationship always seemed to arise.

Luke's question broke into her thoughts. "Do you need me for the other riders today?"

"They don't need extra help, but you're welcome to stay."

"Thanks, but Dad and I are planning a hike tomorrow, along the Trail. So we're going to get some supplies at the supermarket, like granola bars and other healthy snacks."

Maura smiled at his slightly disparaging emphasis of the word *healthy*.

"No problem, Luke. We're happy to have you whenever you're available." She paused a second.

"I guess there's no deadline set for your return to Augusta?" She cringed at her blatant fishing expedition.

He shook his head. "I don't think so. Dad hasn't told me, anyway. It seems like I'm always the last to know."

Spoken like a grown-up, his complaint almost drew a laugh from Maura. Then an idea occurred.

"If you're back before three o'clock, tell him there's a meeting at the community center for anyone interested in helping out at the Fourth of July festival. Maybe you'll still be here for it and either you or your dad would like to volunteer."

Luke's face lit up. "You mentioned that a few days ago, I think. Yeah, that would be cool." Then his excitement lowered. "Except we could be anywhere by then."

She patted his shoulder. "No worries. It's only a thought, and wherever you are, you'll be with your dad, right? That's what matters."

He nodded, but his face expressed some doubt.

"Either way, if you're not doing anything around five o'clock, are you interested in coming over to help groom the donkeys?"

"Definitely!"

Maura watched him work his way through the row of cedars, exactly as she, Maddie and Theo had done years ago. He was a nice kid. Whatever the differences between Theo and his wife, they'd clearly accomplished something good in their marriage.

A stab of envy caused her eyes to well up.

LOOKING BACK, Theo still couldn't explain why his hand shot up when the festival planning committee chairperson—Bernie Watson—asked if there was anyone else who'd like to donate or contribute in some way. It wasn't only Luke's elbow nudge, because he'd already thought of something.

They'd arrived at the meeting shortly after it had begun, missing Bernie's welcome to newcomers and introductory remarks. As he and Luke took two of the last seats in the back row of the hall, he saw Maura wave at him from across the room, closer to the front. Relief washed through him at her smile. He'd been stressed all day about their next encounter after his impulsive embrace last night. He hoped the moment had been special to her, too. As a teen, he'd never been able to predict her reactions.

Bernie gave a big smile at Theo's raised hand. "Theo Danby! Nice to see you here. Folks, for those of you who remember, Theo is the nephew of Vera and Stan Danby, whose farm is located right next to the Stuart place."

Theo flushed as all heads turned his way. He cleared his throat, wishing he'd gone up to Bernie afterward. "Um…I'm happy to have people use my front pasture adjacent to the Stuarts' for extra parking or whatever."

"Terrific!" Bernie's voice boomed across the room. "We can use the extra space, for either parking or vendor tables. Why don't you and the Stuarts get together to discuss how that could work?"

Well, of course he ought to have anticipated that reply. He hoped the Stuarts, one in particular, would be on board with yet more meetings between them. He felt another dig in his side and looked down at Luke, who was grinning. Someone was happy about his impulse, anyway.

The rest of the meeting dealt with reports from various people, which Theo basically tuned out. The last to speak was Finn McAllister and Theo snapped back to attention. The tall, gangly teen he remembered was now even taller but muscular—someone who worked out regularly or had a job that was very physical. He had a vague memory of Mrs. McAllister mentioning a fire department when he and Luke had met her their first morning back in the Glen. Finn was still as self-assured and poised as he'd been when they were teens, and the way the voices in the room hushed as he spoke was a sign the man held a respected place in the community.

His report was mainly about the safety and emergency measures for the festival, which triggered a memory for Theo. One hot summer day they were swimming in the creek when someone—a girl, Theo thought—seemed to be in trouble. Without hesitation, Finn had jumped into the water and pulled her ashore. She was okay, but he'd instinctively known to turn her onto her side and let the mouthful of water she'd swallowed and choked on drain out.

When Finn referred to his team of volunteers from the Wallingford Fire Department and the local branch of the Long Trail Club, Theo thought how appropriate it was that Finn had a career in rescue work. The meeting broke up half an hour later, and Theo stood to leave until he noticed Finn coming his way and stopped.

"So glad I got a chance to say welcome back, Theo. My mother told me you were here, but she wasn't sure for how long. I've been a bit busy and so haven't made it out to the farm to see you yet."

Theo shook his hand, thinking the man was as welcoming as he'd been as a teen, a gift that made him the natural leader he'd been then and clearly was now. "No problem. I'm glad we had this chance today." He heard Luke fidgeting and said, "This is my son, Luke. Do you remember meeting Mrs. McAllister a few days ago, Luke?"

"Yes, and the little girl, but I can't remember her name."

"Kaya, my niece. She and my sister are staying with us for a bit." He peered down at Luke. "Nice to meet you." He held out his hand, which Luke grasped. "Are you two here to organize a move to the Glen or...?"

"A sale," Theo said. "But there's a lot to clear out and arrange first."

Finn nodded. "I wondered if that might be the case. Well, I'm happy we can see more of you before and during the festival, too."

Theo was about to clarify that he might not still be there for the festival, that it depended on many factors, but kept quiet because now he was hoping his tasks would extend beyond the festival, which would be in ten days' time or so. More opportunities to catch up with some of the old gang, but especially to be with Maura. "I'd like that, Finn. Have many of the gang settled here? I recollect most of them vowing to move away permanently."

Finn laughed. "Yeah, me too. My move back wasn't in my plans, but fate intervened."

His pause gave Theo the chance to say, "I was sorry to hear about your father. How's he doing?"

"As well as can be expected. It's a progressive disease, as you know, but he's in a great nursing home. I heard you became a doctor! Not a surprise, really."

"Oh?"

"You were always one of the more compassionate kids. I remember the time we pulled Sue Webster—well, she's Giordano now—from Otter Creek. She had a panic attack after inhaling some water."

"But it was you who jumped in for her, not me."

Finn shrugged. "Maybe, but you and I both knew what to do."

Theo's memory wasn't as clear. Finn was making more of his part than what actually happened. Still, catching Luke's raised face and proud smile, he appreciated the remark. *Any kudos that elevates me in my son's esteem.*

"At any rate, in answer to your question, there are a few of us who've come back to stay, Sue being one. And I'm not sure if you remember Shawn Harrison? His folks lived where Bernie's B and B is now. He's been gone for years, but I've just heard he's taken a job with the Green Mountain Conservancy in the county and is looking for a place to live here in the valley. Maybe in the Glen itself."

Someone from across the room suddenly called out, "Finn!"

Finn turned around and waved. "Gotta see that guy. Let's get together again, before the festival," he said, patting Theo's upper arm and walking away.

Theo felt his heart rate pick up when he saw Maura approaching. Did she know Shawn Harrison was back in Maple Glen?

CHAPTER EIGHT

INVITING LUKE TO go with her to see Walter Ingram on Sunday was a last-minute idea, but Maura thought maybe he'd be interested in seeing Walter's beehives.

"And I suppose you'll probably see Theo again, when you pick up Luke," Maddie teased.

"Give me a break," Maura mumbled as she rinsed out her cereal bowl.

"Just a reminder that he's here temporarily, Mo. I don't think that facade of cool indifference you mastered as a teen works anymore, despite the efforts I've witnessed this week."

"I don't have a clue what you're talking about." But Maura was thinking, *She knows me too well.*

Maddie snorted. "C'mon. You fooled Theo back then, but not me."

"*Fooled?* What do you mean by that?" Maura turned from the sink to face her sister, who was writing the coming week's riding appointments in the calendar.

"The secret crush that you hid by acting as if you didn't like him. It was a successful ploy with all the kids in the group, but you couldn't fool me." Maddie's grin disappeared. "Though I couldn't understand at the time why you went to such trouble to make him think you didn't like him."

"You remember what things were like that last summer he was in the Glen? How some kids in the group became couples? Sue Webster started dating Finn and that girl whose father was the village reverend at the time was hanging on to every word Shawn Harrison said." Maura kept her eyes on Maddie, watching for any reaction to that name from the past.

"Amy something. But you're evading answering," Maddie said, her face unreadable.

"I didn't like having my feelings out in the open for everyone to see."

"You still don't."

"I'm better than I used to be," Maura pointed out.

"You are, but, sis, when Theo left at the end of the summer and he came over to say goodbye, you disappeared somewhere and didn't reappear until after he'd gone. I'm simply reminding you that he'll be leaving again when the farm is sold, and there'll be no reason for him to come back."

"I know that, Mads. I'm not a teenager anymore."

"You still haven't told me why you went to such trouble to make him think you actually didn't like him, when we both know you did."

"Because I thought *you* liked him! The way you two were always whispering together or casting meaningful looks at one another." There, it was out. The doubts and insecurity she'd carried that whole summer.

"For heaven's sake, Mo! We were friends, and most of our talks were about how I could get Shawn's attention away from that Amy. Because I liked *Shawn*. But nothing really worked until Amy and her family moved away from the Glen partway through senior year."

Maura sighed. "Things really were messed up, weren't they?"

"Well, we were teenagers." Maddie paused, then added, "If only we knew then what we know now. Isn't that how the saying goes?"

Maddie's brief smile held a hint of sadness. Maura wanted to offer some words of comfort, but her sister's hopes and dreams about Shawn Harrison had faded a long time ago.

After a short silence, Maddie muttered, "Not much we can do about the past, but we don't have to make the same mistakes again."

"I'm still going to ask Luke," Maura said.

"Suit yourself." Maddie returned to the riding schedule.

Maura pursed her lips and left the kitchen to get her cell phone. *No, I'm absolutely* not *going to make the same mistakes this time*. Yet a voice inside whispered, *Too late*.

THEO AND LUKE stood at the top of the drive watching Maura's truck roll up. When it came to a stop, Luke ran forward. "Dad says he'd like to come, too, Maura. Is that okay?"

Theo almost bowed out at her slight hesitation. He'd been foolish to think their connection the other night was something that might thaw her longtime coolness. He'd even allowed himself an occasional thought that they could be more than friends, though that fantasy always ended with his returning to Augusta while Maura stayed in Maple Glen.

After an embarrassingly long minute, she said, "Of course."

Luke's excitement helped smooth over the awkward moment as he scrambled into the back seat of the truck and Theo climbed into the passenger side.

"I barely remember Walter Ingram," Theo said, buckling his seat belt. "Has he been in the beekeeping business for long?"

"I'm not sure when he set up the apiary. Sometime when we were at university, I think." She headed down the drive to the main road and turned toward Route 7.

"But he didn't always live in the Glen, did he?"

"No, and theoretically, he still doesn't. His place is between here and Wallingford but closer to the Glen, so he's always been considered a resident." She glanced at him and asked, "Were you here when the missing children incident happened?"

The question brought back a vague memory. "The case about the kids lost on the Trail? I remember something about it, but I think it happened after I'd returned to Augusta. What did that case have to do with Walter?" He noticed her check the rearview mirror and half turned to see that Luke was more interested in sticking his head out his open window than in the conversation up front.

"At the time Walter was a firefighter in Wallingford and also headed up the local Long Trail search and rescue volunteer team." She paused, looking at Theo again. "He was the one who found the kids. They were in an off-trail section near the Glen's access point."

He let that sink in and would have commented but she added, "Because of the wide interest in the case, a lot of media outlets descended on Wallingford as well as here. Child Protection Services took the kids, and the foster parents were charged with negligence among other things, so Walter became the focus of all the press attention."

"That must have been a challenge for him."

"For sure. Of course, this all happened—" she paused, her forehead wrinkling "—almost twenty-five years ago, so I'd have been ten at the time. My memory is pretty shaky, but I recall being fearful for the kids, 'cause one of them was about my age. Most of what I know came from my parents at the time, and much later, when I read newspaper accounts. Walter's story is a bit sad, though."

"How so?"

"Every year for a few years after, some reporter would show up here or in Wallingford to interview Walter. Then later they came at every milestone anniversary. He basically had to hide. His marriage fell apart, and he became a bit of a recluse."

"Will he mind my coming, then?"

"I think he'll be okay with it. He keeps to himself but sells his honey here and in the county. Plus, I've seen him at the occasional church potluck over the years, and he came to the festival last year, when it was at the community center. He's been getting more involved in life here in the Glen."

Theo thought about how a life could change so drastically, and his interest in Walter Ingram rose as the truck trundled down a long dirt road off Route 7.

"Just to let you know," she said as the house came in sight, "people here are very protective of Walter, despite his tendency to keep to himself, and no one ever asks about that time."

She didn't need to give him the warning. As a doctor who'd treated a broad spectrum of patients and their individual needs, Theo knew all about maintaining respect and consideration of a person's right to privacy.

"Did you text or phone to let him know you're bringing company?"

"I don't know his number or if he even has any kind of phone. But he does have a dog, with a strong sense of territory, appropriately named Magnus because he's very big." She gave a low laugh. "He helps to keep the strangers at bay."

Sure enough, when she pulled up in front of the two-story, somewhat rickety clapboard farmhouse, a large dog careened around the corner toward the truck. Maura turned off the engine and dug into her jeans pocket.

"Do we wait until Walter comes out?" Theo asked, trying not to sound nervous in front of his son, who was now unbuckled and leaning over the front seat to stare at the barking dog near the front bumper.

"We can, but I think this will do the trick." She held up a small plastic bag.

"Salami?" Luke asked from the back seat. "That should work."

"It did the last time I came, though that was a few weeks ago. Wait till I give the word."

She climbed out, leaving her door ajar, and whistled. The dog stopped barking and, tail wagging, padded up to the salami in Maura's fingers. "Yes, you do remember me, don't you, Magnus?"

The dog delicately lifted the meat from her

hand and wolfed it down, then begged for more. "That's all for now, pal." She turned her head to Theo and Luke. "I think you can come out now."

Her calm handling of the dog impressed Theo, but she'd always loved animals, and clearly even those that seemed scary. As he and Luke got out, a robust, gray-haired man in his mid to late sixties appeared from around the same corner as the dog had. He raised a palm in greeting to Maura and walked their way. Theo noted the wariness in the man's eyes as he drew near, looking at him and Luke.

"Hi, Walter! Do you remember Stan and Vera Danby? This is their nephew, Theo, and his son, Luke."

The guarded expression in the man's eyes disappeared. He nodded and offered a hand to Theo. "Sorry for your loss."

"Thank you, sir."

"Walter," he murmured and, turning to Luke, offered his hand to shake.

Theo felt a flush of pride as Luke immediately shook the man's hand.

"I was wondering if Theo and Luke could see some of your hives."

After a few seconds, he nodded. "Why don't we check out the hives right now?" Without waiting for a reply, he turned and headed in the direction from which he'd just come, Magnus at his heels.

Theo glanced at Maura, who shrugged and grinned. They followed Walter around the house, where an expanse of wildflowers and trees spread out before them. Theo paused to take in the scene—the bursts of color among the tall grasses and the blossoms on the rows of trees.

"Pretty, isn't it?" Maura said as she came up next to him.

"I was expecting pasture, but I guess this makes more sense, considering—"

"Beehives?"

"Yeah."

Luke passed them, catching up to Walter and Magnus.

"Fruit trees," Walter announced, stopping at the start of the orchard. "Pear and peach in blossom now, apple coming later this summer." He resumed walking.

"Not a man of many words," Theo whispered to Maura.

She shook her head. "Not until he talks about bees. They're his passion."

Luke seemed undeterred by the man's taciturnity and, along with Magnus, stuck by his side until they reached several rows of white boxes. Theo raised an eyebrow at Maura.

"The hives," she said.

"These are only a few of my hives," Walter was telling Luke as Theo and Maura caught up. "I've got a hundred or so scattered around this part of the county, at various farms and a few commercial orchards. I visit them every second week, see that they're okay. Take off some honey if I need to or deal with any problems that might have cropped up."

"What kinds of problems?" Luke asked.

Walter peered down at Luke. "Good question, son. Could be a queen has decided to leave a hive with her retinue of workers. That's called a swarm. Sometimes I can catch them and bring them back, and sometimes I can't. Other problems happen when a raccoon or some other creature knocks over a super—that's what those individual boxes are called. You can see that every hive has a different number of supers."

"Are they after the honey inside?"

"Yes. All animals like sweet things, don't they? Not just humans."

Luke nodded. Theo was surprised to see him walk from one hive to another, unfazed by the clouds of bees buzzing around the entrances of each hive. "Um…" He began to warn him to be careful when Walter looked his way.

"He'll be fine, long as he doesn't try to get too close. They've got more important things on their minds than stinging a young lad." Then he added, "But he's not allergic, is he?"

Did he even know that? Now he was worried. "I don't think so."

Luke must have overheard. "I'm not, Dad."

Walter's mouth curved up in a half smile. "Seems to be a confident young fellow," he said to Theo, before going up to Luke, who was standing in front of a hive where a cluster of bees circled the small entry hole.

"Put me in my place," Theo muttered to Maura, who was grinning.

As they joined Walter and Luke at the hive, Walter was explaining what the bees were doing. "They've discovered a great source of nectar and are communicating its location."

Luke frowned. "How do they do that?"

"See them moving in those tight circles, with some moving up and down, or to the right and left? That's called a dance, and the way they move tells the worker bees watching exactly how to get to the nectar and how far away it is."

"Cool!" Luke exclaimed. "Like a kind of sign language, but with movement instead?"

"Exactly. And if we waited long enough, we'd be able to see some of those other bees fly off."

"Do they ever make mistakes?"

Walter thought for a minute. "I can't say for sure, but I doubt that happens very often. They're already familiar with what's available to them here—" he gave a sweeping gesture "—and will travel farther, maybe miles away, to feast on other food."

"Food, as in nectar? From plants and flowers, right? I learned that in school."

"That's right. Summer's the best time for nectar, of course."

"What do they eat in the winter?"

"Good question. I leave them lots of honey to eat. They gather around the queen in a big, tight circle, buzzing their wings to keep her and the hive warm."

"Does it work?"

"Pretty much. After a bit, the circle shifts so the bees on the outside move in and the ones closer to the queen move out."

"I think I saw a TV special about some penguins that do that, too, to keep warm in winter."

Theo saw Walter's eyes light up. "You're right. Nature's pretty amazing, isn't it?"

"A lot of work for such small insects," Theo put in.

"Yes, and they have such a short life span."

"They do?" Luke asked.

"About six weeks."

Luke's face fell. "Oh, that's sad."

Maura caught Theo's gaze and smiled. He noticed that Walter himself was smiling for the first time, too, as the man looked down at Luke.

"True, but it's the way of the world, isn't it? The life cycle all us creatures have." After a moment of silence, Walter said, "I guess you'll be wanting some honey, then. Would you like to come to the honey house with me and see how I take the honey off the frames?" he asked Luke.

"You have a *honey house*?"

Maura and Theo laughed at the blend of disbelief and enthusiasm in his voice.

Walter's smile widened. "I do indeed. Follow me."

Theo hung back, watching his son and the big man head for a wood outbuilding closer to the house. "I think Luke might enjoy this on his own. Then he can tell me all about it later."

"You should know that the invitation is a rare one. I can't say when I've seen Walter so…"

"Open?" Theo searched for the right word.

"Friendly," she said. "Luke has clearly made a good impression."

Theo thought about the Luke from a mere week ago, wondering how his son had changed so much in only seven days. *Or maybe I'm only now seeing him for the first time.* He clasped her hand in his and in a slightly shaky voice murmured, "Thanks for this, Maura. Thanks for today." Then he leaned down and kissed her.

He'd intended it as another thank-you, but the instant his lips found hers he found himself sinking into the kind of kiss lovers enjoyed. And this was Maura, whose lips he'd only dreamed of kissing so many years ago, when he'd known nothing of the magic of a first kiss. Even the adult version of that teenage self couldn't have imagined the sweet taste of her lips now, or the way she clung to him, her body swaying against his. The other surprise was that he pulled away first, breathing deeply and wishing they were somewhere else, anywhere but in an open field with his son a few hundred yards away.

Her smile was as wobbly as his felt. "Wrong time and place?" she managed to say.

He heard the tremble in her voice and knew she was as affected by the kiss as he'd been. "Unfortunately" was all he could say.

A hollered "Dad!" brought another smile. Luke was speed-walking their way, clutching a plastic bag. He slowed down as he approached them, and Theo wondered, from the hesitation on his face, if he suspected something was amiss.

Luke said as he drew near, "Mr. Ingram—well, he told me to call him Walter—gave us two jars of honey, and I got to see him spin some off these frames in a big machine. A centri—"

"Centrifuge?" Maura said.

"Yeah, that's what he called it, but it may have another name, too. Anyway, it was supercool how the honey just flew off these frames in that machine. Then it drips into a big bucket, and from there, he pours it into jars."

"Very cool," Theo said.

"This has been the best day ever." Then, remembering other recent days, he explained, "Not better than riding Matilda or walking with Katie and Sammy, but—"

"In a different way?" Maura helped out.

Luke nodded. "Exactly. And Walter said to come back anytime. Oh, and he told me to tell you that he knows about the festival and is planning to attend."

Maura laughed. "I can see that your father and

I didn't need to come on this errand at all. We could have just sent you."

"Anytime." Luke's nonchalant shrug brought more smiles.

Walter waved goodbye from the doorway of the honey shed as they walked back to Maura's truck. Theo's high from the kiss was short-lived. Maura strode ahead, slowing down only when Luke caught up to her. They chatted together as they walked and climbed into the truck without a glance back. Theo had the sense that they could easily drive off without realizing he wasn't with them. He buckled up in the passenger seat and sneaked peeks at Maura, but she kept her focus on her driving.

Now he was regretting the kiss and figured she was as well. When she turned onto the lane leading to his farm, he waited until Luke had exited the truck, carrying his jars of honey and heading to the door. "Maura—"

"What happened back there?" she voiced at the same time.

"I seriously intended it to be a thank-you—"

"I guess we need to talk, Theo. It's about time, don't you think?" She finally looked his way. "Just that we both have our own plans and expectations, and I'm not sure if any of them include…"

"You and me?"

She nodded.

"Okay. You're right, and I'm sorry if I've complicated things." He swallowed hard over the sudden lump in his throat as he opened the truck door. "We'll talk, sooner than later. Tomorrow is a busy one for me. Maybe Tuesday? I'll text you." He stepped out and added, "Thanks again, for giving Luke the chance to see the hives and meet Walter."

Another nod and she shifted the truck into gear. Theo watched her reverse and head back down the lane. Somehow, he'd have to get his relationship with Maura back on track. Friendship was a more realistic option and probably the best one for them.

Yet, as confused and mixed up as he felt right then, the happiness on his son's face was a sight Theo knew he'd never forget. Long after they'd left Maple Glen, today would still be, in Luke's words, "the best day ever."

CHAPTER NINE

"WHAT'S UP WITH YOU, SIS?" Maddie looked away from the truck windshield to Maura, in the passenger seat.

"Hmm?" Maura shifted her gaze from the scenery on Route 7, heading to Rutland.

"You've been in some kind of other world since yesterday."

Tell me about it, Maura thought.

"Did something happen when you went to Walter's?"

Mads was probing, and Maura refused to get sucked in. "Other than someone getting stung by a bee, what could happen at Walter's place? And by the way, he's bringing honey to sell at the festival."

"Um, okay, I'll put him down for a table. But you're not answering my question. What's going on in that busy mind of yours?"

The memory of Maddie's teenage outburst once, long ago, brought a smile—*Mom and Dad say you're the quiet one, but I know your mind is always busy!* Her sister wouldn't give up until she got a reply. "Just thinking about our loan application," she finally said.

"Fingers crossed." Maddie took her right hand off the steering wheel to demonstrate. "I think we covered everything when we went through it again last night after supper. Though you weren't a hundred percent present."

Maura shrugged. "Worried, I guess. What happens if we don't get as much as we need? Or, worst case, we don't get it at all?"

Maddie's eyes met hers. "Then we'll be making different plans."

And that, Maura thought, was the crux of the problem. Reassessing the plan for Jake & Friends meant a discussion about Maddie's ongoing presence. She'd promised a year, and that deadline was a mere two months away. "I guess," she murmured. Returning her attention to the window again, she let herself drift back to yesterday and Theo's kiss.

Some thank-you, she'd thought in the middle of her restless night. *A thank-you kiss is on the forehead or cheek, not on the lips!* Still, she hadn't averted her face when she'd realized he was aiming for her mouth. She hadn't pushed him away, as she might have when she was fifteen. She hadn't put an end to it, despite the headiness and every nerve in her body wanting more. Theo had.

Theo, the summer friend. Theo, the unexpectedly handsome teenager whose presence caused such fluttering deep inside. Theo, the tall, attractive neighbor—and father—whose time in Maple Glen was limited to days, not weeks.

Maura took a deep breath to calm the anxiety mounting inside. She needed to take up running again. Exercising the donkeys wasn't enough to clear her head and get her mind off all the problems swarming through it. The business, the debts, the loan agreement she'd kept secret from her sister, not to mention the other person directly affected by it—Theo.

When he'd first arrived, she'd hoped his stay would be brief, that he'd sell his farm and leave Maple Glen before learning about the acreage. Then she wouldn't have to face him with what she'd done. Obviously an irrational hope, she told herself. Now old memories and new passions had complicated everything.

"Okay, let's do this!" Maddie announced as she parked in the lot next to their bank.

Maura blinked. They were already here, and she hadn't rehearsed her arguments for the loan once on the drive. Theo vanished from her mind as she followed her sister inside.

An hour later, she climbed behind the steering wheel, taking her turn to drive home.

"It's not all bad," Maddie began. "Half is better than nothing, and he had a point about the slow growth of the business."

The truck engine chugged into life, and Maura

waited until it slowed to a rattle. The truck was one more thing to be worried about, she was thinking. But not today. Today was about the business. "He wasn't even listening when I tried to explain how difficult it was to draw more riders when we only have three donkeys. We need at least one more! Plus, we can't depend only on volunteers. You know that from this past week, with Cathy's absence."

"Don't forget Ashley will be starting in a few days," Maddie murmured as she buckled up. "And there's Luke."

"How long will he be around, though?"

"You'd know that better than me."

"What's that supposed to mean?"

Maddie snickered. "C'mon, Mo! For once, drop the 'I don't know what you're talking about' routine, not to mention your ridiculous pretense about Theo Danby. We've already gone over this, and I'm tired of the way you keep skirting around the very obvious fact that the feelings you had for the guy when you were a teen have resurfaced."

Maura bit down hard on her lower lip. "This isn't about me or Theo Danby. This is about Jake & Friends. My…my *dream*." Her voice broke, and as she shifted into gear, the truck surged forward out of the parking lot onto the street.

Maddie didn't speak until they turned off Route 7. "Be kind to yourself, Mo."

If only she could, Maura was thinking. But

guilt shadowed her every thought. Now they had a bank loan to pay off on top of the ten thousand dollars from Stan Danby. Now she had mere days to tell Theo, as his stay in the Glen was certainly coming to an end. And then there was Maddie, her twin and best friend, who deserved to know the truth. Soon, she silently vowed. *Soon.*

THEO WAITED IN the car while Luke was choosing snacks in the convenience store for their afternoon hike on the Trail, which had been postponed from yesterday due to the spontaneous trip to Walter Ingram's place—the meadow, the hives alive with buzzing under the hot sun, and Maura Stuart, in his arms. *Kissing her.* Several times in the night he'd had to tell himself all of that had actually happened. The sweetness of her lips on his and the way she'd fit so perfectly against him. She'd wanted the moment to go on as much as he had, until he'd heard nearby voices as Luke was leaving the honey shed. Then Theo had remembered where they were. And what they were doing.

The kiss had been at the forefront of his mind all the way to Bennington and through part of the bank manager's opening remarks. Then the woman had said, "I didn't know your uncle well, having transferred here only half a year before he died, but reviewing his file, I see that except for one anomaly, he and your aunt were very conservative and predictable with regard to their savings and expenses. That frugality, along with the blue-chip investments they made years ago, account for the substantial nest egg you've inherited." She looked up from the computer and smiled at Theo.

The amount of his inheritance had been the surprise that shifted his thoughts from the kiss yesterday to the present. "This is news to me because I couldn't get a clear picture of their assets from the scattered bookkeeping system Uncle Stan used." *Maybe now I can simply throw all those papers into the old oil drum in Uncle Stan's barn and have a bonfire.* Then he'd focused on the first part of her remarks. "What kind of anomaly?"

She'd scrolled through the computer again. "Let me see… About four years ago your uncle withdrew a large sum of money." She frowned as she read. "Ten thousand dollars, to be exact."

Theo had blinked. That was a large amount for a man who'd saved every elastic band and plastic food container through the years. He almost missed what she'd said next.

"It was actually a cashier's check. Made out to a Charles Stuart. Do you know him?"

Do I know him? "Uh…yes. He was a neighbor of my uncle's. Is there any mention of why that payment was made?"

"No, we don't collect that kind of information."

"Right, of course not. And…uh…any other payments made to Charles Stuart since?"

"No, just that one."

Theo had intended to close the account at the meeting but changed his mind, deciding to wait and see what more he could find out about the mysterious payment. Had his uncle owed the money to Charles Stuart or purchased something from him? The matter of the money occupied him until they got back to the farm, when Theo decided he should bring it up with Maura.

He quickly texted her a suggestion to meet at the Glen bakery tomorrow afternoon. The place did take-out coffee and maybe they could talk while walking around the village. A neutral and public place, where they could focus on discussion, rather than their physical proximity. Luke climbed back into the car as Theo pressed Send.

"Everything okay?" Luke asked, looking at the cell phone in Theo's hand.

"Hmm? Oh, sure… Let's get a move on. The Trail awaits us!"

Luke rolled his eyes. "Sheesh."

Theo smiled, shifted into gear, and they rolled away from the convenience store. Half an hour later, after a quick lunch, he helped Luke adjust the small daypack they'd bought in Bennington, and he slung his slightly larger one over a shoulder. He started to walk past the car when a thought occurred. He opened the door and bent down to retrieve the small first aid kit he always carried in the glove compartment. When he closed the door, Luke whined, "Aren't we driving to the place?"

"It's only a mile into the village, and the walk will be a good warm-up." He ignored Luke's pout, an expression he hadn't seen for several days. The county road turned into Church Street at the village's Welcome to Maple Glen! sign, and Theo was just beginning to hit his stride when a car approaching from behind slowed down. He turned quickly, checking to see if Luke was safely on the gravel shoulder, then stopped as the car's window rolled down.

Finn McAllister was behind the wheel and nodded at Theo. "Hiking?"

Theo walked over to the passenger side. "Thought I'd show Luke some of the Trail."

"Great idea. Do me a favor? Someone told me a couple of the signs had been either pulled off or fallen in that windstorm we had a week or so ago. The blue blazes. You remember them, right?"

"They mark the off-trail sections?"

"Yep. How far you planning to go?"

"It depends on my son." He tilted his head to indicate Luke, taking his time catching up to them.

Finn chuckled. "Maybe a short one the first time? I'd appreciate your checking the signs, and also, if you see anything unusual, let me know."

"What do you mean by unusual? It's been many years since I've been in this area, Finn."

"Maybe some branches fallen on the trail, from that storm. Any evidence of camping, litter, that sort of thing. The Glen section is off-limits for camping, but some people still do it."

"Okay, and if you don't hear from me, you'll know all was good." He thought for a second. "I'm guessing there's no cell phone coverage?"

Finn grinned. "Not much. Maybe at the start, but once you get into the woods or deeper into the valley, nothing. But you won't be going that far, right?"

"Not planning to, and realistically—" he glanced at Luke, scuffing the gravel as he approached the back end of the car "—not likely to."

"Okay. Thanks again. Saves me a short walk-about today."

"How often do you and your volunteer team do an inspection?"

"In summer, once a week due to the increased numbers of hikers. Less so in early spring and late fall. In winter, maybe once every two or three weeks." He stared at Theo for a long minute. "We could use someone like you on the team. Athletic and with a medical background."

"I haven't worn hiking boots in years, and my walking has been basically limited to hospital corridors, but thanks for the vote of confidence."

"If you plan on staying here for any length of time, would be great to have you. Okay, then, take care!" He rolled up the window, and Theo

stepped back onto the shoulder as the car continued into the village.

"Wasn't that man offering us a ride?"

Theo stifled a laugh. The disappointment in
his son's voice was confirmation that the hike
would probably be a short one. "No, that was Finn
McAllister. He's a firefighter in Wallingford but
heads up a team of volunteers who check the Trail
and act as a search and rescue group if necessary."

Luke stared at the car a moment longer, lost
in thought. "Can we get something to eat at that
bakery before we get into the woods? In case our
snacks aren't enough."

"Definitely." He patted Luke's shoulder, and
they resumed walking.

Twenty minutes later they were standing at
the foot of the pedestrian bridge spanning Otter
Creek. Theo strapped his backpack on properly,
cinching its waist belt. There was water, the bakery purchases, the snacks and the first aid kit,
which he hoped they wouldn't need.

"Remember what I told you last night? About
the blue and white blaze signs on the trees? They
mark the path, and basically, we just have to follow them. I'm thinking we might only go as far
as the junction where the Glen's off trail meets up
with the main one. When we see our first white
blaze, we'll stop, have a look around and return.
Okay?"

"How far is that?"

"Honestly, I can't remember the last time I hiked here."

"Your last summer in the Glen?"

Theo smiled at his son's use of the shortened name, spoken like a real local. "Yeah, probably. All set? We can walk side by side most of the time, but if the trail narrows, stay close, don't wander off. And if you want to rest or if you see anything interesting, speak up. Okay?"

"Okay."

Theo sensed the mumbled response was trepidation, not reluctance. "Let's do this, then!"

Luke snorted, which made Theo smile. They crossed the bridge and stepped out of the blazing sun into the cool, dark woods. A hush descended on them, and Theo stopped, held a finger to his lips and pointed to an ear.

"Listen…the sound of the forest."

Luke pulled a face but after a second whispered, "It's so quiet. It's not even this quiet at night, back home."

"True, but it is here in the Glen."

"I haven't noticed 'cause I'm asleep."

"Which proves my point." He nudged his son and said, "Let's walk."

He led the way past the first blue blaze, still intact, on a tree a few yards beyond the footbridge. Occasionally, he craned round to see Luke, glancing right and left as he kept pace. A good sign, he thought.

They'd just passed the second and third blaze markers when Luke whispered loudly, "Dad! I can hear something rustling over there."

Theo looked where Luke was pointing. A bevy of birds flew up into the air from the underbrush, startled either by them or by some unseen predator. "Lots of small mammals and birds around, and as quiet as we are, we're still disturbing them. It's important to keep one ear attuned, but even more important to watch the ground beneath your feet. See that root sticking up there? If it were dead center on the path, someone could trip over it if they weren't paying attention."

Luke nodded solemnly. "But can we talk once in a while? I have some questions."

Theo's laugh echoed through the woods. "Yeah, let's take a rest and ask away."

"First of all, where are we going?"

They'd been through some of this the night before, but Theo figured Luke hadn't taken it all in. "Well, all of this—" his arm swept a broad arc "—is part of the White Rocks National Recreation Area. Remember I pointed out the parking lot and entrance when we drove through Wallingford, our first day coming to the Glen?"

"Will we see any white rocks?"

"They're on the side of White Rocks Mountain. If you look up, you can see its summit above the tree canopy." He gestured upward.

"Does this path take us there?"

"No, this is the off trail, but it'll connect to the main one, which would take us to the summit. It also would take us down, to the ice beds below the summit."

"Ice beds? Cool."

"Literally."

"Are we going up or down, then?"

He was relieved that Luke was interested enough to try either route but knew going up meant tackling a steep climb and going down, the jumble of icy rocks that, even in summer, could be treacherous. "Maybe for the first time, we'll walk to the fork, where this path meets the main trail. By then we'll be ready to turn around, hike back to the village and maybe visit the bakery again. I noticed some homemade pizzas."

"Sure." Luke smiled. "I might want two. They looked a bit small."

"You're right. Okay, let's get on with it." Theo resumed walking but had to stop a few feet beyond to pick up a large branch across the path. He tossed it into the bush, causing birdcall alarms from the trees.

The next blue blaze sign they encountered was dangling from a nail, partially protruding from a tree trunk. "I'll see if I can fix this," he said, peering around for a stone to hammer in the nail more securely.

"Here." Luke bent over to pick up a large stone, which he handed to Theo.

The sign was quickly fixed, and they continued upward. Later, Theo figured they'd been walking another fifteen minutes when he heard a low sound, unlike any bird or small mammal. His heart rate shot up, and fearing it was a very large animal—like a bear—he held up his hand, motioning for Luke to stop and to be silent.

There it was again. But this time, he recognized it. Low moaning, from a human.

"That sounds like a person." Luke's voice trembled.

Theo stared ahead. The path rose sharply and then took a hard turn at its crest. "Stay here." When Luke was about to protest, he added, "I'm going up to have a look. It could be anything. Don't worry. I'll give you a shout when it's okay to follow me." He kept his eyes on Luke's face. "Got it?"

"Okay."

He kept his backpack with the first aid kit on and topped the hill in seconds. There was no one in sight, but the moaning was louder. Making the sharp turn, he hoped whoever was in trouble was on or near the path and not lying somewhere in the brush. "I'm on the way," he hollered. "Stay wherever you are." Despite his long strides, time seemed to slow down. A trailing vine slapped against his cheek, and he thought he heard Luke calling from below, but Theo pushed on until he rounded another bend in the path and saw a man slumped against the base of a tree ahead.

Slipping out of his pack, he lowered it to the ground and sank onto his knees in front of the man, whose moaning ceased immediately. The man's color wasn't good, but at least he was conscious.

"What's the problem, sir? Have you fallen? Hurt yourself anywhere?" He skimmed over the man's body but didn't see any obvious injuries. His ashen face and the way he held a hand over his chest led Theo to suspect a heart condition. He placed two fingers at the base of the man's neck to feel his pulse. It was racing and erratic.

"Nitroglycerin?" Theo asked.

The man nodded.

"Where?"

The man turned slightly to his left, where Theo noticed a small daypack. He pulled it toward him, unzipped it and rummaged through it. Finding the small vial of pills in an inside pocket, he shook one out. Then he clasped hold of the man's chin again, using a finger to open his mouth, and slipped the pill under his tongue.

"It won't be long now. Try to relax. You're going to be all right."

The sound of footsteps caught his attention, and he swung around, getting up onto his feet at the same time. Luke was standing, wide-eyed, behind him.

Now wasn't the time for reminders about following instructions. "He's all right, son. In a few minutes, when his chest pains have subsided, we're going to help him get to the house at the footbridge. The McAllister place."

An hour later, the man was carried off in an ambulance. Finn drove Theo and Luke back to the farmhouse. Luke still hadn't uttered a word. Theo was reheating dinner from the night before, while Luke sat silently at the kitchen table, watching his every move. Theo guessed the boy would soon speak but was taking his time processing what had happened.

Finally, Luke said, "You saved that man's life, Dad. You're a hero."

Theo took in the dampness in Luke's eyes. "No, I'm not a hero, son. That man might have been able to eventually get to his medication."

"But we don't know for sure."

"It was good timing for him, our being on the scene when he needed help. That's all."

As he moved past Luke to get to the microwave, his son grabbed hold of his forearm. "*I* think you're a hero, Dad."

Theo felt his eyes well up. He bent down to kiss the top of Luke's head. "Thank you, son. Now, let's eat." He opened the microwave door and pulled out the bowl of spaghetti. "Sorry it's not that pizza we saw."

"Tomorrow night, Dad."

And they began to eat.

CHAPTER TEN

MADDIE CAME INTO the kitchen while Maura was listening to a voice mail from Walter Ingram.

Are you and Maddie interested in another donkey? I just got a message from a friend about a farm foreclosure, and the fellow needs to find a home for his donkey. No home means bad news for it. I can truck it to your place this morning. Say ten? Let me know.

"I'm going to order another delivery of hay," she was saying before she noticed Maura's concentration. "What's up?" She moved toward Maura, who was sitting at the table where the bank loan agreement was strewn.

Maura handed her the phone. "Two things. One, Walter definitely has a cell phone, and two—this." She watched as a frown appeared on Maddie's face while she listened to the message. "It's free," she put in as Maddie set the phone on the table.

"We still have to feed it, have it checked by a vet, take care of it!"

"But the whole point of the loan was to expand

the business, even if in a small way. This is what we need to do that."

"More riders are what we need."

"They go together, Mads. You can't have one without the other."

After a long minute, her sister yielded, but with a caveat. "Fine. You're right. As long as another animal doesn't end up costing us too much. We could also wait till the end of the summer."

When you might not be here? Maura was tempted to ask. *No, you've made your point, so don't raise another issue.* She picked up her phone and texted YES before her sister could change her mind. She managed to keep the excitement from her face as she asked, "What do we need to prepare?"

"I'll change the hay order if we're getting another animal, and I guess you'll be prepping another stall. Right now, they're all out in the northwest pasture."

"Any riders today?"

Maddie pursed her lips. "No" was all she said as she left the room.

Maura sat a moment longer, until the brief euphoria of winning an argument passed. The new donkey would have to earn its keep. She'd been so eager to let Walter know they were willing, she hadn't thought to ask for any details. She slipped into her rubber boots in the mudroom and headed for the barn. It was another bright, sunny day, though she could see clouds building in the south. They could use the rain, but she hoped it would hold off until the new donkey was inside getting used to the stall, not to mention the other donkeys.

Maura had always loved entering the barn early in the morning, with its warm, earthy odors. When their father was a boy, his family had horses and pigs, but when she and Maddie were young, there'd only been chickens and a few goats using the same stalls that the donkeys now called home. Gradually, the goats were sold off, leaving the chickens. Maura knew selling the goats, along with most of the farm's acreage, had been necessary after their mother's cancer diagnosis and her ongoing care. Though she'd been unaware of the entire cost of that treatment until she'd found the loan papers. *The loan.*

Her long sigh rebounded around the empty barn. She and Theo were supposedly going to talk about the unexpected shift from friends to… what? Something new and exciting but, she had to admit, scary, too. Maddie's warning about getting too involved had resonated even more after the other day at Walter's. Even now she couldn't explain why she'd responded as she had to his lips on hers. Only that she hadn't wanted the kiss to end.

When she'd received Theo's text about meeting somewhere in the village, she'd snorted at his comment about a neutral, public place. Clearly, he'd forgotten village life, with its hidden eyes and ears, not to mention tongues. No, she figured they could pick up treats and walk back to his place. She had to have Theo all to herself because today she was determined to find out if he knew about the loan agreement.

Half an hour later, the stall was clean with fresh hay and water in its troughs, and Maura was about to go inside to shower when she heard the rumble of a truck. She pulled her phone out of her jeans pocket to check the time. Walter was early. She opened the back door and hollered, "Mads, Walter's here," then walked around to meet him. The instant she saw his face, Maura knew something was amiss.

Instead of unlocking the horse trailer, he strode toward her. "Something I have to confess, Maura, and feel free to change your mind about taking Roger. If you do, I've got someone else who might take him."

So the new donkey—Roger—was a male and company for Jake, she was thinking as Walter went on to say, "I didn't give you all the details because I kinda hope you'll fall in love the minute you see him." He tried for a smile but pursed his lips instead. "The fact is, Roger isn't a young fellow and may need some extra attention."

Maura was about to reassure him that age probably wouldn't be a factor, as a mature donkey would be best for a new rider, when the kitchen door slammed shut and Maddie joined them in time to hear Walter add, "He contracted some kind of infection when he was young and eventually lost the sight in his left eye."

Maura saw her sister frown and preempted any questions by asking, "Is he trained, though? Is his vision good enough that we can use him as a riding animal?"

"Yes, he's trained. He's slow, but calm and patient. A gentle giant compared to your other donkeys. I think you'll be charmed."

"Then I'm sure we'll be fine, won't we, Maddie?" Her sister didn't look as optimistic as Maura was feeling.

"That's great. I'll bring him out, then." Walter went back to the trailer and unhitched the rear door.

Maura stretched her neck over Walter's shoulder to see four sturdy legs. Walter grasped the donkey's lead rope, and Roger ambled nonchalantly down the trailer ramp. His large head slowly swiveled left and right, and he came to a halt a few feet from Maura, raising his head and sniffing the air. He was taller and bulkier than Jake, a good option for adult riders. Maura noticed his left eye was opaque and cloudy, while the other absorbed everything within its range. She slowly moved close enough to stroke his large forehead. He reared his head slightly at her touch, but she didn't withdraw her hand, reassuring him with steady, firm strokes. Then he bared his lips and snickered, making a strange clicking sound, and half turned his head to the right, his good side.

Maura was about to ask what Roger was doing when Walter quickly said, "There's one more thing."

A black-and-white, long-haired dog trotted down the ramp and stood next to Roger. Maura blinked and heard her sister mutter, "Whaaat?"

Walter sighed and raised his shoulders apologetically. "This is Shep. He and Roger are not only best buddies but soulmates. Least, that's my opinion. When Roger lost his sight, the family had just gotten Shep as a puppy, so they trained him as a kind of Seeing Eye dog. The two have been together ever since, ten years now." His eyes shifted from Maura to Maddie and back to Maura again. "Like I said, there's someone else south of Bennington who might take them. But they're a couple. Roger and Shep. A package deal."

Maura peered down at Shep, sitting on his haunches and gazing up at her, every feature on his face begging to be accepted. Roger gave a loud snort, bent his head and gently nuzzled Shep.

"We'll take them," she announced.

THEO FINISHED HIS phone call with the land surveyor when he heard Luke thumping down the stairs. The surveyor had to change his arrival time to late afternoon, which meant that Theo would also have to change his meeting with Maura, and it was already noon. The timing would be tight, but he didn't want to rush his talk with Maura. Nor did he want to put it off any longer. They needed to sort out how they felt about one another if there was any chance of an ongoing relationship, which, after a tormented night's sleep, he was hoping for. Luke would be fine on his own for lunch, and after maybe he could help out at the farm.

"Dad," Luke began as he dashed into the living room, where Theo was sitting at his uncle's old rolltop desk. "Can you text Maura to see if I can go to the farm and see the donkeys, instead of being here on my own this afternoon?"

Theo grinned. Great minds... Now, if only Maura was available. He fired off a text, adding his own message about their meeting. His phone pinged almost at once, and he skimmed her reply, noting her suggestion about getting lunch at a diner in Wallingford instead. Then he saw a reference to the arrival of a new donkey.

"You're in luck, kiddo. Maura says they just got a new donkey and asked if you'd like to meet him and his sidekick." Theo checked the text again. "Hmm, not sure what she means by that. Maura and I are going to get some lunch in Wallingford, so why don't you make yourself a sandwich before we head over?"

"Oh?" Luke hesitated. "Um, sure, but Maddie will be there, right?"

Theo checked his son's puzzled face. He hadn't

told him about the plan to meet Maura, thinking he could do that later. "Yes, Maddie will be there. But remember I told you about my offer to help with the festival? Maura and I need to organize something. We'd planned to do that later this afternoon, except now I have to meet with a land surveyor here. The timing has changed a bit, but you still get to go see the donkeys."

Luke thought for a moment. "Okay." On his way to the kitchen, he suddenly stopped to say, "Then I guess we'll be here for the festival?"

"Is that all right with you?"

"Definitely!" He held up a thumb and ran into the kitchen.

Theo silently blessed the donkeys for the umpteenth time, realizing how problematic the stay in the Glen might have been without that distraction for Luke. He replied to Maura's text and went upstairs to change. Fifteen minutes later, he and Luke were walking up the lane to the Stuart farmhouse. The place was quiet until a sudden outburst of barking sounded from the barn.

He caught Luke's eye and shrugged.

"A *dog*?" Luke asked, his eyebrows raised.

"Guess so." They headed for the barn and were greeted at the door by Maddie, followed by a midsize black-and-white dog.

"Hi, guys, this is Shep. He's hungry, which is why he was barking. He figures Roger's being fed and he should be, too."

"Um, two dogs or…?"

Maddie smiled. "Nope. Roger is the new donkey, and Shep here is his best friend. Come on in. Maura's bringing something to eat for Shep… We don't have any dog food 'cause we didn't know Roger came with a dog. Long story," she added.

When Shep whined, Luke walked up to him and extended his hand, palm side up. Shep sniffed it, wagged his tail and licked the hand. Luke laughed. "I think he smells peanut butter." He stroked the dog's back, which brought more tail wagging. "Can I go see Roger?"

"Sure, but don't go into his stall. He's very calm but is still getting used to his new home and us. Oh, and one thing. Roger can't see out of his left eye, so if you want to pat his nose, approach him from the right, so as not to alarm him."

Luke nodded. "Come on, Shep," he said and headed into the barn, the dog at his heels.

Theo grinned at Maddie. "I'm not sure if Luke will ever want to leave Maple Glen now."

His light remark was met with a serious expression. "I heard you're probably staying for the festival, though," she said.

"It's looking that way." He hesitated, then asked, "Why?"

She glanced to the kitchen door across from the barn. "Mo said you two were going to discuss the plans for it. In Wallingford."

"Uh, yes." Was that *all* Maura had told her, and where was Maddie going with this?

"I've noticed that you both have made some kind of connection over the past few days."

Theo's face heated up. He was about to make light of the matter when she added, "It's okay. Maura told me. She'll hate me mentioning this, but—"

Now Theo was annoyed. "We're both adults, Maddie. We can figure something out. Don't worry about Maura…or my intentions." He managed a half smile, trying to lighten his tone.

Her face relaxed and a telltale blush rose up her neck. "I know, Theo. I trust you, believe me, but keep in mind that Maura will never leave this farm or Maple Glen."

The closing kitchen door got their attention. Maura headed toward them, holding a stainless steel bowl. "I don't see Luke, so I'm guessing he's inside getting acquainted with Roger and Shep?"

Her eyes sparkled, but not as much as her smile. She was wearing a sundress the color of spring lilacs—a perfect match for the fiery red hues of her hair, falling onto her shoulders. She was always beautiful, he was thinking, even in torn jeans and muddy boots. But this…*this* Maura was a vision he never could have imagined. Definitely not as a teen, and not even as a man.

It was Maddie who spoke up, saving Theo from stammering. "Luke's already made a friend of

Shep and is meeting Roger. I warned him about the eye," she added as Maura was about to speak.

"I knew he and Shep would like one another." Maura looked at Theo. "Do you want to go meet Roger now? Or later?"

He cleared his throat. "Maybe later?"

"Sure. Here, Mads, I found some leftover roast chicken in the freezer and added some mashed potatoes from the other night. I'll pick up some dog food in Wallingford." She handed Maddie the bowl, then turned to Theo. "Ready?"

He could only nod, as tongue-tied as he'd been as a teen.

"I'll drive." She headed for the Ford Fiesta parked next to the pickup.

Theo caught Maddie's expression. "Don't worry. Everything will be fine." He meant to set her mind at ease, but as he followed Maura, he wished the confident reassurance in his words matched his feelings.

CHAPTER ELEVEN

"How DO YOU think the other donkeys will respond to Roger?" Theo asked.

Maura was checking out the menu. She guessed he was avoiding getting around to the conversation they'd agreed to have. The kiss—what it meant, what were the next steps and how were they going to make it work.

She hid a smile. If Maddie could read her mind right now, she'd quip, *Getting down to business, Mo, with an agenda that hasn't any items of fun on it?*

No, Maura thought. *Today I'm going to break the pattern.* "He's a male," she answered, raising her head to meet his dark-eyed gaze, a shiver racing down her spine. "So they'll be wary—especially Jake, who might feel he's losing his place in the hierarchy."

"Is that a thing with donkeys?"

"As with all animals," she said. "That's why we gave Roger the stall farthest away. They'll see him and smell him, but he won't be too close. The real problem for the next few days is Shep."

"How so?"

"The others will view the dog as a predator. They don't know Shep and won't want him around them. Walter said Shep is used to sleeping in a stall with Roger, but I think we might have to have him in the house with us until the others are accustomed to him. It'll be a gradual introduction, but I'm hoping all will work out." She pulled a face. "It better, or I'm in big trouble."

"Maddie?"

"How'd you guess?"

"I couldn't help but notice her expression."

"Yeah. She's just worried about…you know… how we can take care of another animal, given our financial situation." She noted his instant frown and regretted mentioning finances, which she knew could lead to a topic she wanted to defer as long as possible. Despite her vow yesterday to tell him about the loan, she knew that money and romance weren't a good combination. *One issue at a time, Maura.* She stared at the menu again, its offerings blurring as her eyes welled up. The server came to take their order, and Maura chose the daily special, whatever that was.

Theo immediately said, "I'll have the same." He toyed with the spoon in his mug of coffee for a second. "I told Luke we were meeting to discuss how I can assist with the planning for the festival, so…"

"We better get around to that. I told Maddie basically the same thing."

"Uh-huh?"

Maura saw a flicker of doubt on his face and recalled how he'd lingered behind, chatting to her sister. "Did she say something to you? About us?" When he hesitated, she said, "C'mon, Theo. Out with it. There's no point having an honest discussion about what's happening between us if we can't be open with one another." She ignored the instant pang of guilt.

"Yeah, you're right. I think she's worried about us getting into something that will probably be temporary and not good for either of us."

Maura pursed her lips. "She gave me the same speech."

"And?"

She noted the combination of hope and dread in his eyes. "I think… I *know* that's a concern for me. I have a lot of serious issues to deal with at the moment, and frankly, a romance will only complicate things." His face fell in disappointment. "But," she quickly put in, "at the same time, I know I need some levity in my life."

"Levity? Sadly, I'm not known for my sense of humor or wit."

"You know what I mean. My family always referred to me as the 'serious' twin, and I think

I bought into that label, especially as a teenager, so I basically—"

"Lived up to it?"

"What can I say?" She sighed, dramatically.

He reached across the table to clasp her hand. "I definitely saw that side of you the last summer I was here, but now…"

"Now?" she prompted.

"Now I see that aloofness as reticence or—" his brow wrinkled in thought "—caution." He pressed her hand. "I think you were afraid of your own feelings back then. We all were! Teenagers and hormones. Not a great situation." He shook his head. "What I'm trying to say is that you shouldn't beat yourself up about how we behaved when we were that young."

"I know all that, but my current worries are adult ones, and totally realistic."

He reached for her other hand, wrapped around her coffee mug. "Here's my idea. Why not take this new situation between us as far as it will go over the next week or so? Let's simply get to know one another as adults. You can't deny that there's already a great dynamic happening, with Maddie, Luke, the donkeys…"

Her laugh raised a few heads in the busy diner.

"So, let's go along with it. Have some fun. Enjoy each other's company. When it's time to leave, you and I can talk. Maybe work something out."

She wanted to believe all that he said, but as she

nodded, part of her mind centered on one word: *maybe*. Still, he had a point. Some fun in her life—*and a little romance*—sounded like a good antidote to stress. "You're right. One day at a time kind of thing, then?"

"One day at a time and no analyzing or predicting as we go along."

"I see you already know things about me," she quipped.

"*Some* things, but my goal is everything."

She felt that shiver again and ducked her head from the intensity in his gaze. There was a rustling at her side as the server placed their order in front of them. Maura stared at the food. "What is this?"

"The daily special," said the server, in a weary tone. "Liver with onion gravy and mashed potatoes."

Catching Theo's expression as the woman walked away, Maura grinned. "Guess I skimmed over exactly what the special was."

He gave a forlorn nod. "The potatoes and gravy look good."

"Maybe leftovers for Shep?"

"Sounds like a plan."

Fifteen minutes later they waited while their server packaged up the remaining food. "Well, there's no other diner here in Wallingford, or even a fast-food outlet, so—"

"Ice cream to finish off?"

"Reading my mind."

They collected their container and headed for the ice cream parlor a block away. "This is one of Luke's new favorite places in the area," Theo said as they entered the busy shop and got in line.

"And the others?"

"One other—your farm with the donkeys." They moved forward a few inches, and then he added, "I'll be eternally grateful to you and Maddie for giving him the chance to help out."

"He's been great, otherwise we wouldn't have been so willing. We're getting a high school student for the summer. She helped out a bit in the early fall, when we were just starting up. The daughter of an old school friend and Bernie Watson's niece. And Ashley, that's her name, is also a second cousin of Sue Giordano, the owner of the bakery. She used to be a Webster."

Theo shook his head. "I'd forgotten—or maybe hadn't realized—all the intertwining of people in the Glen when I summered there. I do remember Sue, but only because Finn McAllister mentioned her when we met up at the festival planning committee. Luke and I've been into the bakery a couple of times but haven't met her in person yet."

"Do you remember the time she fell into Otter Creek and inhaled some water and was choking? You and Finn pulled her out."

"Right."

"See, you were destined for a career in helping people and saving lives." She was teasing but noted his red face.

"That was mostly Finn. I just followed his instructions. Not surprising that he went into search and rescue work. And speaking of that…"

He suddenly stopped.

"What? Speaking of what?"

"He told me that Shawn Harrison was moving back."

"To the Glen?"

"Or someplace nearby. He works for the Green Mountain Conservancy and is taking over the management of the county's section of the Trail."

Maura was speechless, mainly because the way word spread in the village guaranteed rapid public knowledge of every morsel of news or gossip. Did Maddie know? She was about to probe for more information when it was their turn to order, and all thoughts were immediately devoted to eating ice cream.

They were almost at the cutoff on Route 7 when Maura realized the clouds darkening to the south were now hovering directly over the Glen and the farm.

"Looks like rain," Theo remarked, peering out the windshield.

Maura pressed down on the accelerator.

"Is that a problem?" he asked, shifting his attention.

"It may well be. We wanted the donkeys to stay

out for a couple of days, until Roger and Shep are used to the barn and our routines."

"I've seen animals outside in rain."

"Sure, it's not a problem unless there's lightning and thunder. The problem is Matilda. She hates rain."

"Say again?" he asked, laughing.

"Seriously. If she's inside and it starts to rain, she won't go out. We've had to physically push and pull to get her out the barn door."

"Well, what will she do? She can't get out of the pasture and into the barn on her own."

"No, but she'll start braying, which will set off Jake and Lizzie. Then they'll charge toward the gate and press on it. Maddie won't be able to handle them on her own, and Luke isn't big or strong enough to be much help."

"Hmm, I get the picture. Maybe it'll hold off until we get there." He'd only finished the sentence when large drops splattered onto the windshield.

Maura gave the car a bit more gas, and they were driving up the lane when the rain fell faster, with more intensity. She parked, leaped out of the car while Theo was still unbuckling his seat belt and dashed past the barn toward the pasture. She could hear the earsplitting brays above the gusting wind and reached the fence in time to see Maddie struggling to grab hold of Matilda's halter while Luke stood behind the opened gate. Jake and Lizzie were pacing behind Matilda, and Maura's first troubled thought was that, in a panic, they might charge the gate, which Luke was holding.

"Get Lizzie," Maddie shouted when she saw her.

Maura guessed the plan. Lizzie and Jake could be left in the pasture, but unless Matilda was removed, they'd keep pushing at the gate until they, too, were out. She took in Luke's pale face as she squeezed past Matilda and grabbed hold of Lizzie's halter.

Maddie pulled Matilda through the opened gate just as Theo arrived. "Can you close the gate?" she hollered.

Maura saw both Luke and Theo struggling against the wind to push the gate. She let go of Lizzie, slapping her on the rump to encourage her to move away, and managed to slip out just before the gate clicked shut. Jake and Lizzie were still braying and pacing in circles on the other side of the fence. Maura pointed to Maddie and Matilda, heading for the barn.

"We need to go help," she shouted. "Roger and Shep are going to get caught up in all this racket."

The din continued into the barn, where Roger, in his stall, had joined in and Shep started barking. Despite being out of the rain, Matilda kept braying and snorting, now alarmed by the presence of a strange donkey and a potential predator—a dog. Maura rushed to Roger's stall, easing open the door so that Shep, leaping against it from the other side, wouldn't escape and cause even more panic for Matilda. She forced herself to keep calm, making shushing noises to let Roger and Shep know everything was okay. She cautiously approached Roger from his good side, keeping as clear of his legs as possible. Getting kicked by a frightened donkey wasn't how she wanted the day to end.

By now Maddie had secured Matilda in her stall, trying to calm her as well. Maura figured the two animals would quiet down eventually, but she knew some factor in the noise equation would have to change. Theo and Luke, covering their ears, entered the barn. Maura scanned the scene around her—two noisy donkeys, a barking dog, three adults and a boy all holding hands against their ears. It reminded her of a Christmas carol, and she smiled at the random thought.

Luke reached the stall as Maura, stroking Roger's head, grabbed hold of his halter. The kid seemed to know intuitively what to do, she later thought, as he stooped over the closed stall door and beckoned to Shep. "Here, Shep!"

Maura watched the dog trot over to Luke, who held out his hands. Did he have a treat of some kind? Then she remembered the incident earlier, when Shep had smelled peanut butter on Luke's fingers. Sure enough, Shep began to lick them again, wagging his tail. Seconds after Shep stopped barking, Roger stopped braying. Maura exhaled. She let go of Roger's halter and worked her way around him and out of the stall. She saw that Maddie had managed to soothe Matilda and was now latching that stall door.

Except for Matilda's chomping on some hay in her trough, Shep whining for more attention from Luke, and Roger shuffling nervously in his stall, the barn was quiet. After a few seconds, Maura said, "Tea, anyone? Coffee?"

"Something stronger?" Theo suggested.

Maura and Maddie laughed at the pitch in his question. "Some caffeine, I think," Maura said. "Luke, can you try to get Shep to come into the house with you? I want Matilda to get accustomed to Roger first, then Jake and Lizzie tomorrow. After that, we'll see how Shep fits in."

"But he will, won't he? I mean, this is his home now."

The combination of anxiety and optimism in Luke's voice touched Maura. She'd have replied, "I hope so," but knew he was looking for reassurance. "It may take a few days, or even a week, but he will," she said.

Maddie looked out through the large, open barn door. "The rain is tapering off. I'm going to check on Jake and Lizzie. And I'll have tea, not coffee," she said over her shoulder as she left the barn.

"Want me to get the liver from the car?" Theo asked.

"Liver?" Luke's jaw dropped.

"We'll explain over coffee, or tea," Theo said, grinning at Maura.

She watched him walking to the car, thinking about the agreement they'd struck at the diner. His broad-shouldered back and long stride reflected the confident, strong man Theo Danby had become. She could hardly wait to learn more about him—his view of the world, his private thoughts and even his secrets. But was there time for all of that? *Maybe I'll have to content myself with the taste of his lips or the warmth of his hand in mine. Perhaps that will be enough.*

"Maura?" Luke's voice broke into her thoughts. "Will you help me get Shep out of the stall?"

They returned to Roger's stall and Maura slowly opened the door, keeping herself between it and Roger. "Call him, Luke. But quietly."

Luke extended his hands in a beckoning gesture. "Here, Shep. Come."

The dog scanned the stall, his dark brown eyes lingering a minute on Roger, and then walked out to Luke. Maura closed the door. Roger was either unaware of the dog leaving or unbothered. A good omen, she thought, as she followed Luke and Shep.

Theo was waiting by the kitchen door. He held up the Styrofoam container of liver. "Lunch for Shep. And maybe a snack for us humans?"

"I'm starving!" Luke exclaimed.

"Not to worry," Maura said. She smiled at Luke, tousling his hair. "Plenty of food for us, too."

She led the way into the mudroom, where everyone slipped out of their wet shoes while Shep trotted nonchalantly into the kitchen, as if he'd been living there all his life. A sense of contentment washed through Maura. This felt like...*like a family.*

CHAPTER TWELVE

THEO SAT, phone in hand, for a long moment. He had the kitchen to himself, and his sigh was loud in the quiet room. Thank goodness Luke was still asleep, another sign of his soon-to-be teens. The news he'd received from Trish didn't bode well for Theo's improving connection with his son.

When she'd asked him to take Luke for the summer, Theo had suspected she was making plans that involved a move and, possibly, a remarriage. None of that was a surprise for Theo. The affair with a colleague of hers had been revealed a year ago, and after a few months' separation, she and Theo had gotten a divorce—uncontested and polite. Not because he didn't care for her, but by then he'd realized the marriage had begun to dissolve long before.

Everything had moved at a dizzying pace, and Theo, struggling with the stress of running the emergency department along with the unexpected death of a patient he'd come to like and admire, hadn't had the stomach to contest any of her conditions. For Luke's sake, he'd refused to drag the whole sad story into court. She could continue to live in their home in Augusta, Maine, with Luke, whose school was nearby, but when Luke started high school, they'd sell the family home, split the money and discuss with whom Luke would live. They'd been frank with Luke, explaining their plans and assuring him he'd share both parents. But now…

He'd tried to negotiate more time in the half-hour phone call, but she was adamant. The couple were moving out of state next month, and Luke would have to go with them or stay with Theo. There were so many problems with that scenario that Theo couldn't think straight. When she'd hung up, asking him to discuss it with Luke and make a decision as soon as possible, Theo had sat, staring blankly at the run-down kitchen, as if he could find an answer in its cracked walls and worn floor tiles. If his own situation were uncomplicated, he'd reorganize his life and his work. But right now, there were no other career opportunities at his hospital. He'd been granted the six weeks' leave for some much-needed rest and a chance to "clear his head," as the administrative chief had recommended. Ha! If only.

The decision to return to Vermont to take care of his inheritance and show his son Maple Glen, where he'd spent his summers, had certainly improved his sleep and appetite, and taken his mind off the twenty-four-hours-a-day demands of the emergency department. Except the return had also raised an unexpected glitch. *Maura Stuart.*

Last night had been fun. They'd impulsively ordered pizzas that Maddie had picked up, leaving Theo, Maura and Luke to get the animals settled. They'd brought Jake into the barn, after realizing that Matilda had accepted Roger's presence. Lizzie, Maura asserted, would have to wait. By the time the pizzas were consumed, Jake had ceased stamping his hooves on the stall floor and snickering warnings to Roger. Introducing the donkeys to Shep, who'd be staying in the house, could wait a day or so.

The night was quiet when Theo and Luke finally headed home, pushing through the cedar hedges and pausing to gaze up at the sky littered with thousands of twinkling stars. Theo had scarcely listened to Luke's ongoing recount of the day, his mind dwelling on the possibility of some kind of relationship with the person he'd been smitten with years before. He'd been filled with such comforting hopes—even dreams—of the future that his sleep had been deep and restful, a record for him.

Now he went through all the potential reactions from Luke about this new development. Of course, their stay in the Glen had always been finite. In fact, his original plan had been to clear out, sell and leave all in a week, ten days max. That goal had passed without event yesterday, and he was no closer to selling than he had been his first day back. The crux of the problem was that he was no longer in a hurry. He still had four weeks left, and since his talk with Maura, he planned to make full use of every minute of that time. Maple Glen wasn't that far from Augusta. Seeing one another would be complicated, given his work schedule and her responsibilities with Jake & Friends, but not impossible.

The reality that Luke might not be part of that scenario, assuming his son would choose to live with his mother, altered everything. The converse, that Luke would want to live with Theo, was equally problematic. Theo's hospital job meant Luke would be alone a lot—too much, Theo figured, for a young teenager with divorced parents. He could relate, because his own parents had divorced when he was nine, the first summer he came to stay with his aunt and uncle. And how lucky he was to have the couple and their farm as a refuge against the loneliness and insecurity of those early postdivorce years. Who would Luke have, with his mother many miles away and his father rotating through long shifts?

He got up and poured himself a third cup of coffee. When he heard the slam of the bathroom door upstairs, he popped some bread into the toaster and took the peanut butter and jam out of the fridge. Luke's fussiness over food was gradually shifting into teen territory, with a bigger appetite and more willingness to experiment, but PBJ remained a staple. He was spreading those condiments on the toast when Luke came into the kitchen, his hair still damp from a shower. Another milestone of sorts, Theo thought with a smile. No reminding necessary.

Luke snatched a piece of toast and started munching as he opened the fridge to take out the milk. "Are you going to sit for breakfast, or eat on the run?" Theo asked.

"I'll sit but only for a few minutes, Dad. The new volunteer is coming in this morning, and Maddie said I could work with her. She's in ninth grade and worked with the donkeys last fall. Her name is Ashley Watson and guess what? She's related to the man who owns the B and B where we stayed our first night here."

That explained the shower. "You didn't mention you'd be working with her."

"Maddie said it was a possibility, so I decided to—"

"Err on the side of safety by taking a shower anyway, 'cause Ashley is a girl?" he teased.

"C'mon, Dad. Gross." But his blush was telling. "Anyway, can you check your messages and see if Maddie let you know?" He heaved a loud sigh. "If I had my own phone, we wouldn't have to do this!"

Theo peered down at his phone, grinning as he logged in. But the realization that Luke would definitely need a phone in the fall, if he was on his own with him in Augusta, hit hard. His vision blurred as he scrolled to his messages, finding an unread one sent while he was on the phone with Trish. He cleared his throat and waited a second longer. "Yeah, Maddie says come over anytime."

Luke fist-pumped the air. "Yes!" He got up, swallowed some milk, grabbed the other piece of toast and headed for the door.

"Hey, hold on a second. What's the plan, then? Are you there all morning or…?"

"I don't know. Does it matter? When I finish there, I'll just come home."

Home. Theo had no idea when exactly that word first applied to the decrepit farmhouse as far as Luke was concerned, but his son's casual use of the term brought another lump in his throat.

"What about you, Dad? What's happening with you today?"

The grown-up question, coming from the son who could barely utter a whole sentence to him the first week of their road trip, was overwhelming. He couldn't speak until Luke got to the kitchen door. "Um, not sure. Maura asked me to go with her to a planning meeting for the festival this afternoon. And the real-estate agent is coming by this morning with the surveyor's report." He added the last part as a gentle reminder that their stay at the farm was temporary, something he had to keep in mind himself.

Luke didn't turn around, but mumbled something that Theo couldn't decipher, which he figured was just as well. Perhaps his son had the same conflicting feelings about leaving Maple Glen as he had. Theo rubbed his forehead, going back to the early-morning phone call about Luke's future, and felt the energy he'd awakened with that morning draining out of him.

The Realtor arrived an hour later to report that the survey was all in order, as Theo had anticipated. She brought a For Sale sign that she hammered into the lawn near the road. After she left, Theo's outlook on the day took a nosedive. Weeks ago, he'd expected to celebrate this moment—the final resolution of his inheritance. Instead, his whole body seemed to sag under the weight of regret and nostalgia. He thought back to his persuasive message to Maura at the diner in Wallingford. *Let's just enjoy our time together—get to know one another. Have fun.*

If only life—and love—were that simple.

MADDIE NOTICED THE sign first because she was driving, and the Danby farm was on her side. She turned sharply to Maura. "Did you see that?"

Maura craned her neck as they sped by. She was so startled she couldn't speak. Of course, she ought to have remembered that the sign and all it represented was inevitable, like Theo's leaving the Glen. But a big part of her mind, and heart, had resisted accepting that hard fact. *He might have told me*, she was thinking.

"I guess this was inevitable," Maddie murmured, eerily echoing Maura's thoughts. After a brief silence, she added, "Life goes on, doesn't it?"

Maura felt a rise of annoyance. "For heaven's sake, Mads. Cut the corny philosophizing." She averted her head and stared bleakly out the passenger-side window until they reached the community center. The small parking lot was packed with vehicles, so Maddie pulled onto the adjacent side street and parked.

Before Maura could get out, Maddie grabbed her forearm. "I'm sorry, Mo. That was silly. I didn't intend to trivialize what you must be feeling about Theo leaving. Forgive me?"

Maura didn't smile, but she nodded. "If my twin can't bring me down to earth, no one can."

"Thanks, and I'll try not to puncture your balloon of happiness any more than I have to."

This time Maura smiled. "Likewise, sis." Then she recalled Theo's news yesterday about Shawn Harrison. The whole brouhaha with the donkeys had erased that bit of information from her mind. She was about to mention it when a tap sounded at Maddie's window. It was Sue Giordano. Maddie rolled down her window.

"Hey, ladies! Haven't seen you gals in ages. What's up? Not eating carbs these days?"

"You're kidding, of course," Maddie said.

"We've been too busy feeding donkeys," Maura said, leaning forward. She finished unbuckling and got out of the truck.

"I brought some treats with me for the volunteers, so you'll get your fill." Sue held up two canvas bags.

"Can't wait," Maddie said as she followed Maura out.

"I heard Theo Danby's been back in the Glen for more than a week, and I still haven't seen him."

Maura resisted glancing at her sister. "I know he's been into the bakery. His son, Luke, is already a big fan, Sue."

"A son? No kidding. Is there a wife, too?"

Maura kept her eyes on the open front door of the community center, but heard Maddie say, "They're divorced. Sue, are you setting up a table of your bestsellers on the Fourth of July? Because I haven't received your registration form yet."

"You bet! I've even persuaded my niece to help sell. I'll get the form to you right away. How many tables have you got registered now?"

Maddie reached into her handbag and pulled out a small notebook. "Let me see." She flipped through some pages. "About thirty-five so far, and I'm hoping to sign up more at the meeting. Plus, a woman from the co-op in Wallingford told me a few people there have filled out the forms and paid her the fee."

Sue screwed up her face in thought. "So thirty-five tables for sure, times the twenty-five-dollar fee… That's a good start on our goal of a thousand or more for the community center's new roof. Oh, there's Barb," she said, spotting a friend entering the building. "Okay, see you ladies inside."

Maura watched her greet the friend—not a Glen resident, she thought—and turned to Maddie. "By the way, Theo told me—"

"What did I tell you?"

Maura swung around as Theo came up beside her. "Oh…uh…that…you know…you were going to section off the whole side of your frontage for vehicle parking." Theo's arched eyebrow and Maddie's frown caused more hesitation. "And… um…is Luke here? Did he tell you he and Ashley really hit it off this morning?"

"He did and he also said she's going to introduce him to some other kids here. Apparently, there's some kind of youth club every Friday evening, so he's excited about going with her this Friday. Right now, he's just hanging out at the farm. I left my phone with him so he could play some games."

"Uh-oh," said Maura "The slippery slope…"

"Yep. A matter of time, I think."

"Ashley lives on the next street over from this one." Maura pointed to her left and was about to relate some family history when Maddie interrupted.

"Maura, I already knew about Theo's offer of

land for parking. I was at that meeting, too, re-member?"

"Oh, right. Anyway, we better get inside and grab a good seat." She hustled toward the center door, aware that she'd left Theo and her sister with the impression that she was really losing it. And she was, she told herself. Why would she want to blurt out the news about Shawn Harrison right before a community meeting?

By the time the three of them found seats, Bernie was calling the meeting to order. Maura tuned out while people stood to give their updated reports, followed by an occasional round of questions. At last, Maddie stood to give her report—an update on the number of tables, a plea for more registra-tions, and an announcement that the final numbers had to be in by the coming weekend.

"Maura and I will create a map so people will know where their tables will be located, and we're asking that everyone with tables arrive at the farm by nine that morning, which should give every-one plenty of time, as I think we decided the of-ficial start would be eleven. Right?" She directed this last word to Bernie, at the front of the room.

"Yes, Maddie. Folks, try to get your table or-ganized well before that time, though. And you'll have a map of the whole festival area for them, as well, is that right, Maddie?"

"Yes, Bernie. We'll have the layout on a large board, and to be clear, the table area will be our entire front lawn, with spillover onto the northwest pasture. The donkeys will be in the riding ring, for petting and… We haven't decided yet about giving rides. However, some of the shady areas on the front lawn and maybe the veranda will be allocated to parents with small children or seniors needing some quiet time."

"Hey! We seniors are just as hardy as everyone else," someone called out, and the room erupted with chuckles.

Maura caught Maddie's eye and grinned. Then she whispered, "The first aid station?"

"Oh, I almost forgot." Maddie raised her voice, stilling the buzz of chatter. "The first aid station will also be located on the front lawn." A hand shot up from the first row.

Maura couldn't see who wanted to speak until Finn McAllister stood up.

"Guess I might as well step into this conversation now, Maddie, if you're finished?" When Maddie nodded and sat down, he went on to say, "I've got everything organized for our station, with a rotating team of volunteers from the fire department. Oh, and two of my men are bringing our main engine for kids to see and maybe even sit on, so I'll have to confer with the Stuarts and Theo Danby about the best place to park it."

The room broke into more chatter until Finn held up a hand. "One more thing—and this is nice news for us longtime Glen residents. I've enlisted another volunteer who's not only well qualified but will soon be the administrator of the county's Green Mountain Conservancy search and rescue department." Finn motioned to a man sitting at his side.

A swell of dread surged up from the pit of Maura's stomach. She glanced at her sister—calm, impassive and unsuspecting.

"Let's give a hand for a guy some of us remember as a nerdy teenager—Shawn Harrison." There was some applause, a sharp whistle from the back of the room and more talk as a few people stood to see over the heads in front of them.

Maura kept her eyes on Maddie, whose face was now the color of new-fallen snow. She clasped her sister's hand in hers, squeezing gently, as a ruggedly handsome man got to his feet and turned around to wave at the crowd. Maddie's grip on Maura's hand tightened. "It's okay, Mo. I'm fine," she whispered.

But as soon as Shawn sat back down, Maddie got up and began pushing her way across the row of chairs. Maura was about to follow when Theo, sitting next to her, grabbed her elbow. "Better to leave her. She won't want to have any further attention focused on her."

He was right.

The meeting broke up shortly after Maddie left, and when Maura exited the hall, she couldn't see her sister anywhere, nor could she see their truck.

Stifling a curse, she went back to look for Theo, somewhere in the crowd of people mingling outside. She could easily walk home, but a ride with Theo meant another chance to be alone with him, and maybe tell him about the loan.

He was in the last group leaving the center, and as Maura wound her way through the small clusters of people, she spotted him talking with Shawn. She hesitated for a minute, then told herself she was not only being silly, but unrealistic. From what Finn had said, Shawn would be living in the area, perhaps permanently.

As for Maddie…she decided not to think about the possibility that her sister's commitment to staying may now be hinged on Shawn's move. When Theo caught sight of her and beckoned, Maura took a deep breath and walked over to say hello to the man her twin had been madly in love with years ago, and deeply hurt by.

"Welcome back to the Glen, Shawn," she said as she joined them, hanging back just far enough that a handshake or a hug would be awkward.

"Good to see you again, Maura. It's been a long time." His smile was warm, which eased some of her tension.

"Seems like some of the Glen gang have moved back, despite our vows not to."

"You never know the opportunities life will throw at you," he said. "Finn told me that you and Maddie have donkeys and are running a riding therapy program at your parents' farm now. That's pretty awesome."

"Well, it's a business venture and we enjoy it. And congratulations to you on this new job of yours. Have you been in search and rescue long?"

"I got into it when I was in the army, and after my discharge, I took some courses. Started with the Conservancy a few years ago. The chance to head up things here was irresistible."

"And your parents?"

"Enjoying retirement in Florida."

There was a lull after this, and Maura was about to ask Theo for a ride home when she realized she'd also have to mention Maddie leaving with the truck.

As if reading her mind, Theo asked, "Want a lift back to the farm?"

"Yes, thanks." She was about to add that she'd wait for him at his car when Shawn spoke up.

"How's Maddie? I heard her report but couldn't see her from where I was sitting at the front. Is she still here?" He quickly scanned the remaining people.

"Uh, no. She had to get back to the farm for the animals."

Another long pause until Theo said, "Good to see you again, Shawn. Drop by the farm sometime."

"Thanks, Theo. I'm currently staying in a rental unit in Bennington, where my office is located, but I'm hoping to find a place closer to Maple

Glen. The lure of nature…plus the Trail. Have you been out on it yet?"

"I have once, with my son, and will try to get some more hiking in before we leave."

"I'm looking forward to a combination of work and hiking. Finn and I are going out for an inspection tomorrow. You and your son are free to join us, if you like."

"That sounds good, though I'll have to check with Luke. Lately, he's begun to make his own social plans."

Shawn chuckled. "Okay, well, now that we've exchanged phone numbers, text and let me know by eight in the morning," he said.

Maura felt Theo glancing her way but kept her eyes focused on Shawn. His nerdy teenage self had morphed into an attractive man—burlier than, but not as tall as, Theo. His hair was military-style short, and she thought she saw some silvery strands in it, but the thick, horn-rimmed glasses of his adolescence had been replaced by trendier frames.

"Will do. Uh, Maura," Theo said, breaking into her thoughts, "are you ready to leave now, or…?"

"Oh, yes. Thanks, Theo. And nice to see you, Shawn."

As she and Theo began to walk away, Shawn called out, "Say hi to Maddie for me."

She didn't reply, but kept pace with Theo. When they reached his car parked farther up the side street where her own truck had been, Theo said, "Don't get ahead of yourself, Maura."

"What do you mean by that?"

"Just that once Maddie is used to the idea of Shawn being around, there won't be a problem. I'm sure there'll be some tension between them at first. That's only to be expected. But they've both gone on with their lives."

Maybe so, she was thinking as she stopped to get into Theo's car. As for his advice not to get ahead of herself, she already had dozens of questions demanding answers, and she knew Maddie would be grilling her with even more once she was home.

But there was one above all that she needed to know right away. "Is he married?"

Theo was starting the car and shrugged. "I don't know."

Maura sighed. Trust a man not to find out the most important bit of information.

CHAPTER THIRTEEN

MAURA PITCHED THE last forkful of hay into Roger's trough and listened to the other donkeys munching contentedly on her way out of the barn. She'd awakened at daybreak after a restless night and, noting the gray clouds to the east, decided to bring the donkeys in from the field. This way, she and Maddie wouldn't need to corral a panicked Matilda. She couldn't remember the riders booked for today, but if the clouds became a full-out storm, she and Maddie would call them to reschedule.

When Theo had dropped her off at the farm after the meeting yesterday, he'd given her one more piece of advice that she'd heeded. *Let Maddie be the one to start talking about Shawn.*

She'd been grateful for that, because she knew she tended to push people, especially her sister. It wasn't until after a mostly silent supper that Maddie got around to talking, and for the first time Maura heard the full story of the sudden breakup that had blindsided her sister in her freshman year.

"I never got a clear reason from him. I swear there was no sign at all, except he was moody and very distant for a couple of weeks before," she'd told Maura. "I heard through mutual friends that he left university before the end of the year with no explanation even to them." She'd paused to collect herself. "He never wrote or got in touch with me."

She'd stopped then and, after a moment, Maura told her own story—how she'd always measured any potential partners against her teenage memory of Theo. "I know I passed up a couple of chances to have something special with someone, but I knew I'd be making comparisons. How ridiculous is that, right? Clinging to a memory from years before! Now I have this unexpected second chance with him, and there are so many obstacles to the possibility of anything developing that I...I can't even—"

"Don't." Maddie had placed her hand on Maura's arm. "Just let it all play out. Worry about things when...when his farm is sold." Maura had nodded, but she was thinking, *By then it will be too late*.

"I hope you'll take that advice, too, Mads. With Shawn."

"I'll have to, won't I? If he's going to be living here. Unless..."

Maura hadn't wanted to hear what her sister had left unsaid and, yawning, had used fatigue as a pretext to head to bed.

Now Maddie was making coffee when Maura entered the kitchen from the mudroom. "I put the donkeys into the barn because it looks like rain, coming from the east."

Her sister peered out the window over the kitchen sink. "Hmm, good idea. Didn't you say last night that Shawn had invited Theo and Luke to walk the Trail with him and Finn?"

Maura marveled that Maddie could utter Shawn's name with such ease. A good omen. "Yeah. But who knows—the weather could make a sharp right turn and head north to Montpelier."

Maddie laughed. "Oh, I've missed that great line of Dad's, Mo. I remember how he always had some reason for us not to stay home from school, no matter how hard we tried to convince him and Mom that a storm was brewing, and the buses would surely be canceled."

Speaking of Dad, this was a good time. "Did you ever wonder how Dad managed to cover Mom's medical expenses?"

At that precise moment, Maddie turned on the coffee bean grinder. When she finished dumping the ground coffee into the filter, she looked across the room and said, "Sorry, you were saying?"

"Um, just thinking of Mom and Dad, and how they must have struggled to pay for Mom's health care."

"I assume they had some kind of insurance, didn't they?"

"Maybe."

"Well, we just saw his bank manager and there were no outstanding debts from when he was alive, so…"

"True, but it was odd that he withdrew fifty dollars a month like clockwork, always the day he got his pension money. I mean, such a regular amount, and it wasn't for living expenses, because those were obvious in his bank statements," Maura said, wending a circuitous path to her revelation.

Maddie flipped the On button of the coffee maker. She reached into the cupboard for mugs and turned to ask, "Are you having toast this morning or cereal?"

"Cereal," she said. The moment was passing, Maura realized, and she felt some relief as she let it go, rationalizing later that it was Maddie's next comment that got her attention.

"I can't believe Shawn enlisted in the army. Did that happen before or after he graduated?"

"He didn't say. Why? Do you think it's peculiar that he did?" Maura poured milk over her granola and sat down at the table to eat.

"He never seemed the army type, and he's an only child, so he'd have left his parents on their own, which must have been difficult."

"Maybe he just wanted to get away. I don't know where he was deployed, but it could have been Afghanistan. He did mention it was the army that led into his search and rescue work." When Maddie didn't respond, Maura went on to say, "How do you feel about bumping into him, either before or at the festival?"

"It won't be a problem. I'm fine." Her eyes locked on Maura's. "Seriously, Mo, I'm not so fragile. Not anymore. Besides, I may not be around too much longer myself." She finished her coffee and took her breakfast dishes to the sink. "I don't think that storm is going to make a right turn. It's coming our way."

"Guess we should start making phone calls," Maura automatically said, though a large part of her brain was still processing the dropped information she'd feared.

"We had four riders set for today, and one is a newbie. Let's hope we can rebook them all."

"Why don't you do that while I call our volunteers?" Maura waited until Maddie left the room, then got up to take her cereal bowl and coffee mug to the sink. Her hand shook as she rinsed them, and she silently wished Shawn Harrison had never returned to Maple Glen.

The rain started shortly after Maura finished her phone calls. She debated texting Theo to advise Luke that there wouldn't be any riders today but remembered that he might be hiking, too, unless their plans changed due to the weather.

She was restless, hemmed in not only by the rain but by circumstance. She couldn't spontaneously visit Theo to discuss their future, if any, because Luke would be there, and she didn't know what Theo might have told him about their relationship. Merely thinking that word caused Maura to pull a face. It was such a generic term and could mean anything. Or worse, nothing at all.

Still, it wasn't likely that Theo would talk to Luke about her...*them*...considering their time in the Glen was now coming to an end. They'd be staying for the festival, but what would be the point in lingering afterward? Theo didn't have to wait until the farm was sold. If time was running out for Theo, it certainly was for Maura, too.

She heard Maddie on the phone upstairs in her bedroom and went into the den and her father's desk, where she'd found the envelope with the loan agreement. By the time she'd searched through every drawer, looking for any piece of paper or bank statement confirming the loan repayment, Maddie was coming downstairs.

"What're you doing?" she asked, seeing Maura leaving the den.

"I...I was just looking for..." she stammered, thinking of an excuse. But looking at her sister's face, both puzzled and a tad concerned, Maura knew this was the time. "Mads, let's go sit in the living room. I have something to tell you."

When Maura finished speaking, silence fell over the room. Maddie had averted her face partway through, staring bleakly out the bay window at the rain. After what seemed like ages, she rubbed her hands across her face, took a long breath and asked, "Have you told Theo?"

Maura shook her head.

"Do it. Right away." Then she stood up and left the room.

Maura blinked back unexpected tears. She'd never seen her sister with such a grim, unyielding expression. *What did you expect? If you'd told her in the beginning, you both could have dealt with the problem.* She knew Maddie would forgive her, hopefully in a matter of days. As for Theo...the odds of their newfound relationship continuing up to the festival and beyond weren't looking great.

"HAVE YOU GOT rain gear?" Finn asked.

"Nothing good enough." Cell phone in hand, Theo walked over to the kitchen window. The rain was still hammering down. "I'd be up for it, but I wouldn't want Luke to come. He's only been out with me once and—"

"Yeah, not a good idea. I'd cancel myself but Shawn is still keen. We'll probably only walk to the junction."

Where the off trail joined up with the main one, Theo was thinking. "I could leave Luke here on his own, but it's a rainy day and he'd probably get antsy." There was the option of Luke helping out in some way at the Stuarts', but he figured there'd be no riders that day, and it wasn't fair to expect Maura and Maddie to be supervising his son. The other problem, an inescapable one, was that Trish had texted first thing that morning to ask if he'd had the discussion yet about Luke's coming school year.

"Honestly, I think Luke and I should bow out today, Finn. Another time?"

"Can't say I blame you. For sure, another time. Talk to you later," he said, hanging up.

Luke appeared at the kitchen door as Theo was setting his phone onto the table. "Are we still going today or what?" he asked.

"Finn and Shawn are, but I decided it wasn't a good idea for us to go." He saw the disappointed frown and added, "Maybe we could check out another movie in Rutland."

"Sure." He didn't sound enthusiastic.

"Got any other ideas?"

"What if I went next door to see if I can help with anything?"

"I doubt there'll be any riders today, Luke." Theo gestured to the kitchen window.

"Still, there's other work to be done, you know. Mucking out, or grooming, or whatever."

Theo couldn't help but smile. None of those terms would have been familiar, much less of interest, to his son before coming to the Glen. "Maura and her sister might be busy. I know they still have some organizing for the festival, and it's only a week away now."

"Can you text them and find out?"

Theo sighed. Clearly his son wasn't getting his hint about infringing on the Stuarts' hospitality. "I suppose." But when he went to text Maura, the earlier one from his ex popped up in the thread of messages. Perhaps right now, he thought, and the promised movie could help soften the inevitable blow when he told him his mother's news.

"Tomorrow's Friday, and won't you be riding with Katie again?"

"Oh, right. Yeah."

"So maybe wait to visit the farm until tomorrow morning?"

His shrug was half-hearted, but Theo figured he'd be fine with a movie. "Okay, so a movie for sure, after lunch. I'll check what's playing... but first, um...I have something to pass by you. Have a seat."

He'd barely begun when the first interruption came. "She's getting *married*? To *Joel*?"

"I'm sure you suspected that would happen, didn't you?" Theo was a bit worried by the look of horror on Luke's face but kept his voice level. "And, uh, do you have a problem with Joel?"

"He's okay, I guess," Luke mumbled. "But he's really boring, and he talks a *lot*!"

Boring was okay, Theo decided, hiding a smile. He went on to explain Trish's options: move with them to Washington State in early August or live with Theo. After a year, they could renegotiate.

"So if I went there, I'd have to switch schools?"

Theo tried to find something to counter the growing unease on his son's face. "It would only be a year and—"

"I'd be leaving all my friends, that I've known forever!" He leaped to his feet. "And…and if I live with you, that means I'll be alone while you're at the hospital! Like last year, when you had to cancel a lot of my weekends with you because you had to work."

This was the dilemma Theo had struggled with since getting Trish's ultimatum. His position in Emergency meant long, unpredictable hours. Luke was twelve, going on thirteen, but would still need some kind of supervision and, especially, companionship. "I'm hoping to figure that out, Luke."

He cringed at the pessimistic tone of his voice and took a deep breath, about to aim for a more positive note when Luke shouted, "No way for any of this! It's not fair!" He ran out of the room and thumped upstairs to his bedroom.

Theo decided to let Luke have some time to himself and was about to make sandwiches for lunch when his phone pinged. It was the real-estate agent.

"I have an interested party," she told him when he answered. "It's a property development firm in Burlington. They want to know if they can send a couple of people out to have a look at your place. Probably an engineer of some kind and an architect. I'm not sure. Is there a day early next week when they could come?"

"I think so. Hang on." Theo checked his phone calendar, noting only the festival on the Thursday, which was a holiday anyway. "Any day but obviously not the Fourth."

"Great. I'll get back to you as soon as I know."

After she hung up, Theo sat for a while, thinking that despite living in the idyllic bubble of Maple Glen, events in the outside world were ticking along at normal speed. He'd simply forgotten that, although Trish's news should have been a reminder. He closed his eyes, his mind suddenly going back to Luke's last words—*"It's not fair!"*—as he left the kitchen. *My sentiments exactly, my boy.* It didn't seem fair that his return here should raise so many conflicting emotions, the strongest being a desire to stay.

There was no way around the problem, he knew. Leaving the Glen was inevitable, and it was time he and Luke accepted that reality. He picked up his phone again and, wandering into the living room, browsed movie options and times. There were a couple that might appease Luke.

When he returned to the kitchen to make lunch, he noticed the back door was ajar. Frowning, he peered out to the yard before closing the door. Then a gut instinct led him to the bottom of the staircase. "Luke? You ready for lunch?"

No answer. He took the stairs two at a time

and strode down the hall to Luke's room, which was empty. Swearing under his breath, he phoned Maura. The call went to voice mail, and he left a brief message asking her to let him know if Luke had gone over to their place.

Almost ten minutes later, she called. "Hi, Theo. Sorry I didn't get back to you sooner, but I was charging my phone, and yes, he's here. Is everything okay? He seems a bit out of sorts."

"He's upset about some news I had to share with him. Um, I'll come over and get him, okay?"

"Sure, but he's fine. He and Maddie are grooming the donkeys. Do you want him home?"

Theo figured that donkey grooming would work better than a movie. "No, no, it's okay. We'd talked about a movie but obviously he'd rather be there."

There was a brief pause. Then she said, "You're welcome to come by, too. An extra hand with grooming and all."

Her light laugh sounded a bit strained. Perhaps he ought to go over, make sure Luke hadn't arrived there at an awkward time. He recalled Maddie rushing out of the meeting yesterday after Shawn's introduction. Perhaps there was some emotional aftermath she was dealing with. He'd check out the situation and bring Luke home if necessary. Besides, looking ahead to the future, there would be fewer opportunities to spend time with Maura.

"Sure, okay. Thanks."

He wrapped up the sandwiches he'd made and was about to head for the car, but noting the rain was still teeming down, he ran upstairs to get a change of clothes for Luke. The fact that the boy had run off like that worried him. It might be no big deal here, because other than the Stuart farm, there were few places for him to go. But in Augusta…one more issue to deal with, he figured, as he drove next door.

Despite his instant apology to Maura when she opened the kitchen back door, Theo saw that something was troubling her. Perhaps Luke had told them about the plans for the coming year.

"Come on in," she said. "I told Luke you were coming over but…"

"Was he unhappy about that?"

"Not exactly, and it seemed he was expecting you to show up."

"We had a bit of a…not an argument, more like a tiff."

"Oh? Do you want to talk about it?" She motioned to a kitchen chair and sat opposite.

He set the bag of sandwiches on the table and slumped onto the chair. "It had to do with an ultimatum from my ex—Trish." He saw the gleam of interest in her eyes. "She's getting married and moving out of state. What she wants is for Luke to either decide to go with her for a year or stay with me."

"Ouch. That's a tough one for a twelve-year-old."

"Tell me about it. I've heard his arguments. Anyway, I'm sure he'll get used to the idea eventually, and at least there's the festival next week. We're definitely staying for that, now I've committed my land for parking."

"That's great, Theo. I was hoping…you know… that you'd be around a bit longer."

"I was, too, Maura." He reached across the table for her hand. "I think staying for the festival has always been in the cards after our…you know…our decision to get to know one another more. To enjoy being together."

She squeezed his hand before withdrawing hers. "Yes," she murmured.

Her lack of enthusiasm was puzzling, but Theo guessed she might be thinking about the For Sale sign at the front of his property. "And you'll let me know if there's anything Luke and I can do to help you and Maddie—for next week, I mean."

"For sure." She got up and went over to the counter, staring out the window over the sink.

Theo wondered if she and Maddie had had a difficult conversation about Shawn, after the meeting yesterday. That could explain the flat response to his offer of help. This obviously wasn't a good time for entertaining unexpected visitors.

"Say, you know what? I'll take these sandwiches out to Luke and give him and Maddie a hand with the grooming. Then we'll head out, as there's a movie we might see in Rutland."

That seemed to rouse more energy from her. "Sure, okay. It's just that Mads and I still have to assign people to tables and map out where they'll go."

"No problem." He stood to leave, but some impulse made him add, "I have some work cut out for me, too. There's a potential buyer coming early next week, and I have yet to finish going through everything in Uncle Stan's office. Okay, well…see you tomorrow?"

He waited a few seconds before she finally murmured, "Sure."

Theo decided that was all he was going to get from her and headed to the barn. Something was definitely amiss with the woman he cared for, and the dark cloud hanging over him since Luke's outburst was just getting bigger and bigger.

CHAPTER FOURTEEN

"I UNDERSTAND WHY you didn't tell him yesterday," Maddie said, "but don't leave it any longer. Especially if people are coming to look at the property. They have a right to know about the possibility that the acreage will be different."

"I know that, Mads, but first I think you and I need to go through every bit of paper left in the house to find out if Dad repaid the loan." Maura slipped her boots on and followed her sister out the door to the barn.

"We've seen his accounts and there's no record of any payment."

"What about the fifty-dollar withdrawals every month, right up to Dad's stroke? He could have been giving that money to Stan and Vera."

Maddie snorted. "It would have barely made a dent in the total amount."

"Still…"

"Which is why you need to tell Theo, so he can search for any papers, too," Maddie said as she headed for Jake's stall.

Maura scanned the barn, looking for Shep. She'd let him out of the house earlier and figured he'd go to the barn, where he usually parked outside Roger's stall. Both Shep and Roger had adjusted to the change in their routine at the farm. Shep spent the day with Roger, either in the barn or wandering the fields. Nights he slept in the kitchen and was always ready and waiting at the door every morning, just past daybreak. She and Maddie were now used to having a dog around and had talked about getting another one. That idea would have to be on hold, though, given recent developments. *Like Shawn Harrison living in the Glen. Like Maddie deciding to stay...or not. Like if our business keeps going.*

She whistled, and seconds later Shep came running into the barn. His feet were covered with mud. "Uh-oh," Maura said. "Have you checked the riding ring this morning?" she called across the barn to Maddie. "It might be too muddy."

"What next!" Maddie muttered as she closed Jake's stall door and stomped outside.

Maura knew she wasn't off the hook for keeping the loan a secret, and Shawn's return was the other curveball thrown Maddie's way. She'd have to make amends somehow—for her part, at least. If only her sister and Shawn could strike some kind of friendly rapport, something like the one she and Theo had agreed to. *Though the connection between us is more than friendly. Our kiss when we were at Walter Ingram's place was hardly platonic, and now...*

Maddie returned seconds later. "It's muddy, but not overly. I think we can go ahead." She went to Jake's stall and led him out of the barn.

Maura knew what was on her sister's mind. They couldn't afford to lose bookings two days in a row. Of course, the regulars canceled yesterday had rebooked, but not the new client.

She got Roger ready, and she and Shep led him out to the field. They hadn't used Roger for riding yet because she and Maddie had decided one of them needed to ride him first, to see how he handled their weight. Walter had said Roger was used to working, and his previous owner had ridden him. But considering his vision problems, she and Maddie wanted him to get used to carrying one of them.

She met her sister leading Lizzie into the ring. "What time did you ask Ashley to come?"

"About nine thirty. Katie's due at ten, but I figured Ashley could spend that time with Lizzie, so the two can get used to one another."

"How is she working out?"

"Fine. She walked with Matilda on Wednesday."

"And Luke, too?" Maura grinned.

"Yeah. They definitely hit it off. Speaking of Luke, didn't he promise Katie he'd be here today?"

"I'm sure he'll show up." Maura thought back

to the dark mood the boy was in yesterday and hoped he and Theo had worked something out. "Who else is coming? Cathy or Nancy?"

"I thought we'd manage on our own today with Ashley and, hopefully, Luke. I'll lead Lizzie and you can monitor the two kids from behind."

Maura knew Cathy had mentioned changing or even canceling her volunteer hours because of the summer holidays and having to arrange childcare. She and Maddie had discussed hiring one of the volunteers part-time, figuring wages might be more incentive. But that was another option that would have to be put aside until they worked out a loan repayment to Theo.

"Plus, Luke won't be around for the whole summer, right? And come September, Ashley will only be available on weekends. Then we'll need Nancy and Cathy during the week, assuming both will be able to help," Maddie said.

One more complication to deal with, Maura thought. At least her sister didn't mention the possibility that she might no longer be involved then.

The sound of a vehicle coming up the drive diverted them from more serious talk about the future of the business, something Maura was happy to shelve for another day. She left Maddie and walked around to the front, where Ashley's father, Ed, was dropping her off. He was backing up his pickup when he stopped at Maura's approach and rolled down his window.

"Hey, Maura! Just want to tell you that Betty hasn't signed up for a table yet, but she wants one. Can you set one aside for her? She's bringing along some of her art."

"Of course. I'll phone her with details since I don't have her email."

Ed and Betty Watson were a few years older than her and Maddie, and their group's teen exploits in the Glen had provided inspiration for Finn and the gang—like the annual summer bonfire at the end of August and stealing jack-o'-lanterns at Halloween.

As she watched Ed reverse and drive away, she couldn't help but think how the Glen was such a unique place with its lore and traditions continuing through the generations. She was grateful to be part of that cycle and she wished Maddie could stay permanently and be a part of it, too.

Ashley headed for the riding ring, where Maddie was waiting with Lizzie. Minutes later, another car turned onto the driveway. It was Katie and her mother, a bit earlier than planned. Fortunately, at that moment, Luke pushed his way through the cedar trees.

Luke gave her a quick nod but greeted Katie with a big smile, so Maura figured the ride should be okay.

Ashley returned to greet Katie and pushed Katie's wheelchair, the three chatting all the way to the riding ring, oblivious to the adults trailing behind. As soon as the group reached the gate, Shep spotted them from the adjacent field and ran to greet them.

Katie squealed with pleasure as the dog leaped up to lick her face. "When did you get a dog?"

"It's a long story," Maddie began. "See that donkey in the far field? His name is Roger, and he and Shep here are best friends."

"Walter Ingram brought them because their owner had to sell his farm and couldn't keep them," Luke added. "And Roger can only see out of one eye, so Shep is like his Seeing Eye dog."

Katie mulled this over. "I think I'm going to like Shep and Roger."

Katie's mother smiled at Maura and whispered, "Another happy experience for Katie, and thank you. Is it okay with you if I make a quick run to the bakery here? My hubby loves their cinnamon rolls."

Maura nodded and watched her dash off as soon as they'd helped Katie up onto the saddle. It was a good sign that Katie's mother had the confidence to leave her daughter with them, even for a brief period. She noted Luke, Katie and Ashley were deep in conversation about something and was about to say, "All set?" when a loud barking ensued, and she swung around from her position feet away from Lizzie's hindquarters to see Shep pacing on the other side of the riding ring. Then she noticed the gate was slightly ajar. Shep was as observant as Maura, and he slipped through the gap into the ring, running eagerly toward them.

"Maddie!" Maura called out to her sister, who turned around and immediately tightened her grip on Lizzie's bridle.

The three kids had been pleased at Shep's arrival, but not Lizzie, who reared her head up and snorted a warning. Shep appeared oblivious to this and trotted up to Luke, eager for a pat or a treat. Maura tensed, watching Luke casually reach down to run his hand over Shep's head and then grasp the dog by the collar and slowly lead him away from Lizzie.

Maura felt herself relax. Luke was taking Shep out of the ring, but Lizzie wasn't appeased. She snorted again, pawing at the ground with her front right foot. She was making a point, Maura figured, and was about to tell Maddie that perhaps they ought to get Katie down before Lizzie's mood worsened.

But it was Katie who solved the problem, as she began stroking Lizzie's neck and mane, murmuring soothing sounds and whispering words that only she and Lizzie could hear. The gate closed, leaving Shep whining on the other side of it. Luke returned to his position, and Maddie raised an eyebrow at Maura, who nodded. *Don't underestimate the power of kids*, she thought.

Then Maddie said, "Let's walk, people."

The rest of the ride was uneventful, and Maura

even had a chance to mentally replay yesterday's talk with Theo in the kitchen. Her instinct to cheer him up and reassure him came automatically. For a few seconds she could forget about her promise to Maddie and the sickening possibility that telling him about the loan would threaten any hope of a future together. She'd be facing that hurdle soon enough, though, because Katie was the only rider that day, and there'd be no excuse to procrastinate further.

THEO COULDN'T REMEMBER the last time he'd seen Luke so animated.

"And Ashley said this youth club is kinda divided into age groups. Like twelve to fifteen forming one group, but the older teens—sixteen and seventeen—mostly doing their own thing." He shrugged. "Whatever that is."

Theo looked down at the sandwich on his plate, hiding his smile. "And you're going to check it out today, at the community center?"

"Do you mind? The meeting starts at four, and then after the talking and so on there's pizza and a movie. Ashley said she and her dad will pick me up and bring me back here."

Do I mind? It was sweet of Luke to think of his father, maybe sad and alone on a Friday evening, but plans were forming in Theo's mind. "That's great, son. I'm glad you'll get a chance to meet some of the Glen youngsters."

Luke frowned. "Preteens and teenagers aren't youngsters, Dad!"

"Oh, no, of course not. Did I sound like an old fogy there?"

"Definitely. Anyway, do you want me to help you bring up the rest of the boxes from the basement before I go?"

Theo was feeling as if he and Luke had stumbled into some alternate universe—a metaverse or whatever it was called, and he planned to take full advantage of the unexpected opportunity. When Luke went downstairs for the first load of boxes, Theo texted Maura and invited her for dinner. A home-cooked meal, he wrote, but nothing gourmet. He was about to go help Luke when she replied, Sure, thanks. What time?

He puzzled over this apparent lack of enthusiasm, but reasoned text messages could be misleading. Though she had seemed out of sorts yesterday. *No, don't make assumptions about people's moods, Theo. You've been led down that path too often. Especially when you were just a few years older than Luke, and decided the girl you dreamed about nightly wasn't at all interested in you.*

"Dad? There's a big one I need help with," Luke hollered from the foot of the basement stairs.

"Coming." He set his phone on the table and went downstairs.

"THAT WAS DELICIOUS," Maura said as she set her fork down on her plate. "But seriously, too much for me."

Theo eyed her leftover steak and salad. The meat wouldn't go to waste, anyway, not with a growing preteen in the house. Still, something wasn't right... She'd arrived fifteen minutes late, with no excuse or apology, and had turned down his offer of a predinner glass of wine. An early start in the morning, she'd claimed.

"How about coffee?"

"Okay, thanks." She peered around the kitchen. "I haven't been inside this place since...I don't know...I think when your aunt and uncle celebrated an anniversary, maybe, when I was on break from college."

"It hasn't changed since I used to come for the summer," he said, getting up to start the coffee.

"I suppose whoever buys it will want to renovate— maybe even gut it and start over. What do you think?"

Theo thought about the people from a development company coming on Monday and figured a teardown was more likely. But that was in the future and not a topic he wanted to raise with a kid-free evening ahead.

"I guess. Luke and I are gradually getting things cleared out. We brought up the last of the boxes from the basement today, and all that's left down there are some rusting tools and general stuff that can go to a dump or wherever people take things in the area." When she failed to reply, he turned away from setting up the coffee maker. She was staring blankly at the basement door, as if expecting someone—Luke?—to pop up any second with another box. Theo shook his head. *You're making too much out of this, pal.*

He switched on the machine. "Let's have it in the living room—or the parlor, as Aunt Vera used to say." He reached for her hand as she got to her feet. A waft of some unknown but heady fragrance rose up with her, and he put his arms around her, drawing her against his chest. She tucked her face into the crook of his shoulder and time stood still, until the coffee maker beeped, and she slowly pulled away. Regretfully? he wondered, noting an unreadable expression on her face.

"The coffee smells good," she said.

Small talk? What's going on? He stifled his impatience. This was the teenage Maura he remembered—unaccountably shifting from one mood to another. "Why don't you go into the living room while I get the coffee, and there are cookies from Sue's bakery."

"No sugar in my coffee."

"Hey, do you think I'd forget?"

Her smile was the most genuine of the evening, and Theo thought maybe the dinner date wasn't going to be a bust after all. Not if she was remembering the same rainy day he was.

"How old were we?" she asked.

"Twelve. Luke's age."

"And how come the three of us were alone?" Her brow wrinkled in thought.

"Your parents had to go pick up something at the co-op in Wallingford."

"But why did we make coffee? That's so random."

"We didn't. It was in the machine, left from breakfast."

"No wonder it was so awful."

"Yeah, and all the sugar we dumped in to make it taste better—"

"Didn't work." She laughed with him. "I swore I'd never drink coffee again."

"Yet here we are."

"Yes, Theo. And here we are."

Her soft voice and wistful look filled his heart with a longing he hadn't had in so many years he could barely identify it. *Love?* He pulled her close again, kissing her gently at first and then urgently. Forget the mystery moods and the memories of an unreachable teen. This was adult Maura—beautiful, tender, compassionate.

This time he broke away, lifted by the hope that the night was still salvageable. That whatever was on her mind would be resolved. "Living room," he murmured, letting her go.

His hands trembled as he poured coffee. But by the time he was taking the two mugs with a well-balanced plate of cookies into the living room, he was calm and steady—except for an increased heart rate.

She was standing in the center of the room, looking thoughtfully at the papers strewn on the side table next to the sofa and the pile of boxes stacked against one wall.

"Oh, sorry about this," he said. "I decided to keep everything on the ground floor, to simplify hauling it away once I've gone through it all."

He was shoving aside papers to set down the coffee when she said, "Theo, I have something to tell you."

Her face told him two things: more romance that night was not going to happen, and he wasn't going to like whatever she had to say.

CHAPTER FIFTEEN

PROCESSING IT ALL was a challenge for him, and Maura's anxiety was shifting to impatience. He finally believed her when she handed him her phone with the photos of the loan agreement. She paced the room, her hands curled into tight fists, while he read.

Then he looked up from where he was sitting on the sofa. "This explains the cashier's check. When I went to see the bank manager about Stan and Vera's accounts, I found out my uncle had withdrawn ten thousand in a cashier's check, made out to your father."

"Why didn't you say something?"

"It was only a few days ago. I figured your father had sold Uncle Stan something, or that the debt was the other way around and my uncle was repaying your father. I've been searching for a record of it." He handed her the phone. "How long have *you* known about this?" His eyes fixed on hers.

She averted her face, uncomfortable under his cool appraisal. "A couple of months before you arrived. I suppose I was hoping all of this was just a mistake or—"

"A bad dream?"

He smiled for the first time since she'd blurted her secret minutes ago. But it was a sad smile, Maura thought. "It's just that we don't have the money to pay back the loan, Theo."

"I assume Maddie knows?"

She nodded but refrained from telling him her sister had been in the dark until yesterday.

"I'm not too worried about the money, Maura, but there's another problem. From what I can see in those pictures, the agreement was signed by a notary, making it a legal document. There's probably a record somewhere, which means that if I'm going to sell this property—"

"Our pastures would be included in your tract." She'd figured that out herself, when she first found the papers, but her focus had been on how to repay the loan.

"I'll need to get another survey done to include the land in question, and also let my Realtor know. I have a prospective buyer coming after the weekend."

Maura watched him rub his forehead, stress obviously mounting inside him. She wished she could turn back time to the decision she'd made weeks ago. For now, she was grateful that he wasn't angry.

"This may complicate our timeline here. Luke

and I planned a road trip after leaving the Glen, but that wouldn't be until after the festival anyway, so…"

So his plans would be delayed but not changed. That reality hurt. "Maybe there's something we can do, before you contact your Realtor." She suddenly thought of the monthly withdrawals from her father's account. "My dad might have paid back the loan or was in the process of doing so. Your uncle must have a record, too. Why don't we start looking?"

"Worth a try. Let's each take a box."

She heard him sigh as he slowly got up from the sofa. He seemed drained of energy, and she felt another pang of guilt. "I'm sorry, Theo. I knew I'd have to deal with this, but I suppose I unconsciously chose to forget about the whole mess until you came back."

"I've been back almost two weeks, Maura."

There was no good response to that, other than to tell him his return had raised feelings she hadn't had for many years. She'd been content to drift along with the possibilities of what his presence in the Glen could mean for her, without considering the impact of her secret.

Rather than reply to this, she lifted a box from the pile and took it into the kitchen, where she set it on the table. Seconds later he joined her, and they worked silently, wary—or so Maura thought—of continuing the discussion about why she hadn't told him sooner. When she finished with the first box, she returned it to the living room, placing it against the opposite wall.

Four boxes later, with no luck, she asked, "Can you think of any place your uncle might have stored valuable papers? You told me he was a pack rat, but there must be someplace in the house where he kept important things."

"Seriously, I don't really know. When they went into the nursing home, I hired a company from Rutland to check on the place every couple of weeks."

A horrifying thought occurred to her. "Haven't you already had boxes hauled away?"

He held up his hands, as if in surrender. "Yes, and I've been thinking these last few minutes that what we're looking for may already have been sent to recycling."

Maura blew out a mouthful of sour breath. "We may as well finish going through what's here, just in case." She left the kitchen and returned with another box.

"This isn't turning out to be the night I'd anticipated," he joked.

His faint smile brought one from her, though she refrained from saying that the night *she'd* envisioned after deciding to confess could have been so much worse. She stopped counting the number of boxes they rummaged through, but each time she went back for another, she noticed the piles were shifting from one side of the living room to the other. Her hope of finding any mention of the loan was fading fast. She was about to suggest they call it a night when the kitchen door flew open and Luke rushed into the room.

"What's going on?" he asked, looking from Theo to Maura, then at the boxes and papers scattered across the table.

"We're searching for some important papers that my uncle might have had," Theo explained. "Uh…Maura was here for dinner and I…uh… asked her to help me."

"What kind of papers?"

"Relating to a legal document Uncle Stan signed, years ago. So how was the youth group?"

"Great, Dad. And guess who the speaker was tonight? Finn McAllister!"

Maura exchanged grins with Theo.

"You mean *Mr.* McAllister?" Theo teased.

"He told us to call him Finn. Anyways, he was telling us some cool stories about rescuing people on the Trail and how he got into it. Did you know he and his father went hiking on it when he was really young? Like eight or nine."

"No, I didn't know that, but I went with him a few times, when we were teens. Sounds like you had a good time."

"I did, but the pizza wasn't as good as the one we got from Wallingford." He was staring at the boxes on the table and asked, "Do you want some help with that?"

Maura smiled at the half-hearted question. "We're good, Luke," she said. "I'll be going in a few minutes anyway."

Luke nodded and was about to leave the room when he turned to say, "Oh, and by the way, Finn told me to ask you if you and I want to go walking with him tomorrow, to make up for yesterday when we had to cancel because of the rain."

"Uh, sure, if you want to."

"I do because he told us about some interesting things to look for when we hike on the part leading out from the Glen."

"Okay, I'll text him before I go to bed."

"And he said that another guy...Shawn?...might come, too." He paused a second before saying, "I'm going to bed now. I'm beat. G'night, Dad. 'Night, Maura."

"Wonder of wonders," Theo murmured after Luke left. "If we were in Augusta, I'd be lucky to get him off the recliner and away from his PlayStation console to come for a meal."

"The miracle of Maple Glen." Maura met his gaze for a second and then turned her attention to the table. "And...um...I'm beat myself, Theo. Can we continue this tomorrow after your hike?"

"Sure. I'll let you know when we're back."

She plucked her cardigan from the back of a kitchen chair and headed for the door.

"Wait," he said, as she opened it. He crossed the room in three strides. "Look, don't worry too much about all of this. We'll deal with whatever happens when…well…when it happens." After a minute, he added with a wry grin, "Worst-case scenario, I just forgive the loan." He placed his hands on her shoulders, and she felt her tension give way as he drew her close against him, his arms a refuge from the turmoil of questions and self-doubt. But her certainty that he was going to kiss her faded as he gently pulled back. "I'll call you tomorrow," he whispered.

When he closed the door behind her, she stood in the yard a moment longer to collect her thoughts and calm the surge of longing. The night hadn't been as awful as she'd expected and there was a plan to meet again. But he hadn't kissed her when he could have.

"DAD? DAD!"

That voice has no place in my dream about Maura. Theo opened his eyes, squinting against the sunlight streaming from the bedroom window, then turned over to see Luke hovering in the doorway.

"It's late," his son was saying, "and we slept in. You have to hurry." Then he vanished, his footsteps thudding downstairs.

Have my son and I traded places, he wondered, *as in some old movie?* He swung his legs out of bed and sat on its edge, rubbing his eyes. He hadn't slept well. After Maura left, he'd gone through a few more boxes until fatigue and despair forced him to stop. For a couple of hours in the night, he'd made a mental tour through the farmhouse, thinking of possible hiding places. Then he'd segued to Maura, her pale face and trembling lips as she'd told him about the loan, her weak answer when he'd pressed her about keeping the information from him.

And always, lurking in the shadows of his mind, was the question *why didn't she trust me enough to tell me sooner?* Okay, maybe not the first few days he'd been back, but surely after that pact they'd made to enjoy one another's company, to renew a kind of friendship and see where it might lead. Which begged the question, could that lead anywhere now? Could he trust her to be transparent with him in the future, if there even *was* a future with her?

He dressed quickly, shying away from that last question, and hurried into the kitchen as Luke was swallowing the end of a piece of toast and peanut butter. Crunching loudly, Luke pointed to another slice of toast on the counter.

Another first, Theo thought. The wake-up, and now breakfast. *We* have *traded places!*

"We better take the car," Luke said after he gulped down a mouthful of milk.

"Right. I packed some sandwiches last night before I went to bed. They're—"

"I put them in your pack." Luke pointed to the small backpack on a kitchen chair.

"Great, thanks. Where's yours?"

"In the car. And there's your fob. I took it from the hallway table. To save some time."

Theo had no idea how long this version of his twelve-year-old son would last, but he intended to enjoy every minute. "Okay, well, let's go!"

He was turning onto the county road when Luke spoke again. "So…uh…is Maura like… your *girlfriend*?"

Theo kept his eyes on the road ahead, giving himself some time to find an answer. "Well, she's not a girl anymore, but—"

"Dad, c'mon."

"We…we're getting to know one another again. It's been a long time, so we like being with each other and…well, we'll see what happens."

"What about Maddie?"

Theo turned to look at his son. "What do you mean, what about Maddie?"

"You told me the three of you always hung out together. Is it different now? 'Cause you seem to be around Maura more than Maddie."

Theo stopped the car at the crosswalk before the church. The McAllister place, where they'd agreed to meet Finn and Shawn, was several yards ahead, but Theo figured he needed to wrap up this discussion now. "I like Maddie very much, as a good friend. What I feel for Maura is a bit stronger, more special."

"Like what you used to feel for Mom?"

Theo winced. It was a loaded question and one he'd prefer to discuss anywhere else but in the car minutes before hiking with friends. "Luke, I think we need to talk about this later, all right? When we have more time."

"Sure," Luke mumbled and stared out the window.

Theo took his foot off the brake and continued along the street, feeling the silence pressing in. He hoped the day's hike wasn't going to be ruined. He pulled up in front of Finn's place where the two men were standing by the gate and turned off the engine. Luke waved, then glanced with a quick smile at Theo before jumping out the door. Theo's mood rose a notch. Everything was going to be okay.

Finn spent a few minutes going over some rules with Luke. Basically, the same ones Theo had mentioned days ago, on their own walk. He noted that Shawn was quiet, smiling at Luke's chatter with Finn about last night's youth club meeting. But once they crossed the bridge into the woods, Luke fell silent. Theo was proud of his son's intuitive sense that small talk could wait until their guides indicated otherwise. When they reached the first blue blaze, Finn stopped and held up a finger.

"Hear that? A mockingbird, you think, Shawn?"

"Could be. If Walter Ingram was here, he'd know for sure. Right now, I'm seeing some tracks." Shawn pointed to the side of the path. "Deer. And see that?" His finger moved beyond, off the path to his right. "Deer scat," he added at Luke's frown.

Luke moved closer to the cluster of almond-shaped droppings nestled among some mossy plants. "Oooh, weird."

The men laughed. "Not much for such a big creature," Shawn agreed.

"Will we see a bear?"

"I hope not." Shawn's grin took the edge off his answer. "Okay, let's keep going." He led the way up the first sharp incline, which Theo recalled would bring them closer to the junction of the off trail and the Long Trail itself.

For a long time, there were no other sounds in the forest but their breathing and the crunch of boots on vegetation. When they reached the first white blaze, indicating the main trail, Shawn stopped and, looking at both Finn and Theo, asked, "Up or down?"

"What's your preference?" Theo asked.

Shawn glanced quickly at Luke. "Maybe up and avoid the ice beds. The White Rocks cliffs trail?"

It was the right call, Theo knew, given the presence of two inexperienced hikers—he and his son.

"I know a good lookout where we can rest and have lunch. Maybe decide there to go on or go back," Finn said.

By now Luke was at the end of the group. Theo slowed down and waited for him to catch up. When he did, he patted him on the shoulder and murmured, "You're doing great." Then he fell into place behind Luke. If his son needed to quit before the lookout Finn had mentioned, they would.

There were a few more stops along the way, as Finn and Shawn indicated types of flowers or trees. Once a coyote fled from the path ahead, and they watched silently until it disappeared into the brush. Theo was beginning to question his own ability to reach the lookout, wherever it was, when Finn rounded a curve in the path ahead and suddenly halted. He was taking his backpack off and Shawn was gazing through binoculars as Theo and Luke caught up to them.

Theo remembered the view at once, though he'd only seen it a couple of times as a teenager. White Rocks Mountain, across the shallow valley, its namesake white rocks sprawling down its northwest side as if some mythical titan had scattered them in a game. Or in a rage, Theo thought, for their appearance was both awesome and frightening. No one spoke for a long time, until Finn said, "Lunch?"

Then packs were opened, and the sounds of containers popping open or sandwiches being unwrapped echoed in the quiet. Theo sat next to Shawn, enjoying the sight of Luke wolfing down his lunch while keeping his eyes on the scene across from them. Theo ate half his sandwich before taking a break to ask Shawn if he'd found a place to live.

"I gave up my place in Bennington, since it was a bit too far away. For now, I'm staying at Bernie's B and B."

That seemed appropriate, Theo thought. "Is it a bit like going home for you?"

"Not really. Bernie's changed it around so much, but I guessed which room used to be mine when we lived there, and it was available, so that was pretty cool."

Theo noticed Luke turn their way, listening to the talk. He was about to mention that his farm-house was for sale, but Shawn would know that already from the posted sign. Besides, the proximity to the Stuart place might be problematic for Maddie.

As if on the same wavelength, Shawn suddenly said, "I still haven't seen Maddie around. I was sorry I missed her at the festival meeting."

"Had to leave early to feed the donkeys, I think," Theo said.

"Donkeys!" Shawn smiled and shook his head. "Who'd have thought?"

"Yeah, right," Theo murmured. He saw Luke edge closer to them.

"That was Maura's idea, wasn't it?" Finn put in. "When Maddie came home after Mr. Stuart died, Maura convinced her to help out with the riding therapy program she'd set up."

"Oh?" was all Shawn said.

Then Finn added, "Maddie promised to stay for a year at any rate, and that'll be coming up by the end of the summer, I think."

Theo was taken aback by what Finn knew, but then he thought of the Glen grapevine. He opted to keep eating.

After a moment, Shawn asked, his voice husky, "How *is* Maddie?"

"She's great!" Luke suddenly interjected.

The three men exchanged smiles, and a few minutes later, Shawn stood. "Keep going or head back?"

Finn said, "Maybe head back? I'm on dinner duty tonight and have some shopping yet."

Theo wasn't about to argue. He and Luke gathered up their lunch remains, and as Luke was slinging his small backpack on, Theo bent down to say, "Good job today, son. Pizza again tonight or...?"

Luke grinned up at him. "Yeah, but from the bakery. And, Dad, why don't we invite Maddie and Maura?"

Why not? Theo asked himself. He smiled, elated by good exercise, the beauty of nature and his son, who never ceased to surprise him.

CHAPTER SIXTEEN

MAURA SAT BACK in her chair, her gaze drifting from Shep, curled up in front of the kitchen door, to Luke, midway through his account of the hike that afternoon, then to Maddie's smile as Luke described the deer scat they'd found, and last of all, to Theo. His face shone with love and pride as his son spoke, and for the first time in her life, Maura wondered what that unconditional love of a parent for a child would feel like. Would she ever have the chance to experience it? She closed her eyes against the question, not liking what the answer might be.

"Mo?"

She blinked and sat upright to see her sister smiling at her from across the table. "Hmm?" Maura's face heated up as she realized everyone had not only finished their ice cream but also their stories of the day. Theo's grin was irksome. Almost indulgent, like parent to child. Or maybe he was thinking back to last night, the two of them in this very kitchen, rummaging through boxes.

"I asked if you and Theo could clear up while Luke and I go check the donkeys. They're still out in the field, but Roger's with them, so I figured if everything's okay we can leave them all out for the night. Weather looks good. No rain to spook Matilda." As soon as Maddie uttered Roger's name, Shep leaped to his feet and began whining.

"He knows you're talking about Roger!" Luke exclaimed.

Now Shep was barking.

Maura grinned at Maddie and Luke. "I think you're committed to checking on Roger and the others now. And I guess you'll be taking Shep, too."

More barking and whining from Shep, standing at the door with a somewhat impatient expression on his face.

"Okay. Well, Luke, we better get going, and I'll walk you back when we're done," Maddie said, getting to her feet.

"I can find my own way," Luke protested.

Theo frowned and was about to say something when Maura interjected, "Maddie can text when you're finished over there, and I'll meet you at the break in the cedar trees. You know the one, Mads." She saw that Luke was about to protest further and added, "I'm sure I'll be ready to leave by then anyway. Maybe we should consider making a bigger gap between the two properties before the festival. That would enable people who'll be parking on Theo's land to pass through rather than walking along the road to us." She knew it was a good idea, but Theo took his time replying.

"Let's discuss that after my meeting with my Realtor. For now, I think Maddie's plan to walk Luke partway is a good one," Theo said with a tone of finality.

Back to reality, Maura was thinking. Of course, Theo was reluctant to change things on his property, which even a temporary path linking the two farms might do.

The prospect of a sale and permanent move fell over the room, and for a moment, no one moved. Then Maddie prompted, "Luke? Let's see how Roger's doing." When she and Luke stood up, Shep began leaping at the closed door. "Hold your horses, Shep!" she cried.

"Or maybe hold your donkeys," Luke suggested, and they all laughed.

The scene was almost like family but not quite, Maura was thinking. A new and different version of family, and she was struck by a desire to hold on to this moment for as long as she could. But the door closed behind them, and the room fell silent.

"What are your plans for Roger and Shep?"

Theo's unexpected question startled her. Did he have to ask? Or was he thinking they might not be able to keep them, given the possibility of Maddie leaving when her year was up?

"We're hoping to attract more riders like teens

and adults, not necessarily for therapy, but for fun," she said, "and Roger is our largest animal, so he's the best candidate. Jake can handle bigger people, too, but he's younger than Roger and not as docile."

"I can attest to that." Theo grinned.

She had to smile at the image of Theo trapped between Jake and the barn door, the day he first arrived back in the Glen. Was it only a couple of weeks or so ago? How everything had changed since that day, when she'd feared her whole world was toppling down on her with the possibility of having to repay a huge loan. Not to mention the emotional equivalent of a tidal wave—meeting up again with Theo Danby, her teenage crush.

As Theo started clearing dishes, Maura felt the line of tension between them tighten. Something was bugging him, and she knew her confession last night was the reason. She got up to remove the rest of the plates and carried them over to the sink. "Do you want to talk, Theo?"

He looked up from rinsing. "We need to, Maura, but maybe we should hold off on making decisions about the loan and the land until after I meet with the agent on Monday. Does that make sense to you?"

Was he having second thoughts about their pact to enjoy one another's company, she wondered, or worse, regretting that he'd even come back to Maple Glen? "I guess so," she finally said. She set the stack of plates and cutlery onto the counter and was turning back to the table when he grasped her arm and pulled her close.

"We'll figure something out, Maura. Try not to worry too much. I have a lot of things to work out as well."

She rested her head in the dip between his shoulder and neck, closing her eyes and trying not to imagine how this moment could go if...

Theo's cell phone chimed from the table. "Luke's probably ready to come back." He began to pull away but suddenly stopped, clutching her tighter for a second before kissing her forehead. "We *will* continue this discussion tomorrow or Monday, okay?"

"Okay."

He picked up his phone and replied to the text, then turned to Maura. "Luke's ready to come back, and I'll go with you to meet him at the cedars." Then, tucking his phone into his jeans pocket, he reached for her hand and clasped it in his as they went out the door into the quiet night. They walked quickly across the front lawn to the gap Jake had forged almost two weeks ago. "I remember doing this when we were teens. Sneaking into our mutual homes after curfew," he said in a low voice.

"Yes, though it was always the three of us."

"True, but I tried my best that last summer to have you to myself."

His light chuckle warmed her, despite a fleeting wish that she'd been more responsive back then, when she was fifteen and feared revealing her feelings to the sixteen-year-old boy next door. When she saw a flashlight's beacon bobbing their way, she dropped her hand from his.

Maddie waited on the other side of the cedars as Luke crossed through. "They're all okay," he announced, "but Shep wouldn't go inside, so we left him in the field, too." He turned briefly to Theo to say, "Maddie asked me to help out tomorrow morning 'cause the rider I helped with before—Sammy—wants to come for another session."

This was a new development, Maura thought, as Sammy had been riding every two weeks. Whatever the reason, the change was good for him and for business.

"That's great, Luke, and I have more clearing out to do." He shifted his gaze to Maura. "Talk tomorrow, then, when you're finished with your rider?"

"Okay." She pushed through the weeds around the cedars and joined Maddie, waiting with flashlight in hand.

"That was a nice evening," Maddie said as they walked across the lawn.

Maura knew her sister was fishing for an update on the status between her and Theo, but she refused to be drawn in. She wasn't ready to talk about the situation without giving in to emotion. And emotion wasn't going to help solve the problem. She glanced to the field on their right and the silhouettes of grazing donkeys. "Think we should leave Shep out for the night?"

"Worth a try. He absolutely refused to go inside when I walked Luke back."

"So this is a new development," Maura said, changing the subject. "Sammy wanting another ride after his session last week."

"Yeah, his mother phoned when Luke and I were checking on the donkeys. She said he had such a great time he didn't want to wait another week. She thinks a weekly ride will be better through the summer, to give him a break from the day camps she's enrolled him in. She also said he asked if 'that boy' who was here last time was going to help again."

"Aw, that's sweet and so nice for Luke."

"He literally swelled with pride when I repeated that to him."

Maura thought how much Luke had changed in the short time she'd known him and hoped the inevitable parting wouldn't be too hard on him, or on all of them. She'd miss him.

Once inside and on the way up to their bedrooms, Maura suddenly hugged her sister. "Thanks for being so patient and understanding with me, Mads, about keeping the loan a secret and…well… basically everything." She closed her eyes. They hadn't hugged like this since their father died, and Maura had forgotten how wonderful it was to have someone who'd understand and forgive, no matter the transgression. Or so she wanted to believe.

Maple Glen without Theo and Luke would be painful, but the village without her sister—her twin—would be devastating. She decided to do everything she could to ensure that never happened.

THEO WAS AT loose ends. He had the place to himself and had been plugging away at sorting the rest of the stuff in the basement while Luke was next door, but now his energy, as well as his resolve, was flagging. What was the point of all this work, when he could easily hire one of those companies that swooped in, gathered everything for a flat fee and took it away? He doubted there was hidden treasure in any of the boxes, cabinets, drawers or cupboards in the entire farmhouse—unless you wanted to count a piece of paper regarding a loan made five years or so ago.

Ten thousand dollars! It wasn't a fortune but definitely not to be dismissed, as he'd so blithely done when Maura had confessed. He couldn't explain that blurted reassurance, except that she'd looked so darn sad and forlorn. And forgiving the loan was obviously a solution to the problem but, realistically, not one he could afford. He'd be paying child support—if Luke decided to move and live with his mother—until the boy was eighteen and even after that because Theo wanted his son to be able to go on to whatever postsecondary education he wished. He also had a mortgage on his condo in Augusta and a few more car payments on the impulsive purchase he'd made right after Trish left their home, and the sports car was definitely not going to stay in the family, either.

Family. Last night had felt so natural, so good. Better than any family experience he'd had since Luke's early years when he and Trish were still in love. After Maddie and Luke left to check on the donkeys, he'd been half hoping the illusion of family might continue. But then Maura had suggested they talk, and Theo'd had a bad feeling where that would lead. What he'd really wanted at that moment was to keep her in his arms and fantasize about keeping her in his life.

Long after Luke had gone to bed, he'd sat in the dark living room and mentally played through possible scenarios: forgive the loan, which meant shrugging off money he knew he himself could use, or ask the sisters to pay him back in installments, which obviously would have an impact on their business.

If he sold his property to that developer—his agent had implied a big-name company—he wouldn't have any financial problems for a long time. The only win-win solution was to forgive the loan, contingent on selling his land. He knew Maddie and Maura would be grateful. He might even be a hero in their minds. But right then, he wanted none of that. He didn't want to be that kind of hero and he didn't want gratitude, especially from Maura. The money—repaid or forgiven—would inevitably be a wedge between him and the sisters.

The best immediate course of action would be to check county records for the notarized loan agreement, and he could do that after the prospective buyers came tomorrow morning. Then he'd sit down with Maura and Maddie to discuss next steps. He scanned the room, littered with boxes. Tomorrow he'd hire a company to collect and dispense with everything.

Maybe Luke would be interested in keeping some of Uncle Stan's mementos. There was a small box of medals garnered during his uncle's military service and photograph albums meticulously collated and captioned by his aunt during Theo's summers in the Glen. Skimming through it, he'd grasped how important his visits had been to the childless couple. Most people didn't keep actual photo albums anymore, but perhaps when Luke was an adult, he'd want to share memories of Maple Glen—both his and his father's—with a child of his own.

Theo groaned. This kind of sentimental thinking wasn't like him. He'd always been a "calm under pressure" kind of person, which fit with his career. A bit like the adult Maura he was beginning to know better. For some reason she'd kept her emotions in check at a young age, though, which had resulted in the Glen gang of kids thinking she was cold. He hadn't understood her when he was a kid himself, but as an adult he figured her behavior was a defense mechanism against being hurt. Perhaps if he'd been able to realize that about her when they were teens, he might not have been deterred by her aloofness.

Back then, the dynamics of the group had seemed so complex, but in hindsight, the drama of those last two summers was plain silly.

He got up from the sofa and went into the kitchen and poured a glass of water, which he drank standing at the sink and staring out the window overlooking the rear of the property. Although he'd gone through just about everything in the basement and bedrooms, there was still the barn and tool shed. He groaned again. He checked the time, thinking that Luke might be finished helping with today's rider, the young boy Maddie had mentioned last night.

He marveled at the connections Luke had already made in the village, in a mere two weeks. Either he'd been misjudging his son or hadn't seen his potential, and the thought saddened him. Long hours at the hospital and the missed teacher interviews and school events had exacted a heavy toll on his marriage, but also on his bond with his son. That wasn't going to happen anymore, he decided, clanging his empty glass onto the kitchen counter.

The sound of a vehicle's horn pulled him back

to the moment. He went out the kitchen door and rounded the corner to the front, where Walter Ingram was getting out of his pickup.

"Theo." The older man's gravelly voice broke the silence of a Sunday morning. "Came to see if Luke would like to come and help me extract some honey today for the festival."

Theo was touched by the man's thoughtfulness. "I'm sure he'd want to help, but he's at the Stuart place right now."

"Okay. I'm heading over there anyway to talk to them about the tables for the festival."

As Walter was about to get back into his truck, Theo impulsively blurted, "I'll come with you. I'm finished cleaning up here for now and feel like I need a break."

"Climb aboard," Walter said. "Guess sorting through your aunt and uncle's things has been challenging."

"No kidding," Theo agreed as he sat in the passenger seat. "My aunt and uncle were complete pack rats."

Walter chuckled. "Yep. I sometimes offered to help them remove anything they didn't want or need, but their answer was always that they were saving it all for their great-nephew." He shifted the truck into gear, made a sharp U-turn and headed back down the drive to the county road.

Theo moaned. "What I figured. Say, do you know of any local trucking companies that I could hire to haul stuff away? It needs to be sorted for recycling or donating to any charities. And then there are some things that simply need discarding somewhere, I guess."

"Sure thing. I'll contact a guy I know in Wallingford." After a slight pause, he turned Theo's way and asked, "Any word on the property sale?"

"My agent is bringing some people tomorrow to have a look at it." He decided that was enough information to pass along at the moment.

Walter nodded. "Hopefully good people who'll fit into the community."

Theo kept his thoughts about that to himself. He doubted a development company would be interested in preserving the tone of a small village. That thought nagged until they were parking alongside a car in front of the Stuart farmhouse. He was about to head toward the riding ring behind the barn when he noticed Walter getting something from the back of the truck.

He was carrying a bright green ball about the size of a large beach ball as he walked toward Theo. Up close, Theo saw that the ball was made of heavy-duty rubber.

Walter grinned as he held it aloft. "Thought it'd be good for us all to have some fun today."

Some fun would definitely be a good thing, Theo mused, as he followed Walter.

CHAPTER SEVENTEEN

MAURA'S HEART SKIPPED a beat when she saw Theo walking her way. She and today's volunteer, Nancy, were helping Sammy down from Matilda while Luke and Maddie, with Shep's assistance, herded the other donkeys into the northeast pasture. When Sammy was safely on the ground and heading for his mother at the riding ring fence, Maura took a few minutes to remove the saddle and bridle from Matilda, setting them on top of the riding ring fence. She looked toward the barn again and this time saw Walter Ingram behind Theo. Right. He had phoned yesterday to say he'd pop around to discuss the setup for the tables on festival day.

She was a bit relieved that Theo wasn't alone, not yet ready for the talk he'd mentioned last night—the loan and what the three of them could do about it. When the men reached the riding ring, Walter spoke briefly to Sammy and his mother. Then all four headed toward her and Nancy, who was holding on to Matilda's halter. Sammy's face was lit with excitement, and Maura soon found out why.

Walter was carrying a very large green ball. As he drew near, Maura noticed Nancy tighten her grasp on Matilda's halter. She, too, had noticed the ball.

"Thought a bit of fun was in order before getting down to work this beautiful morning," Walter said.

Sammy's whoop sounded all the way to the pasture, catching the attention of not only Luke and Maddie, but the other donkeys.

"Roger and Shep played with a ball like this at their old home, so they'll get into the idea right away," Walter said. He led the way to the pasture, followed by the procession of Maura, Nancy, Matilda, Theo, Sammy and his mother. By now Maddie and Luke were waiting at the pasture gate, their faces creased with curiosity.

Maura nudged Matilda through the gate and was about to close it when Shep ran out to greet them.

"Best leave Shep with us for now," Walter advised. "He might get kicked inside there."

When everyone was lined up at the fence, Walter hurled the ball into the center of the field. It was Roger who trotted after it, braying raucously. The other donkeys watched, suspicious of this strange green object that now was flying through the air after Roger's kick. Jake got the hang of it quicker than Matilda and Lizzie, running after the ball and flicking it with a deft hoof.

"They're playing soccer!" Luke exclaimed.

"How did they learn that?" Sammy wanted to know.

"I met Roger's former owners while shopping in Wallingford the other day and they told me about this game he used to enjoy. So I went and bought a ball right away. Thought it'd be fun for the others and us." He was staring at the other donkeys when the ball suddenly landed at Lizzie's feet. "Will she get into the game or is she too ornery?" he asked.

"I'm betting she'll want to," Luke said, joined at once by Sammy's "Me too."

Everyone waited. Maura caught Theo's eye and grinned. As if sensing the audience was expecting something from her, Lizzie slowly lowered her head to the ball, sniffed it, poked at it with one hoof and then, with a bray that must have carried all the way to the Glen, kicked it to the far side of the pasture. Roger quickly galloped after the ball, flinging it up into the air with a hoof, but when Jake tried to intervene before the next kick, Roger pivoted to nip at him.

"Uh-oh," Walter said, chuckling. "Maybe it'll take a while for them to play fair."

"They have to learn to share," Sammy affirmed.

The adults and Luke smiled at his solemn tone.

"Who's going to be brave enough to go in and

retrieve the ball when they're finished with it?" Theo asked.

"They'll tire of it eventually," Walter said.

"Maybe donkeys have a short attention span, too. Right, Mom?" Sammy peered up at his mother.

"I think so," his mother said, smiling.

"We'll take away their new toy later, when the excitement has died down," Maura said and began walking toward the barn.

Theo caught up to her as the others lagged behind. "I didn't plan on coming over this early, but Walter showed up at my place to see if Luke was available to collect honey, and then he mentioned something about a fun event, and I was all set for that."

Fun. Maura could hardly recall enjoying some of that the past year, yet despite her initial misgivings about Theo and Luke's arrival in the Glen, there'd been fun times and, underlying those lighter gatherings, a sense of contentment.

"I thought maybe we could discuss the loan after lunch, if Luke goes to Walter's place."

So much for the fun part of today, she was thinking. "Sure. I'll let Maddie know. Our chat with Walter about the tables will probably be brief, so call or text after lunch."

"It's a deal," Theo murmured.

His pat on her shoulder was warm and reassuring, and Maura watched him move away, joining up with Luke and Sammy. His tall, straight physique was so familiar now she could barely remember her response to the adult Theo Danby when he'd first arrived days ago. She'd grown accustomed to the man he'd become since those summers. His strength, his purposeful walk, his quick decision-making, even his unexpected silences and hard-to-read expressions. If she'd mentally carried the teenage Theo around for so many years, how long would it take to shake the memory of this man when he eventually left for good?

The morning's fun disappeared at that thought. Maura stopped to take a long, deep breath. One day at a time, she reminded herself.

The goodbyes at the front of the house took some time, with Luke promising Sammy he'd look for him at the festival and the boy's happy face eliciting more smiles. Nancy reminded Maura that she, too, would be on hand to assist with rides on festival day. And watching her drive away, Maura thought again how lucky she and Maddie were to have volunteers. It was a situation that could change with a substantial increase in clients, as volunteer hours were always finite. *Another potential financial complication.* Okay, Maura told herself, no more thoughts like that. Not today. She joined the others standing by Walter's pickup.

"Walter and a friend will deliver the tables on Tuesday," Maddie said at her approach, "so I suggested we plot locations and match table to vendor

on Wednesday, mainly because you and I have yet
to figure out where everything will go."

"I can help with that, too," Theo put in. "Maybe
when I drop by later this afternoon?"

"Theo's coming over to discuss…you know…"
Maura said quickly at the question on her sister's
face.

Fortunately, Maddie got the hint. "Oh, right.
Sure."

There was an awkward lull until Walter said,
"Okay, then. Luke is keen to help with honey and
maybe Theo can drop him off after lunch."

"What about the ball?" Luke asked.

Walter chuckled. "I've a feeling they're more
interested in grazing right now. I'm sure Maura
and Maddie will extract it at a convenient time."

"That was so much fun today! Thanks for bringing it, Walter."

They all smiled at Luke's grown-up voice.

After Walter's pickup chugged down the drive,
Theo said, "I'm ready for lunch. How about you,
Luke?"

Luke nodded. "It was a good morning, but now
I'm starving."

When they were out of sight, Maddie asked,
"What's this talk Theo mentioned?"

Maura caught the sharp tone of the question
and felt her face heat up. "Last night he said the
three of us should discuss—"

"The loan?"

Maura nodded. Her sister's expression was daunting. "Sorry, I meant to tell you last night but—"

"You were busy apologizing again for keeping it a secret."

Maura expelled a loud sigh. "Seems my go-to state of being these days. Apologizing."

Maddie allowed a brief smile. "Better than keeping everything to yourself, Mo."

Relief surged through her. She was forgiven—again.

Then Maddie went on to say, "Remember that after the festival, when real life takes over again." She turned away and headed for the kitchen door.

Maura stood awhile longer, her thoughts forging ahead to the day after all the hoopla, when, as Maddie warned, real life would take over once more.

THE FUN PART of the day was over, Theo thought when he tapped on the door and entered the Stuart kitchen. Maddie was sitting at the table where a handful of papers lay among leftover lunch plates, glasses and cutlery. Maura was brewing coffee and turned around as he came in.

"Coffee?" she asked. "I can make instant decaf, too, if you prefer."

He figured he'd need all his senses to be alert. "Regular, please. I brought some cookies." He held up a paper bag. "Made a pit stop at Tasty Delights because Luke wanted to pick up a couple of their specialty doughnuts for him and Walter."

"He was excited about helping with the honey," Maura said as she clicked on the coffee maker and began to clear away the lunch dishes.

Theo sat down on the chair nearest the door, opposite Maddie. "Yeah. He told me they might be working late because Walter had hundreds of jars to fill. 'Don't hold supper for me,' he said." Theo laughed. "As if."

"Hopefully he's as enthusiastic after pouring fifty jars, let alone 'hundreds,'" Maura said.

"I can't remember the last time he hauled out his video game console. Certainly not since our second night here. He hasn't even asked to use my phone to contact some of his friends." Theo shook his head, frowning. "I worry a bit about that. Not keeping in touch with his school friends."

"Did you, when you were here all those summers?"

"Well, no cell phone but—"

"Stan or Vera had a landline."

He thought for a minute. "Funny, but I never thought about contacting my school buddies. Maybe because I knew we'd all be together again in the fall."

"Or maybe because you were here, cemented in the community of Maple Glen, and that other world was too far away," Maura suggested.

"Yeah, I think you may be right. This place is a bit—"

"Otherworldly?" quipped Maddie.

Maura snorted a laugh as she brought the coffee to the table and sat on Theo's right. "Anyway," she said, "it's great that Luke will have so many different memories of this place—and all good ones."

"Amen to that," Theo murmured as he sipped the dark brew. He hoped that his son's memories would carry him through the inevitable emotional tumult of a possible move at the end of summer.

"Okay," Maura announced, setting her mug down on the table with a decisiveness that put him on guard. "Here are the hard copies of the loan agreement, plus statements from the bank account in our mother's name where Dad deposited the money. Have a look." She gathered the papers in the middle of the table and pushed them his way.

Reading the actual documents rather than skimming the photos on Maura's phone made everything real. The language might be prosaic, but there was the notary's signature and stamp. "Have you found out anything about this person? The notary?"

"I googled him," Maddie said. "He's the town clerk at city hall in Rutland."

"After my meeting with my Realtor tomorrow, I'll go there just to confirm this is on file. As I see this, we have a couple—maybe three—courses of action." He paused, wanting to get his message right. "One, I forgive the loan entirely and find out how I go about doing that." He waited, but neither sister glanced up from her coffee mug. He felt a stir of impatience. Did the Stuarts always have to be so hard to read?

"Two, we work out a repayment schedule. If I sell my property for a good price, I'll have enough equity not to have to worry about getting the money back all at once. The payment schedule could be spread out in small amounts to accommodate your business plans." Now Maddie was looking at him from the other end of the table. Her face was pale, but she was nodding. Maura, on the other hand, seemed engrossed in some breadcrumbs scattered around her coffee mug. Theo bit down on his lower lip.

After a long minute, she looked up and asked, "And three?"

Ha, he thought. *She's already dismissed the two most likely possibilities and is going for a third.* The problem was, he actually didn't have something specific in mind for number three. He swigged some more coffee, his head now buzzing more from what to say than the caffeine because a lightning-strike thought had just occurred. What if he didn't sell the land after all but kept the place as a holiday getaway for him and Luke?

His surge of optimism dropped almost immediately. The idea was preposterous. Luke would have summers off, but he wouldn't. Luke might not even be living with him after the fall. Could he even afford the luxury of a summer home? Wouldn't he have to hire someone to care for the place? Or maybe the sisters could extend their business onto his land. Random thoughts and questions scattered across his mind like playing pieces in a board game.

"Number three?" Maura repeated, her eyes steady on his, bringing him back to the moment.

"Um, well…" He cursed his stammering, but the intensity in her expression was unsettling. If Maddie hadn't been present, he'd have sprung to his feet and wrapped Maura in his arms and told her…*what exactly?* Nothing about the loan because the issue here wasn't really the loan. The issue was that he was desperate for a way to have it all—her land, his land, *their* land—and her.

But none of that was going to happen. He had important work in Augusta, a son who might be wrenched from his childhood home and shipped off to a new school, bills to be paid and now a piece of land to be dealt with.

He took a deep breath. "I'm not sure yet about number three. It's a work in progress." He added a light laugh that fell flat. He saw the immediate disappointment on Maura's face and wished he'd never raised some bogus third option.

"Okay." Maddie's voice broke the mood. "Those two options are doable, but Maura and I need to discuss them alone because, frankly, Theo, it isn't fair to expect you to forgive this loan. We're not talking a few hundred dollars here!" She got up from the table. "I'm going to retrieve that ball now before it's destroyed by the gang out there."

When the door closed behind her, Maura said, "She's right, Theo. You deserve to have that money or the land, whichever you prefer." She stood up to carry coffee mugs to the sink.

Theo rose to help, but when they nearly collided at the sink, he grasped hold of her forearms and drew her close. "I'm sorry we even have to consider a solution here. My choice is to wait and see. If I get an offer on the land, well, then we'll have to decide. If not, we can—"

"Wait and see some more?" she asked, pulling apart from him. Her brow was raised teasingly, but her face was serious.

He shook his head and groaned. "I'm cursing my uncle's disorganization this very minute."

"His money gave my mother another year. That's pretty special, and...I'll be forever grateful to Stan and Vera for that chance. I'm sure Dad was."

Theo thumbed away the tears spilling onto her cheeks, stroked down and onto her lips, which were trembling now. "Maura, I...I..." The words were stuck in his throat. She brought her hands up to his face and gently lowered his head to hers, setting her mouth on his in a long, slow kiss.

What seemed an eternity later, the shrill blare

of a truck horn ended the moment. Maura gave a breathless sigh as they separated, and Theo was about to jokingly ask if she felt like she'd been running a marathon because he definitely did when she peered through the kitchen window and quietly swore.

Theo ducked his head to see a pickup parked in front of the house. Finn McAllister stepped out of it, followed almost at once by Shawn Harrison.

He caught Maura's eye. "Expecting them?"

She shook her head. "Can you greet them while I sneak out to warn Maddie? Just give her a heads-up. You know?"

Theo ran his palm down the side of her cheek. "I do know, Maura. Not to worry."

Her mouth twisted in a half smile. "My dad used to say that, and though I chafed at it as a teenager, I knew deep inside I wouldn't really have to worry."

"You *don't* have to worry."

"Thanks, Theo," she whispered.

Then she was out the door, running toward the barn, before he could say another word.

CHAPTER EIGHTEEN

MADDIE WAS STOWING the rubber ball in the empty stall where they kept the riding tack when Maura rushed into the barn.

"What's up, Mo? Has Theo left already?"

"No, he's still here. But…um…did you hear that horn?"

"Nope, but I've just come from the pasture and Shep was barking about something. Maybe that was it." She paused, frowning. "Come to think of it, Roger started braying at the same time. Weird, eh?"

"Maybe we have a guard donkey as well as a guard dog now," Maura quipped, prolonging the inevitable.

"So who's here?"

"Finn McAllister…and Shawn's with him."

Maddie was rooted by the stall door, her hand on the gate. "Were we expecting them?"

"No, but I'm assuming they're here about the festival. Do you want me to give you an excuse? You could sneak into the kitchen while Theo and I talk to them."

Maddie shook her head. "No, that's silly, Mo. Maple Glen is too small to go on avoiding someone, but thanks for the warning. Just…um…give me a minute, okay?"

What Maura wanted to do was to give her sister a big hug, but she feared that might result in tears for both of them. Besides, Maddie was right. Shawn had moved back to the area and encountering him was inevitable.

"Okay, see you out there." She hesitated a second. "By the way, there's a smudge on your left cheek and a strand of straw in your hair…right there, by your ear."

Maddie laughed as she pulled a tissue from her jeans pocket and rubbed at her cheek. "Okay?"

"Gone. Here, let me." Maura moved closer to brush off the straw. "Once a farm girl, always a farm girl. Isn't that what Dad used to say?"

"I think that was Mom, out of frustration."

"Makes sense. She did her best to get us into frilly clothes occasionally."

"At least they weren't matching outfits."

"Only that one time, those dresses Grandma sent one Christmas."

"Ugh! There's a photo of us somewhere."

"Yeah, with our scowling faces." Her sister's laugh was reassuring. "Okay, see you outside," Maura said.

Theo and the other two men were standing by Finn's truck as Maura headed over to them.

"We've come to check out a site for the first aid tent," Finn said. He scanned the large front lawn extending from the house to the road. "Have you allocated any places, yet? I believe you and Maddie were organizing that."

"Yeah, we are. I mean, we're working on it." She avoided Theo's amused gaze. "But right now, the area is pretty much free. What about over there, by that oak tree?" She pointed to the giant old oak centered in a cluster of other trees at the far west side of the property.

"Won't you want that shade for some vendors' tables?" Finn asked. "We have a tent, so it doesn't matter too much where we go. Just someplace visible."

Maura bit her lip. She wasn't presenting a credible image as one of the festival's organizers.

Theo rescued her by saying, "How about there, closer to the front veranda? That way anyone with a minor issue—dehydration, heat or whatever—can be treated under the tent and then move up onto the veranda to sit a bit longer if necessary. That would free up spaces in the tent."

Finn and Shawn looked at one another before Shawn said, "That'll work." He turned to Maura. "We've also booked a table to display pamphlets from the Green Mountain Conservancy, and Finn has some about Wallingford Fire Department's new search and rescue initiative."

"Do you want the table for the flyers to be

near the tent?" Maura asked, finally getting her thoughts focused.

"If there's room, that would be the logical place," Finn answered. "And I haven't organized a volunteer to man it yet, so whoever's on duty in the tent can replenish the stock." He hesitated a moment, then turned to Theo. "I hate to ask because I know you're on holiday, but would you be able to relieve our first aid volunteers if necessary? I've got a lineup of people from the fire department, but you know how these things play out with volunteers. Stuff happens and they have to cancel. It would just be on a 'needs must' basis."

"Of course. But I don't have any supplies with me," Theo said.

Finn waved a dismissive hand. "We're well equipped, and thanks, Theo—that's great. All right, then, that's about it for now, isn't it, Shawn?"

Maura was intrigued by Shawn's shrug. He hadn't spoken much, but she'd noticed his attention shifting now and then to the house. *Wondering where Maddie is?*

As if on cue, the slamming kitchen door answered the question. Maddie must have sneaked inside to change from jeans and T-shirt to slim-fitting capris and a floral top. There was an air of breathlessness about her as she strode their way, and Maura guessed that she'd taken a few seconds to summon her courage. She sneaked a peek at

Shawn and saw he was captivated by the image breezing toward them.

"I thought I heard people talking out here," Maddie called as she approached.

Yeah, right, Maura thought. She turned slightly and caught a quick wink from Theo.

"Hi, Maddie," Finn said. "We came to have a look at where we can set up our tent on Thursday." He gestured to Shawn. "I don't think you two have met up yet. Shawn was at the community meeting last week."

"I had to leave early, so no, didn't get a chance to say hello." She shifted slightly to look directly at Shawn. "Welcome back to the Glen, Shawn."

"Thanks, Maddie." He cleared his throat. "Good to see you again…and Maura, too."

Maura didn't dare look at Theo, guessing he'd be grinning at the awkward afterthought. She admired her sister's composure, though the split between Maddie and Shawn had happened so many years ago surely painful emotions were long gone. But then she remembered her own gut reaction to Theo's return. Was there an expiry date on a broken heart?

"I saw your sign out front, Jake & Friends," Shawn was now saying, "and Finn's told me you and Maura are running a riding therapy program but with donkeys instead of horses. How did that come about?"

"It's a bit of a long story," Maddie answered.

"I'd love to hear it sometime," Shawn said, his eyes glued on Maddie.

"Sure, whenever you like."

It was Theo who broke the moment. "Think it's almost time to pick up Luke from Walter's place."

Everyone stirred into action then.

"Let us know if you need any more help before the big day," Finn said as he got into the pickup.

Theo began walking to the cedar hedge to get his car while Maura stood still, transfixed by the tableau of Maddie and Shawn reconnecting.

"Maura?" Theo beckoned from the hedge.

Reluctantly, she moved toward him, keeping her sister and Shawn at the edge of her vision.

"You're both funny and obvious," he murmured when she reached him.

"Huh?"

"That." He nodded toward Maddie and Shawn. When Maura pivoted, she saw that they were now saying goodbye.

"I don't know what you mean," she blustered, aware of heat rising up her neck into her face.

"It's good that they're talking. What happens next is beyond your control, so…"

"Are you saying that I'm meddling in my sister's affairs?" She saw his wince and backtracked. "Sorry, I didn't mean that to sound so blunt. I'm just—"

"Looking out for your twin sister. I get that. But she's an adult now, and so is Shawn. They'll work something out between them." He set his palm against her cheek. Reassuring her. Telling her he was on her side.

He was right, Maura knew. She leaned against his hand for a moment longer, then drew back.

"I'll call you tomorrow when all my business is dealt with." Then he pushed through the hedge and disappeared.

Maura turned around to see Finn driving out to the road. Maddie was still standing where she'd said goodbye. She glanced over at Maura, her eyes shining. With tears, Maura wondered, or happiness?

Then she smiled. "It's all right, Mo. I'm fine. The first awkward meeting has come and gone, and you know what? It wasn't nearly as bad as I'd expected." She started toward the house but stopped to add, "He's coming over Wednesday morning to help set up tables." Steps away from the side door she shouted, "I'm changing my clothes and then we have to feed the donkeys." The kitchen door closed behind her.

Wonder of wonders, Maura was thinking. Theo's words from the other day resurfaced. *Don't get ahead of yourself.* She needed to keep that in mind. But if the problem that broke apart Maddie and Shawn could be resolved or at least mitigated, that could be a game changer. Her sister might decide to stay in Maple Glen—and Maura would do whatever she could to make that happen.

THEO WATCHED THE flashy black SUV and his Realtor's compact car drive away. The interested buyer, a statewide construction company, had sent a team that included three engineers, an architect, a surveyor and a lawyer. He'd spent their two-hour inspection of the entire property tucked inside the house—the one area they weren't interested in. He'd found the visit stressful but couldn't explain why. The farm had to be sold, and although he figured it shouldn't matter to him who the buyer was, the fact was it did.

His Realtor had informed him that the company spokesperson liked the location, and his acreage, though not as big as they'd envisioned, would suffice. When she added that she'd indicated the adjacent farmland might also be available, Theo's anxiety rose. "They have no plans to sell," he quickly asserted.

She'd shrugged. "You never know. People make surprising decisions sometimes."

When the vehicles hit the county road, Theo went back inside. The place was a shambles because he'd spent the nerve-racking hours before the team's arrival conducting another search for any documents, memos or Post-it notes regarding the loan.

Luke, on his way to help clean out stables, had scarcely noticed the mess. After downing breakfast, he'd lingered long enough to tell Theo that he and Ashley Watson plus two other kids from the youth club had planned a short hike on the off trail leading out of the village that afternoon.

This news had buzzed around Theo's mind like a confused hornet. When and how were these plans made? he'd asked.

"Ashley and her mom came when I was finishing up working with Walter yesterday. Her mother is a pretty good artist, and she'd made some labels for Walter's honey jars. So all of us wiped the jars clean and then stuck the labels on. We didn't finish, though, 'cause there were too many jars and not enough labels."

"Okay, but the hike thing?" Theo had prompted.

"That's when Ashley said I could go with them if I wanted to, and I said yes."

So much for seeking parental permission, Theo thought. He'd have pointed out that Luke might have mentioned this last night but decided not to make an issue out of it. Besides, Luke's absence would give him some alone time with Maura and Maddie to report whatever he found at Rutland Town Hall.

Luke returned from stable cleaning just as Theo finished making his lunch. "Can I take that with me?" he asked, eyeing the sandwich.

"Sure, but I thought you were hiking after lunch."

"Ashley texted Maura to tell me that they're meeting at the bakery earlier 'cause one of the kids wants to buy his lunch there."

"That sounds like a complicated network... Ashley sending messages to you via Maura."

"What happens when I don't have a phone of my own."

Theo would have laughed if he hadn't been struck by the realization that this kind of interchange would only increase as Luke went from preteen to actual teen. "True. Maybe we can negotiate a phone in the fall, if you're with me in Augusta."

"Seriously?"

Theo pursed his lips. The instant perk in his son's expression was both charming and unsettling. Would the kid choose which parent to live with based on the availability of a cell phone? That saddened him because he knew Trish would allow Luke to have a phone.

"Sure," he mumbled, accepting defeat.

"Cool. I'm going up to change. My clothes kind of reek from you-know-what."

"Good idea. Maybe some deodorant, too?"

"Jeez, Dad."

Theo grinned as he packed a lunch. There would certainly be adjustments for both of them in the months ahead. Trish needed a decision by the end of July, and Theo knew he and Luke would have to make plans that could potentially affect his long-term relationship with his son. But not until after the festival, he told himself.

When Luke returned in clean shorts and a T-shirt

and carrying his small daypack, Theo handed him the paper bag lunch. "How far you guys going?" he asked as Luke sat in a chair to put on his hiking shoes.

"To where the blue blazes meet with the white ones. Where you and I were heading the day we found that man."

"Right. Good. And I take it someone will have a cell phone, just in case."

"Of course. They probably all will!"

Luke's head was bent as he tied his shoes, but Theo guessed he was scowling. "And just a reminder that cell phone access in the woods is—"

"Unpredictable. Ashley told me. But they're taking theirs anyway." He stood up and reached for the daypack.

"Water bottle?" Theo asked.

"Oh. Right."

Theo hid a grin while he reached for the bottle on the counter and passed it over. As Luke was stowing it in the pack, Theo said, "Have a good time, son, and get one of the kids to text me when you're back in the village, so I'll know everything worked out okay."

"You'd know right away if I could text you myself."

Theo ignored the gibe. Best to send him off without any more conflict. A car's engine ended the matter.

"That's Ashley," Luke said. "Her mom's giving us a ride to the bakery."

The information just kept trickling in, Theo was thinking, as he watched his son head out to the car. This was going to be life with a teenager. Everything on a need-to-know basis, which actually meant the teen decided who needed to know, how much and when. Theo sighed. Was he really up for this, on his own, given the long, unpredictable hours in urgent care? Yet if he didn't try to make it work, he'd lose the opportunity to be a real part of his only child's life. And that was something he couldn't stomach.

The best- and worst-case scenarios for the end of the month's decision filled Theo's mind as he drove to Rutland an hour later. Getting what he wanted at the town hall was relatively easy, and soon he was on his way to the Stuart farm to tell them that the loan transaction was indeed on record and therefore would have an impact on any sale of his property.

His Realtor had told him the company needed the rest of the week to come up with an offer, as there were other properties they were considering. This was the first indication she'd given that his land wasn't the only choice for the company, and surprisingly, the news was almost a relief. He might have time to look at other options than selling. He wasn't sure what those might be, but maybe he could ask Maura to be part of the brain-storming. And Luke, too.

By the time he reached the outskirts of Maple Glen, the weather was changing. The sunny day that had been promised by local forecasts was shifting as dark, ominous clouds formed over White Rocks Mountain. Theo glanced up at the sky through the windshield, then checked the time on the car dashboard. Luke had been gone for a couple of hours and hopefully would now be back.

He exited Route 7 onto the county road and impulsively turned into the Stuart driveway. As soon as he parked the car, he checked his cell phone for any messages and, finding none, let out a frustrated groan. He was heading for the kitchen door when Maura emerged from the barn.

"Hey, Theo, are you returning from Rutland? What did you find out?"

Theo smiled. Getting right down to business, as Maura was wont to do. "Yes, I am, and all of us should discuss it. Is now a good time?"

She nodded. "Mads and I've been bringing in the donkeys, and she's getting Roger right now. There's going to be a storm."

"Yeah." He peered anxiously up at the sky. "Problem?"

"Luke's gone hiking on the trail with some kids from the youth club."

"How long ago? When are you expecting him back? Did they take cell phones?"

Her questions flew at him, like the ones he'd peppered Luke with hours ago—a shift that might have been amusing if a sudden lightning bolt and crack of thunder hadn't made them both jump.

"Inside maybe?" Maura said.

"I should check on Luke. Do you have Ashley's mother's number?" The question was followed by another crack of thunder, and rather than a reply, they dashed for the kitchen. The rain pelted down the instant they closed the door.

"That was close," Maura gasped. "I hope Maddie made it into the barn. Do you want me to contact Ashley's mother, see if the kids are back yet?"

"Please." But his phone rang as soon as he spoke—it was Luke, using Ashley's phone.

"Hi, Dad, we just got back, and we're waiting out the storm inside Mrs. McAllister's house."

"Oh, great. I was worried. Do you want me to pick you up?"

"No, Dad, please. Mrs. McAllister's making us hot chocolate, and she baked cookies today. Ashley said her mom will drop me off later, after the storm."

Theo was chuckling as he hung up.

"All's well?" Maura asked, smiling.

Theo nodded. "I've had some interesting parenting situations today."

"Good ones?" She turned to look at him as she went to the counter.

"Learning ones."

"Hmm, maybe the best kind. I'm making coffee, by the way. For our talk."

No backtracking now, Theo told himself. Though what he'd really like to do was to brush back the tendril of hair that was clinging to her damp cheek, which would mean he'd have to take her into his arms and then…

Maddie rushed into the kitchen, the door blowing shut behind her. "Just made it. They're all safe and sound." Her attention shifted from Maura to Theo. "What's up?"

"I went to Rutland Town Hall and confirmed the notarized record of the loan."

Minutes later the three of them were sitting at the table, drinking the hot brew and still postponing the talk. Finally, Theo said, "This is what I think. We don't need to worry about the loan until I know for sure I'll be selling the property. My agent tells me the interested party will likely wait until after the weekend, considering the holiday this Thursday. If the offer is a good one, and I'm compelled to take it, we still have options."

"You forgive the loan on paper, for the records, and we repay you in installments every month until it's finished," Maura preempted.

She and Maddie had clearly been discussing this, and Theo figured that course was the best

one for all of them. "Looks like we have a decision, then."

The silence in the room spoke volumes. Maura
and Maddie nodded, stone-faced.

Theo wished he could tell them to forget about
the money completely because he knew how money
could drive a wedge between people. He and Trish
had spent several months hassling over money, and
unnecessary acrimony had resulted.

Now they had a plan—something to act on—
but he had a bad feeling this was a risky situation
when it came to a future with Maura.

CHAPTER NINETEEN

THE BLARE OF a horn shook Maura from a deep sleep. She shot up, rubbing her eyes, and saw that it was eight o'clock. Walter was here with the tables. If she was lucky, Maddie was already up and had breakfast on the go. They'd stayed up late, making a huge map of the festival grounds and assigning spots to all the registered vendors.

Last night they'd both skirted around the money talk with Theo until Maddie had commented, as they headed upstairs, "We're lucky we owe the money to Theo, and not some stranger."

Maura had to concur, though she'd lain sleepless for a long time, thinking that owing money to someone you cared for deeply, someone you wanted to have some kind of future with, might not be such a good thing. Would it always be between them, a deterrent to open and transparent conversation? Plus, he'd implied there were other options but hadn't specified what they might be, instead agreeing at once to their payback plan. Of course, they were obliged to repay, but what were the other options he'd hinted at? She had no answers by morning.

As she got into shorts and a T-shirt, she peered through her bedroom window to see Walter and another man chatting with Maddie. *Saved by my sister, and not for the first time*, she thought as she finished dressing and ran downstairs. Coffee was brewing in the machine, and Maura smiled at the loaf of bread, with jars of jam, peanut butter and honey on the table. Entertaining Maple Glen–style.

The three glanced up as Maura exited the side door.

"Maura." Walter nodded. "This here is Bill Moyer, from Wallingford. He's helping transport tables with me today and can come tomorrow, too, if need be."

Bill, a man approximately the same age as Walter, shook hands and then said, "Nice place you've got here. I was just telling your sister that my granddaughter would love to ride one of your donkeys, so I'm bringing her on Thursday."

"That's great," Maura said, "and thanks for helping." She turned to Walter. "Maddie and I've put together a site map, which we've mounted on a plywood board, so feel free to help yourself to breakfast in the kitchen while we get it from the barn."

"Maybe we should do some unloading first, but thank you," Walter said. "How about if we lean the tables against the barn for now? Or were you thinking of arranging them in their assigned spots for folks?"

"We thought we'd place them today or tomorrow. We've asked people to come as early as possible on Thursday to find their table and set up. The official starting time isn't until eleven."

Walter nodded. "Sounds good. When we finish with this lot, we'll pick up the tables from the church, and then we can help organize them where they're supposed to go, if you like." He and Bill began lifting the folding tables out of the back of the truck and carrying them to the side of the barn.

Maura signaled Maddie and went to get the plywood board. "Thanks for letting me sleep in a bit, Mads, and also for organizing breakfast."

"I figured you had a late night. Your light was still on when I turned mine out. Personally, I slept very well," Maddie said.

Maura smiled. No anxious thoughts about Shawn Harrison, then, she figured. A good omen.

"By the way," Maddie added as they were lifting the heavy board. "Ashley and Luke are coming over sometime today or maybe tomorrow to braid red, white and blue ribbons in the donkeys' tails, and also to help decorate the riding ring."

"What a good idea!"

"It was Ashley's, and her mother is providing the ribbon. I'm thinking just do Jake and Matilda, Lizzie if she's in a good mood, but maybe not Roger."

"I guess we should bring them into their stalls, then, make it easier for the kids."

"That's what I thought."

Maura grasped one end of the plywood board and Maddie, the other. "Ugh, this thing seems heavier than it was yesterday," she grunted as they lifted the board up, carrying it out to the front yard. On the way they passed Walter, who was adding another table to the stack leaning on one side of the barn door.

"Want us to help with that?" he asked.

"We're good, thanks, Walter."

They'd already decided to prop the board up on the veranda where vendors could check it on the day, and the board would be out of the way of children dashing about. After they lugged it up onto the veranda and leaned it safely against the house, they surveyed the map.

"Still a few empty places," Maura pointed out, "which means we can accommodate last-minute vendors." She watched Walter and Bill, who didn't even live in the Glen, finish unloading. "The Fourth of July Festival has been happening in the Glen ever since we can remember, right? Did you ever think about all the people in the village and even beyond who worked to make it happen?"

Maddie shook her head. "Nope, as kids and teens we just enjoyed it. We're lucky, though, to have such community spirit in the Glen."

"Let's hope it never changes." Maura instantly

thought about the sale of the Danby land. "And let's hope whoever buys Theo's property gets involved in our community, too." She noticed Maddie's frown. "What? Do you think that couldn't happen?"

"I was in the northeast pasture yesterday when some people came to inspect it. There was a bunch of them, and they all looked like professionals. Not regular people. I watched for a while and not a single person went into the house."

"Which means—"

"They weren't interested in the house."

"Why didn't you bring this up when Theo was here to discuss the loan? We could have asked him about this potential buyer."

"Wasn't the loan repayment enough of an issue?" Maddie huffed.

True, but Maura found this information disturbing. Although their land would still be theirs thanks to the loan repayment plan, the future of Jake & Friends could be affected by whoever bought Theo's place. Maura held up two crossed fingers. "Wishing for a nice, friendly family."

"Same here but…" Maddie pivoted at the sound of an engine chugging up the drive. "Guess we've got company."

Walter was closing the rear end of the pickup as an old-model Volkswagen camper van rolled to a stop yards away. Maddie glanced at Maura and quipped, "That looks like something from the sixties."

The multicolored van bore a single large blue eye on the side door behind the driver. An array of calligraphic words spread across and around the van's panels. Near the roof, a painted black sign read Clair Voyant, Palm and Tarot Card Reader.

Maura noticed Walter and Bill exchange smiles, and she grinned at Maddie. "Cute!"

When the engine shut down, the driver door creaked open, and a petite woman with short, gray-streaked dark hair and wearing a pair of faded jeans topped by a tie-dyed T-shirt stepped out. "Morning, folks. I'm Rita Moretti, and I'm hoping it's not too late for me to sign up for a spot for your festival."

It was Maddie who moved first, smiling broadly. "Great! I'm Maddie Stuart. My sister and I—" she gestured to Maura "—are hosting the festival this year."

Rita nodded at Maura as Maddie went on to introduce the two men.

"How did you hear about the festival?" Maura asked, thinking of all the flyers they'd delivered and posted throughout the area.

"The internet. Isn't that how everyone gets information nowadays?"

Maura heard Walter chuckle. "I guess someone on our planning committee posted it," she quickly said.

"There are dozens of websites devoted to local and state events, as I'm sure you know, and they're a great guide. I spend most of the year traveling from one place to another to participate in celebrations of all kinds. That's my work." A smile lit up Rita's face.

"Well, we do have places available," Maddie said. "Will you be doing…um…readings from the van or a table?"

"Normally I use the van, parked in an accessible spot." She peered around. "But it looks like this area is going to be for tables only?" She looked at the last pair of tables leaning against the bumper of Walter's pickup.

"Right. People who arrive in vehicles will be parking them on the property adjacent to ours," Maura said, pointing to Theo's place.

"Okay. I'm happy to use a table if there's one available, and I guess I can park my van over there, too." She scanned the area once more and said, "You've got donkeys. I noticed the sign driving up. I'd love to see them."

"Sure. My sister can find you a place on our map while I show you the donkeys," Maura said.

"Anywhere suits me," Rita told Maddie. Then she turned to the men and said, "Nice to meet you two," and followed Maura.

As they approached the side door, Maura heard Shep barking inside the kitchen. They'd left him there while the men were unloading, to keep him from getting in the way. "Hang on," she said to Rita, pausing to open the door.

Shep bounded out, jumping up on Maura and then turning his attention to Rita. The dog's love of attention could be overwhelming, Maura had learned, but Rita didn't mind his eagerness to please as she leaned down, stroking his head and back, while Shep lavished love on her.

"Lovely dog," she said, standing up. "I used to have one, but after he passed away, I didn't replace him. Nomadic life and constant contact with strangers aren't always the best things for a pet. I miss him," she added, her face clouding over.

Shep ran ahead as they rounded the corner of the barn, and Rita stopped when the pasture came in sight. "Donkeys can be pets, too, right?"

"For sure." Maura liked the woman already.

They walked to the fence where Shep paced, whining at the gate. Maura opened it, and he raced inside, heading straight for Roger. Matilda and Jake wandered over to greet the humans, while Lizzie stood motionless in a far corner of the field. Shep was now running circles around Roger, greeting him as he did every morning when he was first released into the field.

"They're gentle creatures and very intelligent," Rita commented as she stroked Matilda's long face and snout. Jake was vying for attention, too, and Rita chuckled as she rubbed his head and neck at the same time. "Have you had them long?"

Maura briefly recapped how Jake and Matilda ended up at the farm and her decision to set up the riding program. She liked the fact that Rita listened quietly, without asking questions or tossing off a comment. Instead, the woman simply kept administering affection to Jake and Matilda as Maura spoke.

When Maura mentioned Lizzie's aloofness and penchant for nipping, Rita said, "She was ill-treated, but I bet there's someone she can connect with."

Maura thought of Katie and her almost magical bond with the unpredictable Lizzie. She was about to tell Rita this when the woman said, "I can see that Shep and the big donkey out there—Roger, you said?—are best friends." After a moment longer of watching them, she turned to Maura. "Thanks for letting me have a sneak peek at them, and I'm looking forward to maybe riding one before the festival's over." She paused to survey the field and the donkeys. "I've a feeling this is going to be a new and wonderful experience for me."

Shep ran up to the gate, and Maura let him out. They followed the dog around to the front, where Maddie was saying goodbye to Walter and Bill.

Rita made for her van, but paused to ask, "Is there a campground close by?"

"Um, I don't think so. What about Wallingford?" Maura looked at Walter, who was leaning out the driver-side window of his truck.

He shook his head. "Closest one I can think of

is to the south of here, toward Bennington. A bit far for a commute, though."

Rita was frowning, and Maura was about to offer her some space at the farm when Walter suddenly said, "I've got lots of property and an electrical outlet as well as a water supply in my honey shed. You're welcome to camp there, if you like."

"A honey shed? You keep bees?" Rita was beaming.

"I do. But the hives aren't anywhere near the shed, so if you're worried about getting stung—"

"Not at all. And thank you, that would be wonderful. I'm happy to recompense you."

"My pleasure. Be nice to have another human around for a couple of days."

"Perhaps I can repay you in kind," she said, gesturing to her van. "A reading?"

Maura hid a grin at Walter's expression but admired his discretion as he merely shrugged.

"Bill and I are going to pick up the rest of the tables, and I'll meet you back here in about twenty minutes or so." With that, he turned on the ignition and reversed to make his turn before heading back to the village.

Maura glanced at her sister, thinking she might be having the same idea right then. "Would you like some breakfast, Rita, while you're waiting?"

"Lovely, my dear."

They trooped into the kitchen accompanied by Shep, who dashed for his food bowl next to the door. As they ate, Maura and Maddie told Rita more about their decision to establish Jake & Friends and gave her a snapshot summary of growing up in Maple Glen. It seemed like only moments had passed before Walter's truck horn sounded.

Waving goodbye, she thought how quickly Walter, notoriously private, had offered Rita space on his property. He'd been actively helping with this year's festival, something he hadn't done previously. She also realized that despite the ease she and Maddie had felt talking about themselves and the locals, they'd heard almost nothing about Rita Moretti herself.

THEO HAD INTENDED to pop next door and help with the tables but was interrupted by a series of texts from his Realtor fielding queries from the company about the property's water and sewage mains, as well as gas and electricity lines. They were simply confirming details the team must have already investigated, but Theo's irritation notched up at each message. He rationalized that was probably the reason for his abrupt reply when, later that day, Luke asked him about the people who'd come to see the farm.

"We were in the pasture with the donkeys when we saw some people wandering around here. They had clipboards and stuff and didn't look like ordinary people," Luke reported.

"They work for a company that's interested in buying this place."

Luke's eyes widened. "What kind of company?"

Theo sighed. Hadn't they discussed this already? Or maybe they hadn't. "It's a development company. You know, building."

"Like condos and apartment buildings?"

"Or houses."

Luke frowned. "So not like a family that's going to buy the farm and renovate or something."

"No." He could see the distaste in his son's expression and felt impatience rising. "My Realtor hasn't had a single inquiry from anyone wanting a farm."

"But wouldn't a lot of buildings and people change Maple Glen? It wouldn't be a village anymore."

There was nothing Theo could say because Luke was absolutely right.

"You can't sell this place to just anyone. That's… that's a horrible thing to do." He stomped out of the kitchen and up to his room.

Theo was anticipating negative reactions to a possible sale to the company, especially from Maura and Maddie, whose land would be most affected by development, but he hadn't considered such a strong response from Luke. He'd seen his son's growing attachment to the Glen but figured their stay would eventually fade into a vague memory once life in Augusta resumed.

Of course, he'd been in denial about the consequences of selling the land to a company, or even a family. Once it was gone, what would draw him back? He knew the answer at once. *Maura.* But would she want him if he sold out to big business?

CHAPTER TWENTY

MAURA WAS UP at daybreak. She'd had a good sleep, likely because she'd been exhausted when she'd finally collapsed into bed. After Walter and Bill had moved the rest of the tables from the church, all four of them had set up the tables on their assigned sites and numbered them to correspond to the map.

During all this, her mind had been fixed on Theo's absence. Why hadn't he come to help as he'd promised? Even Luke had failed to turn up in the afternoon, a break in his daily routine of hanging out with the donkeys and helping with chores. Something was off, and she wondered if it might be connected to the people who'd inspected the Danby property. Business types, Maddie had said.

It was her turn to make breakfast, and the coffee was ready when Maddie came into the kitchen and slumped onto a chair. "I'm beat already," she said, "and today is going to be a marathon of work."

"True, but thanks to Walter and Bill, we don't have to set up tables."

"What else do we have to do?"

"Clean the stables, feed and groom the donkeys. Let's see if Luke and Ashley can help with that, as well as braid their tails. Plus, we've got streamers to decorate the fence around the riding ring, remember? They're in a box in the barn. Nancy said she was available today and Cathy texted to say she could help with riders on the day itself." Maura sat down and poured cereal into a bowl. "It's funny that neither Luke nor Theo came by yesterday, though," she added seconds later. "In fact, I didn't notice any activity there at all."

Maddie laughed, sputtering coffee onto her cereal bowl. "Are you the Glen's neighborhood watch now?"

Maura felt her face heat up. "No, but the place is pretty visible from the northeast pasture, so…"

"Maybe we should look for Dad's binoculars, to help you with this new job of yours."

"Ha ha." Not a bad idea, she was thinking.

They ate in silence for the next few minutes until Maddie asked, "What are your thoughts on the days after the festival, when Theo and Luke will be making plans to leave, assuming he sells the property?"

Maura kept her eyes on her cereal bowl. "Today and tomorrow will be far too busy to think about anything beyond the festival."

"I know you too well, Mo. Hedge all you want—I'm sure you've been playing all kinds of scenarios in your head about what happens after Thursday."

"What about you? In two months, your promised year working with me will be up. Surely, you've been considering your options, too."

"I guess we're both on the same page regarding our futures, then."

"As always. We're twins, right? We don't look alike, and we don't always think alike, but deep down, we're bound by something…indefinable." She managed a smile despite the unexpected threat of tears. "And can we agree to preserve that bond, no matter what?" She stretched her arm across the table, setting her hand on top of Maddie's.

"Yes." Maddie's smile was wobbly, too, as she turned over her hand to clasp Maura's. "For us and for Mom and Dad, because they'd want us to stick together…no matter what."

Maura took a deep breath. "And we won't let any…" She searched for an appropriate word. "…entanglements with men come between us."

"Entanglements?" Maddie grinned.

"You know what I mean."

"And these unnamed men?"

"You know who they are. Deal?"

Maddie gave a mock salute. "Deal."

"Pinkie swear?"

Maddie's laugh startled Shep, who was dozing

by the kitchen door. He gave an obligatory bark and settled back down onto his piece of carpet. "I think that's one childhood tradition we can forget."

"All right, then," Maura said, standing up. "Let's get to work." But as she began to clear dishes, another question stopped her.

"Are you in love with Theo, Mo?"

Maura was afraid to turn around, to reveal the anxiety on her face. She stared bleakly out the kitchen window. "I think I am."

"Have you told him?"

"No. What's the point? He has an important job in Augusta and a twelve-year-old son to support. There's nothing in Maple Glen for him, except a decrepit farmhouse and acreage that he can't do anything with other than sell."

"*You're* here."

"No kidding."

"But you don't have to be. We've never discussed the possibility, but we can always sell the donkeys or give them to a shelter and get rid of the farm."

Maura swung around. "Is that what *you* want?"

"We're talking about you, not me."

Maddie's shrug irked her. Hadn't they just had an emotional moment between them, a pledge of solidarity? Now her sister was suggesting an extremely unpalatable idea. "I...I absolutely couldn't do that," she blustered. "I've put so much into this business, and I love those animals, Mads! They're a part of my life."

"I know that, Mo. But would you sacrifice a chance for a future with Theo and even Luke, out of…I don't know…some kind of fixation on this place?"

"How about you? What are *your* current feelings for Shawn, and would *you* sacrifice a second chance with him because you feel restless here?" She regretted the retort at the pained expression on Maddie's face, but the question was as valid as the one Maddie had hurled at her.

They stared at one another until Shep's whine and pawing at the door distracted them. Maddie got up to let him out and, turning back to Maura, said, "We're doing what we swore we wouldn't do."

"What?"

"Letting two men come between us."

Maura gave a sharp laugh. "True." Her phone pinged just then, and when she picked it up from the table, she noted a text from Theo.

"Speaking of men…"

Maddie raised a querying eyebrow.

"Theo and Luke are heading over after Finn and Shawn arrive with the fire engine."

"So it begins," Maddie murmured, getting up from her chair. She carried more dishes to the kitchen counter, and as she stood next to Maura, she added, "Let's not allow these men to get in our way today. We can deal with them tomorrow."

Maura's smile felt tentative. "Agreed. Let's have some fun." She threw her arms around her sister in a tight hug.

THEO MADE A full breakfast for Luke, knowing a normal lunch might not happen, as the day before the festival promised to be busy. In the middle of the rough patch yesterday with his son, Theo had realized going next door to help with tables might not be a good idea. He'd managed to strike a truce with Luke over the two main problems that had precipitated the blowup between them: the potential sale of the land to a development company, which could ruin the tone of Maple Glen, and the looming deadline regarding where and with whom Luke would live next year. Theo had promised to discuss these two issues with Luke right after the festival.

He'd even managed to extract a wan smile from Luke when he told him they'd shop for a cell phone when they left the Glen and had added that they both needed to try harder to communicate their feelings in an appropriate way. The irony of such a pact wasn't lost on Theo. He was the adult, after all, and there'd be many more conflicts when Luke was a teen, but at least the current situation was stabilized.

When he heard Luke coming out of the bathroom, he went to the foot of the staircase and hollered, "Pancakes and bacon are ready!"

By the time he was plating the food, Luke was sitting down, fork in hand. "Juice?" he asked.

Theo rolled his eyes. *Yeah, he's a preteen all right.* "You know where it is."

After pouring himself a glass of orange juice, Luke stood in front of the open fridge door a second longer.

"What're you looking for?" Theo asked, dishing out his own pancakes.

"Is the syrup all gone?"

"I don't know. You're the syrup fan here." He sat down to tackle his breakfast, adding, "It was only a small bottle, so yes, maybe so." There was a trace of a pout as Luke plunked down onto his chair. "Look in the pantry—that narrow closet next to the fridge. There might be some kind of substitute, like jam or sugar."

Luke pulled a face but got up to check. Seconds later, he was bringing a large porcelain canister labeled SUGAR. "Better than nothing," he muttered and unsnapped the lid. He peered inside and frowned.

"Well, is it sugar?" Theo teased.

"Nope." He stuck a hand in and pulled out a plastic bag, which he dropped next to his pancakes.

Theo stared at the bag, not really understanding what he was seeing, until Luke untied its knot and dumped elastic-bound rolls of bills onto the table. "Money," Luke whispered. "And a lot of it."

Theo gawked at the small pile and knew instinctively what this was. The regular monthly withdrawals Maura had mentioned, missing from her father's account. The bills were fifties, and he counted as he spread them out across the table.

"How much is there?" Luke asked, wide-eyed.

"I think about twenty-five hundred dollars."

"That's a fortune!" Luke exclaimed.

Not compared to ten thousand, Theo was thinking, but it would help Maura and Maddie.

"There's something else," Luke said. He pulled out a scrap of paper and flattened it on the table.

Theo recognized his uncle's handwriting and skimmed the note. *From Charlie Stuart, for the loan. He's struggling. I'll forget about the repayment.*

Theo looked at the date, realizing it had been written only months before his uncle, newly diagnosed with dementia, went into the nursing home. Aunt Vera had followed soon after, and their mutual decline had accelerated. Neither had had the chance to follow through with this, much less tell Theo about it. At least now there was evidence of intent to forgive the loan, and Theo hoped Maura and Maddie would no longer feel indebted to him. Perhaps the awkward shift in their relationship that he'd felt since suggesting a payback scheme would disappear with this find.

"What's this all about, Dad?" Luke asked after reading the note.

"It's a long story, Luke, and I'll for sure get around to it later. For now, we're due next door and…" He paused, hearing a roar of engines. "I think that might be Finn, parking his department's fire engine for the big day tomorrow."

Luke dashed for the door, his interest in the money already fading. Theo scooped up the bills and replaced them in the canister, a hiding place that had proved to be a good one. He stacked the unwashed plates and cutlery in the sink and went out to join Finn and Shawn standing next to the fire engine.

The day had begun, and it was already an auspicious one.

CHAPTER TWENTY-ONE

MAURA FIGURED SOME mischief-maker had messaged the Glen's residents to arrive at the same time on festival day, because as soon as she and Maddie closed the kitchen door behind them, leaving Shep whining inside, she saw a stream of people walking along the road from Theo's place, toting baskets, bins and large bags.

As she approached the gap in the cedar hedge, she saw that Theo's entire front lawn was almost filled with cars already, at eight in the morning. Then she spotted Theo and Luke heading her way and felt a burst of happiness.

Luke rushed ahead. "Is Ashley here?"

"Honestly, Luke, I've no idea. When we came outside after breakfast, people were already checking the site map and looking for their tables. Maddie has gone to bring the donkeys into the barn because we decided braiding their tails in their stalls was the least distractible place. Why don't you…?" But he was already racing toward the barn. She grinned at Theo. "Someone's super excited."

"Yep. Listen, Maura, I want to say, first of all, that I love you. And also, that—"

"Theo, I love you, too, and—"

He laughed with her. And she was about to tell him that she hoped for some kind of future with him when someone spoke from behind. She swung around to see Sue Giordano from the bakery, her husband and their teenage son, holding baskets and trays of baked goods.

"Maura? We can't find our table."

Maura caught Theo's wink and mouthed a silent "later" as she led them to their table. Knowing they'd be selling baked goods, she'd purposely given them a shady location in a place suitable for a lineup of buyers. When Maura returned, Theo had vanished into the growing crowd.

On her way to help Maddie with the donkeys, she was held up several times by people with questions and requests—some wanted a better site for their table, while others wanted to trade places. By the time she reached the barn, she was ready to run and hide in one of the stalls. She peeked inside to see Ashley standing next to Jake as she braided his tail, while Luke was with Matilda in the next stall.

"Are they being good?" she asked as she got closer.

"Matilda is," Luke said, "but Jake wasn't into it at first."

"He's okay now," Ashley added. "But I had to relax him with some pieces of turnip."

Maura laughed. "That'll do the trick. You might need some for Roger. He's still a bit wary of people."

"We think Roger's upset at all the commotion and also missing Shep—he was braying," Luke told her.

"Where's Maddie?"

"She's bringing Roger inside anyway, and Lizzie's going to stay in the pasture today," Ashley replied.

"All good," said Maura. She pivoted round at the clatter of hooves as Maddie led Roger into the barn. His nostrils were flared, and his eyes seemed to be rolling around in his head. Maura saw that Maddie was having trouble holding on as he kept jerking at his halter. She ran over to help, grabbing hold of the lead rope along with her sister.

"He'll settle down now that he's inside," Maddie gasped. Together they steered him into his stall and Maura kept her distance as Maddie unclipped the rope. She had no idea what to expect from Roger. He hadn't been with them long enough for her or Maddie to predict or understand his moods, though she bet Shep could.

"I'll get Shep," Maura said. "Maybe he'll help

settle Roger. Keep talking quietly to soothe him but stay out of kicking range." She waited until Maddie backed away from Roger. Then Maura sidled along the stall's partition and out its gate. Seconds later she was tugging at the kitchen door, but as soon as she flung it open, Shep bounded out.

Confused by the people milling about in the yard, he ran away from the barn and toward the front of the house and the driveway. Maura chased after him, hoping he wouldn't make it to the road. She ignored the voices calling out to her for assistance or tossing questions at her as she jogged around people, trying to keep Shep in sight. When she finally spotted him, he was yards away from the end of the drive. There was no point in shouting his name, for the place was echoing with all the noise people generated. Heart in mouth, Maura picked up her pace, dodging a couple hauling goods in a wagon, and hoping someone would stop a runaway dog. Thankfully, someone did.

Rita Moretti was on her knees, patting and stroking Shep, when Maura finally caught up to him. Once her breathing was under control, she thanked Rita.

"He must be wondering what's going on, poor thing," Rita murmured. Shep whined as if he understood exactly what the woman had said.

The multitude of bracelets, along with strings

of love beads around Rita's neck, jangled and swayed as she stood up. She was wearing a long floral skirt and a filmy batik-style blouse over a camisole. A scarf matching the skirt was wrapped around her head, its ends dangling down Rita's back. She looked exotic and a tad out of place compared to what others were wearing, but Maura figured the outfit was exactly what her customers would expect.

"Were you able to park your van over there? The space is filling up pretty quickly." Maura pointed to Theo's place.

"Yes, thanks. I found a great spot. So, lead me to my table!" She hoisted a large cloth tote bag farther up on her shoulder and gave a low sharp whistle that caused Shep's ears to perk up. The dog trotted behind as they walked up the drive to the front lawn, where people were organizing their table displays.

"I've put you over there," Maura said, pointing to the same shady area where Sue Giordano and her family were arranging tablecloths and signs.

"Hmm, so if people want treats, they can consult with me either before or after they've indulged. That'll work. I need at least one folding chair for clients to sit while I perform my magic." She beamed another smile.

"Okay, I'll see about that chair. I think we might have some in the basement. Oh, and I should take

Shep with me." She peered around and noticed Shep curled up under Rita's table.

"He's fine here with me. If he gets restless, I'll bring him to the house or put him with Roger."

Maura thought that might be too much responsibility and was about to insist on taking the dog now when Rita said, "Shep seems to be the kind of dog who likes to stick with his own people. There's Roger, and you and your sister. I think I'm on the list now, too." She gave a light laugh. "You have lots to do today, so off you go."

Maura had lots to think about, especially the one task that she was determined to make happen that day—the talk with Theo. "Okay, thanks."

As she began to walk away, Rita called out, "Come for a reading—on the house!"

Maura waved, thinking she already had an idea of what her future might look like, and it wasn't great.

THEO STOOD GAPING at what seemed like pandemonium. When he'd attended the Fourth of July Festival all those summers as a kid and teen, he'd never witnessed the prelude to the actual festival. Although it appeared that people were moving about in random patterns and bumping into one another, he began to see that they were simply carrying out their individual tasks of finding and arranging their tables.

He'd agreed to meet Finn and Shawn to help

put together the first aid station and was heading in that direction when he spotted Maura talking to a small woman dressed in flowing, multicolored clothes. Walter intercepted him before he could reach them.

"Theo," he said, "I heard some interested buyers were looking at your land the other day, and rumor has it they didn't seem to be the type to work a farm."

Theo stifled a groan. *The Glen grapevine.* "Just a visit to see what's what, Walter, nothing serious."

Walter pursed his lips and frowned, too polite to push the matter. "Okay. Hate to have this place go the way of far too many other small villages these days."

Theo figured Walter's remark was only the start of negative reactions from the Glen's residents, should he sell to the company. But everything was still up in the air, and there had yet to be an offer. There might not be one at all, he rationalized, recalling his agent's comment about another possible site. No need to rush the explanations.

"Hey."

Theo flinched as someone tapped him on the shoulder but rallied a big smile when he found Maura standing behind him.

"I've been looking for you."

Her smile erased all the doubts and confusion plaguing him the last couple of days. He'd have taken her into his arms right away but for the passersby. "Same here. This scene is…"

"Chaotic?"

"Maybe not that but extremely busy. Have you seen Finn? I'm supposed to meet him where his tent is going to be erected."

"Um, no, I haven't." She looked in the direction of the first aid site.

Rather than follow her gaze, Theo kept his eyes on her. She seemed remarkably relaxed for someone who was hosting the festival, but her pale face and the light blue pouches beneath her eyes told him otherwise. They seriously needed to talk, and he had news to pass on about the cash Luke had found.

Reading his mind, she said, "Maybe we can find some time today to discuss…you know… what's going to happen with us."

He reached down to clasp her hand. "It's a deal."

"Later, then," she murmured, loosening her hand from his.

As he watched her walk away, Theo was overcome with a kind of despair. Sure, they could talk, but to what avail? How would talking change anything? He had an albatross of acreage on his shoulders, a stressful job to return to and a child custody arrangement to settle. Not one of those factors would be easily resolved.

A sharp whistle got his attention. He swung

round to see Finn and Shawn, loaded with equipment, heading his way.

"Give us a hand?" Finn asked as they approached. A long canvas bag hanging over his shoulder had begun to slip, and Theo quickly intercepted its fall, grunting at its unexpected weight.

"The tent," Finn explained as he rotated his shoulder, wincing. "There's a lot more in my truck over there, so I'm very happy we found you in this crowd."

The next hour had Theo realizing that although his hospital work frequently involved physical activity, he wasn't as fit as Finn and Shawn. By the time they'd erected the tent and transported the portable stretcher, gurney, two crates of bottled water, a large folding table and a couple of plastic bins that held an array of medical utensils, bandages, cotton swabs, tissues, latex gloves—all the paraphernalia necessary for first aid treatment—he was exhausted.

"I think we're good to go!" Finn announced, wiping his brow with the cuff of his shirt. He pulled out his cell phone from his back pocket. "Gates are open at eleven and it's almost that now. Shawn and I are taking the first two hours. Want to come about one to relieve us for lunch, Theo?"

"Perfect. I'm going to find Maura to see what else I can help with," Theo said, "but if you need me sooner, give me a buzz on my phone." He was about to leave the tent when Finn stopped him.

"I know you'll be heading back to Augusta soon and your life there, but I feel I have to tell you this. There's going to be a medical clinic in Wallingford. All the permits have been approved and funding granted, but it'll be a year before it's up and running. I'm on the citizens' planning committee, and we'll be hiring staff in about five or six months' time. The hope is that our medical teams will consist of local professionals." He shot Theo a meaningful look. "People like you."

Theo was flattered. "Well, I do have—"

"Commitments. Right. Just giving you a heads-up, that's all. Folks here in the Glen would love to have you."

Theo saw Shawn nodding agreement. The unexpected offer threw him. Of course, as Finn said, the timeline was a long one, and Theo had many obligations ahead. "I appreciate your thinking of me," he said, "and will for sure consider it." He was about to ask when they'd need an answer when one side of the tent's flap lifted, and Maddie came in.

"Hi," she said, her face flushing as the three men stared at her. "Can I help with anything?"

"Um, I'm just leaving," Theo said and was partway out the door when he heard Shawn reply, "Sure. That'd be great, Maddie."

They'd already finished the work, Theo was thinking, but the smiles of pleasure on both Shawn's and Maddie's faces made him happy.

He found Maura minutes later, helping Luke, Ashley and a younger boy Theo didn't know decorate the fence around the riding ring with red, white and blue streamers.

"Can I help?"

Maura's face lit up, and Theo felt a surge of pleasure. He also felt Luke's eyes on him and immediately turned his attention to the kids, complimenting them on their handiwork.

"I think we're good here," Maura said. "But Walter and Bill are trying to string up some LED fairy lights around some of the trees to make the area look pretty after dusk. Maybe they could use an extra hand. Oh, and by the way, I've invited the few people who might still be around after it's all over for hot dogs and burgers."

Theo figured he and Luke would definitely be assisting with some cleanup, and that could be a good time for their talk. He nodded and waved goodbye, off to find Walter.

Much later, when the crowds had thinned and Theo, Walter and Bill had finished stringing lights and were taking a break on the veranda steps, the woman he'd seen chatting with Maura a while earlier approached. As Walter made the introductions, Theo realized that the two had only met the day before.

When he shook hands with Rita Moretti, she

seemed to hold on to his a fraction of a second longer. She told him she'd already met his son and what a fine boy he was. He thanked her, filled with parental pride.

"Come to my table," she said, "and I'll give you a reading."

His frown prompted Walter to explain. "Rita is also known as Clair Voyant, palm and tarot card reader."

It took Theo a few seconds. The others, including Rita, chuckled when he exclaimed, "Aha!" Then he added, "Thank you, and, um…maybe I will."

She smiled before saying to Walter, "And don't *you* forget to come for your reading, either."

Theo saw the spark in her eyes at Walter's harrumph, along with the rise of color in his neck.

"Well, I should get back to my table. Nice to meet you, Theo," Rita said and walked away.

An interesting woman, Theo thought, but even more intriguing was how Walter's need for privacy had eased enough to offer such hospitality to a stranger.

"Looks like the crowds are arriving," Walter said, standing to peer down the driveway.

"Guess I'd better look for my daughter and her family," Bill announced. "They're coming soon, and here's hoping they get a parking space."

"I've put up a sign indicating overflow spots in my north pasture," Theo said. "A couple of Bernie

Watson's nephews came first thing this morning to direct people and assist with any parking issues."

"I'll go over and see if they can use more help, or even a break." Walter hesitated a second, adding, "It's great to have you and your son for this, after all these years. I'm hoping it won't be your last Fourth of July here." He gave a brisk nod and walked off with Bill.

The lump in Theo's throat caught him off guard. Years of medical training had instilled in him the ability to hide certain emotions in difficult situations, yet it suddenly occurred to him that some of that training seemed to have vanished since his return to the Glen. What that meant, he had no idea. Except he felt there was a new and different Theo Danby emerging from his former self and suspected that a return to the Glen was only part of the answer. The other, larger part? *Maura Stuart.*

He decided to look for Luke, and perhaps if he was lucky, he'd find Maura, too.

"Hey, Dad, come see the donkeys!" Luke cried when Theo reached the barn. He grasped Theo's hand and led him inside. "We brought them into their stalls to give them some quiet time before the rides start."

All of the donkeys, except Lizzie, were munching quietly in their stalls, their swiveling ears following Theo's and Luke's footsteps.

"At first we weren't sure about braiding Roger's

tail," Luke chattered away, "but Ashley had treats and we figured we could try. And guess what? He was just fine with it. In fact, he stood still better than Jake did."

Luke's animation tickled Theo, and he wondered if he'd see more of this Luke after they left Maple Glen. "If you need help giving people rides later, come and find me. I'm on duty in the first aid tent at one o'clock, for at least a couple of hours."

"Okay. We're starting the rides about noon, Maddie said, but Nancy and Cathy will be helping, too." Suddenly he threw his arms around Theo. "I'm glad you're helping in the first aid tent."

Theo closed his eyes for a second, reveling in a rare hug from his son. Then he pulled away, patted him on the shoulder and left before Luke noticed his damp eyes.

CHAPTER TWENTY-TWO

MAURA STOOD AT the top of the veranda stairs, shielding her eyes against the sun as she surveyed her land. Well, her and Maddie's land, she silently amended. It was almost midday, and the festival had yet to reach its peak, judging by the steady stream of people from Theo's place to hers. The county road itself was lined on both sides with parked vehicles, though many people were still driving onto Theo's far pasture.

Despite the stress and work of hosting the festival, she felt proud that she and Maddie had pulled it off. Their parents, longtime community supporters in Maple Glen, would be proud, too, and for a split second her eyes filled with tears. She swiped them away. Today wasn't for nostalgia but new beginnings. That was her hope when she finally had Theo to herself, to tell him how her feelings for him had changed—deepened—the last two weeks.

She'd also promised herself some free time to explore the festival as a regular attendee and not an organizer. It would be an opportunity to determine the success of the event for future planning committees. Not that she wanted to actively participate again, she thought, her mouth turning down at the idea, though she might feel differently in a year's time. A year... So much could happen by the next Fourth of July. *Best not to go there, Maura. One day at a time, as Theo would say.*

The first aid tent was straight ahead, and she could see one of Finn's paramedic volunteers talking to an elderly man sitting in a chair. Luke had told her Theo would be working in the tent, news that had raised an improbable scenario in her mind—Theo discovering the benefits of country medicine and moving to the Glen permanently. She'd have laughed at the highly unlikely fantasy if, deep inside, she wasn't yearning for some version of it to come true and change her life. *Not today, though, and maybe not even tomorrow.* She sighed and rounded the corner of the veranda to see what was happening at the riding ring.

Maddie had set up a small table with a shoebox for cash, and Katie was handing change to a young woman at the front of the short line of would-be donkey riders. Katie's mother, sitting next to her, was supervising, but Maura saw right away that the twelve-year-old was managing just fine. She waved, marveling at the growth in Katie's self-confidence since beginning the riding program last fall.

The ring was festooned with red, white and blue streamers, tightly wound so as not to alarm the donkeys, and someone had stuck colorful plastic flowers into the streamer knots. Nancy, Maddie and Ashley were leading Jake, Matilda and Roger slowly around the ring. The riders included two teens, aiming for a casual look, and a gray-haired woman whose gleeful face suggested she might be a future customer.

Luke was standing at the gate next to another small table on which sat a motley collection of helmets—some borrowed, some belonging to her and Maddie—and speaking to a boy his own age who was waiting a turn. She gave Luke a thumbs-up and his instant smile warmed her. What a change from the slumped shoulders and scowl that first day she'd met him and Theo!

Turning to leave, she noticed a younger boy marching around the far side of the ring's fence, fastening the plastic flowers onto the fence. Maura squinted in disbelief. Sammy, focused and actively participating. Another surprise. She scanned the area for the boy's parents, but he seemed to be on his own. Perhaps they were enjoying some of the festival for a few minutes on their own, reassured by the presence of Sammy's riding team. Passing the queue again, Maura couldn't help thinking that maybe all the work she and her sister had devoted to Jake & Friends—her dream!—was finally paying off. The people lining up to ride a donkey were potential clients and customers that would grow the business. Casting a last glance at Katie and Sammy, Maura was filled with pride. However things turned out with the program, she and Maddie already had two success stories.

As she passed the side kitchen door, she heard Shep whimpering inside and had a pang of guilt. The last time she'd seen him he was dozing under Rita's table, and Rita had mentioned she'd return him to the house if he got restless. She went into the kitchen and was almost knocked over by a very excited dog. His water bowl was full, and the kibble she'd left on the counter earlier sat on the floor beside it. Maura picked up his leash, draped over the door handle. "So sorry, fella, but it's all good now. Let's go for a walk."

Shep pulled her out the door and headed straight for the barn, where he thought Roger might be. "Oh, no, not yet, and he's busy now anyway," she told him. She tugged on the leash, forcing him in the opposite direction, toward the tables where buyers and browsers were clustered. It was her first opportunity to check out the variety of goods being sold, and though she'd attended many past festivals, she was still in awe of the talents and initiatives of the Glen residents, as well as the many vendors who'd come from Wallingford and beyond.

Ashley's mother's table featured a variety of handmade cards and miniature, framed watercolor scenes of Maple Glen. Maura bought one of the small paintings of the Otter Creek bridge leading into the woods and the Long Trail. She'd give it to Theo as a memento, though she still clung to the irrational hope that he might not leave. The cloying, sugary fragrance of cotton candy from a cart nearby reminded her that breakfast had been consumed hours before, and judging by the sun, beaming directly onto her, she figured it was noon. Time for lunch. Then perhaps a drop-in visit to the first aid tent, where Theo might be on duty. She veered away from the drive toward the trees on the far west side of the front lawn.

The line in front of the bakery table was long, but Maura decided the wait would be worthwhile. She'd only been standing at the end a few minutes when she noticed Rita waving to her from her table yards away. The woman gestured to the empty chair at her table, and Maura thought, *Why not?*

"By the time I read your cards, that bakery line will be much shorter," Rita told her, smiling, as Maura sat down. "And I'm happy to see you enjoying today as well."

"The festival's been a real memory trip," Maura told her. "My father passed away just before last year's festival, so I only made a very brief visit. Otherwise, this is the first Fourth of July I've attended in years."

"Compared to many fairs and festivals, Maple

Glen's is smaller and more low-key. I like its strong community involvement and especially the lack of outside businesses with their mass-market products."

"We do have a strong community here," Maura agreed. "As teenagers, though, my sister and I yearned to escape its closeness, if you know what I mean."

"I do, and I commend you for recognizing its value now. Many people leave their happy places and never return."

Maura thought instantly of Theo and how lucky he was to have had a chance to come back, even if temporarily.

"All right," Rita said, placing a deck of cards in front of Maura. "You shuffle."

After she shuffled, Rita fanned out the cards face down across the table.

"Before I start," she said, her voice now solemn, "I want to remind you, in case you don't know, that tarot cards don't reveal your future. Instead, the cards you choose may tell you something about yourself or indicate something that's been on your mind. Something you may want—or not want—to explore."

"Okay." Now Maura was curious.

"Please pull any two cards from this spread and move them aside but keep them face down."

Maura hesitated, then slipped one card from the end of the fan and another from the center.

Rita gathered the rest of the deck and pushed it aside. She stared at Maura's choices for a moment, then deftly turned one card over. "Hmm," she murmured. "This card is called the Wheel of Fortune."

Maura stared at the stylistic drawing of dragons and other mythical creatures surrounding what resembled a compass, but without any cardinal points.

Rita looked at Maura. "Does it connect with you in any way?"

"Well, I wish I had one," she quipped. "A fortune, I mean."

Rita smiled. "A natural thing to wish, though I've found that people often misunderstand what a fortune can mean."

"As in *good* fortune," Maura asked, "rather than money?"

Rita nodded. "I think that over the next few weeks—or even days—you will decide which fortune has significance for you." Then she turned the other card over.

Maura stared at the title above the man and woman, dressed in what looked like medieval clothing, their arms intertwined and their heads together. *Lovers.* She glanced up at Rita and felt heat rising into her face.

"Maybe this card has special meaning for you, as it has for many people." Her smile was tender.

She picked up the two cards and set them atop the deck. "You have much to think about, Maura."

What Maura was actually thinking was, *This is it?* But she merely smiled. "Thanks for this, Rita, and..." She looked in vain for a sign listing the reading fee next to the glass fishbowl at the end of the table.

"On the house, Maura! But if you want to make a donation..."

Maura dug into the pocket of her capris and pulled out a five-dollar bill, which she added to the collection of coins and bills in the bowl. "Thanks, Rita. This was very...interesting."

"It was indeed, for both of us. Have a great day, Maura, and good luck with your decision."

My decision? Maura wondered as she walked away. *Which one?*

IT WAS LATE afternoon by the time Theo was free to leave the first aid station. He was tired, but in a good way. There'd been a variety of conditions, mostly minor ones: dehydration, dizziness, headaches, a stubbed toe and a couple of superficial cuts. They'd been easy to handle—water, food, acetaminophen, bandages and rest. The idea of using the shady veranda as an auxiliary site for the tent had been a good one.

He left when Finn and one of his fire department colleagues relieved him. "Thanks again,

Theo, and please give some thought to what we were discussing earlier," Finn said on parting.

The Wallingford medical clinic and a potential job. All up in the air for now, Theo figured. Still, the option of staying in the Glen was, as far-fetched as it seemed right then, compelling. He'd liked the novelty of quietly chatting with patients as he treated them, no rushing about to insert IV lines or run for a defibrillator. The pace had been refreshing.

Finn's proposal stuck with him as he went to check on Luke. If he was lucky, he'd find Maura, too. Maybe he'd have a chance to tell her what Finn had said, see her reaction. Or maybe not, he quickly decided, realizing there were far too many factors to consider before a decision about his future—and Luke's—could be made.

That sobering reality was at the forefront of his mind as he made his way around the tables, so he didn't at first hear his name being called. He stopped, scanning the crowd, and noticed a woman beckoning from a table. Rita, he remembered, though the name on the large sign leaning against the table read Clair Voyant. A couple were walking away from her table, and Theo was tempted to do the same, but something in the woman's welcoming smile drew him to her.

Despite his intention to make an excuse, he found himself sitting down and watching her spread cards across the table as she spoke. Her patter barely registered, as Theo's mind shifted back to Maura again and, inexplicably, the company interested in his property. He needed to tell Maura about that before she heard it through the Glen grapevine.

When Rita told him to draw two cards from the semicircle in front of him, he did so without much deliberation, impatient to get through the reading as quickly as possible. Theo only caught a quick glimpse of their colorful illustrations, but Rita studied them for what seemed a long time.

Finally, she pointed to one and said, "This is called The Juggler. Also known as The Magician. An interesting choice, Theo."

Curious now, he wanted her to say more but remembered her words at the start of the session. This wasn't about his future but about his connections. Whatever that meant, he thought. "Well, I'm constantly juggling priorities, as well as my time, when I'm working," he said, offering an explanation.

She nodded. "Perhaps decisions, too. And working some magic, I'm guessing."

Maybe, he thought.

She upturned the second card, and Theo leaned forward to stare at it. *Lovers.* Definitely an easier one to figure out than a juggler.

"Most people like this card," Rita said, studying his face.

Theo's indifferent shrug didn't seem to bother

her as she added, "But it's a card not too many people draw, in my limited experience. Only one other today."

He waited for further explanation, but when none came, he felt a tad disappointed. Okay, he thought. Definitely not a fortune-telling, as she'd asserted at the beginning. He stuffed a bill into the fishbowl and stood to leave.

"Thanks, Rita. That was…well…interesting."

Later he thought her expression had been slightly amused by his comment. But what dominated his thoughts much longer were her last words.

"Don't be afraid of the *M* word, Theo. And good luck with your juggling!"

The *M* word. Did she mean Maura? Because that was the first *M* word that came to mind. Except it wasn't a word, really, but a name. An alternative suddenly popped into his head—*money*—a word that had consumed his thoughts recently. The loan and the potential sale of his land. Another interpretation occurred—one that stopped him in his tracks as he went looking for Luke.

Marriage? He shoved aside that connection right away. His life was already far too complicated. What else had Rita, or Clair Voyant, said when he was leaving? Something about juggling and decisions. Those were two words he could relate to because they were constants in his working life in Emergency. But of course, the card and her reference to decisions were simply coincidental.

Theo knew coincidences were random events that people wanted to attach meaning to, and he was no exception when it came to accounting for the random things that had happened since his return to Maple Glen: the discovery of a mystery loan that jeopardized a possible future with Maura, Shawn's unexpected return just when Maddie was faced with a decision to stay or leave the Glen, the offer of a potential job in a new clinic, and the hard fact that the only possible buyer for his land was a development company that could ruin the Glen. He was at a loss to explain any of it. He headed for the riding ring, where he hoped to find Luke and maybe Maura.

When Maura saw him and waved, her smile almost had Theo changing his mind. Walking from Rita's table to here, he'd concluded that he must tell Maura about the potential buyers now, rather than wait until after he heard back from them. But as he drew near, he realized why Maura had been smiling. Luke was in the ring, riding Jake.

Theo stood beside Maura, his heart bursting as he watched his son ride Jake around the ring. When he spotted Theo, Luke waved, and Theo's eyes welled up at the proud grin on the boy's face.

"He told me after his first donkey ride that his goal was to ride Jake," Theo said to Maura. "And he did it."

"He did, and you're obviously as proud as he is." She smiled and reached for his hand, squeezing it. Then she added, "You're finished in the first aid tent?"

"Yep. Fortunately, it wasn't very busy. Um…" He peered around. "Do you have a minute?"

"We're shutting down the riding ring shortly. The donkeys need a break and so do we! How about you? Do you need a break, too?"

The question, posed with arched eyebrows and a coy smile, was flirtatious, and he wanted to fold her into his arms and bury his face in the crook of her neck. But no. He'd made a decision and had to proceed.

Pulling her off to the far side of the ring, he said, "I need to tell you a couple of important things."

Her smile faded at the tone of his voice.

He kept his eyes on hers. "First of all, Luke and I found a hidden stash of money at the farm. Rolls of fifty-dollar bills and a note from Uncle Stan saying he was going to forgive the loan to your father. I think that he forgot, or maybe all this happened just before he and my aunt went into the nursing home. I'm not sure."

Maura's eyes widened. "That explains the monthly withdrawals from Dad's account." She paused, clearly processing what this meant to her and the business. "And you also said?" she finally asked.

He was happy at the relief on her face, but knew he had to go on to the next part that might not be so welcome. "The potential buyer for my property is a company. A big one, known for commercial and residential construction."

The words seemed to take a long time to sink in. Her light frown gradually deepened as her lips moved without speech, as if she were underwater. "I'm not sure I understand," she finally began to say, "but when you say *potential* buyer, do you mean there are others or...what, exactly?"

"*Potential* because they haven't made an offer. But so far, the company is the only interested buyer."

She took another long moment.

"And your thoughts?"

He tried to ignore the tremor in her voice but couldn't. Instead, he looked toward the ring, where Maddie and the other women were now leading the donkeys out and to the barn.

"Theo?" she prompted.

He sighed and faced her. "As I said, they're the only interested party."

"And?"

He swore silently. She was pushing him to say it. "I may not have a choice."

"People who say that almost always do have choices, Theo. Are you seriously telling me that you'd consider selling your land—right next to ours—to a construction company that will be building on it? Houses? Condos? In Maple Glen?" Her voice pitched in disbelief.

"I don't know, Maura. I...I have decisions to make and—"

"You're not the only one with decisions to make, Theo. I just hope you'll make the right ones."

At that she spun around and marched away, faster than Theo could catch his breath.

CHAPTER TWENTY-THREE

THE REST OF the day was a blur for Maura. She scarcely remembered later how she endured it, pasting a fake smile on her face while inside she was seething. She knew Maddie suspected something because her sister kept flashing concerned sidelong glances her way, but there was no opportunity to tell her what she'd just learned. But she'd recalled Maddie's remark the other day about spotting people walking around Theo's land. "Not regular people," Maddie had said, and Maura wished now that she'd followed up on that with Theo at the time. Perhaps she could have confronted him right away, instead of having today ruined. That was what it felt like.

Were they always going to fall into this cycle of keeping something from one another? What did that mean for the chance of a future together? The specter of her tarot card rose up—Lovers. Ha! Perhaps she should see Rita for another reading.

"Maura? Got a minute?"

She swung around, only then realizing that she

was standing near the kitchen door staring blankly at the festival crowd, now in various stages of leaving.

Walter smiled. "You were so deep in thought I hesitated to disturb you. Is there a problem? Anything I can help you with?"

Her mood lightened a tiny bit at his kind face. "No, but thanks, Walter. I'm just wishing all this would end soon."

"You must be tired, but I'd say the festival's been a great success and a tribute to the hard work you and Maddie devoted to it."

"All of us, Walter. The committee. The people of Maple Glen."

"True. Anyway, I was about to say that many folks have had enough and are packing up. I know our volunteers will be here in full force early tomorrow, but I'm happy to get a start at some of the cleanup now. Collecting trash or recycling that didn't make it into our bins, for example. You don't want to draw any animals in the night."

Her thoughts, still fixated on Theo's bombshell, hadn't gotten as far as cleanup. Did Walter know about the possible sale? "Thanks, Walter, a good idea. And…um…have you heard that a potential buyer for Theo's property is a big construction company?"

Walter's face creased and he shook his head. "No, though I heard the people who inspected it were definitely not farmers, or even hobby farmers."

"He told me an offer hasn't been made yet."

"Hmm, makes sense he'd want to keep that close to his chest, then, rather than upset everyone for no reason."

"But they're the only interested buyers so far." She felt tears well up and looked away.

"I guess he'll have some tough decisions to make." He patted her shoulder. "Let's wait and see what happens."

She nodded, grateful for the advice, though she knew following it would be a challenge.

"You and Maddie will appreciate a relaxing evening later on, unless you're planning to go to Wallingford for the fireworks."

Years ago, the Fourth of July organizers had decided not to host fireworks at the end of the day. The fireworks in Wallingford and beyond drew most of the Glen's residents anyway, and the village wouldn't have to spend more money or to compete with those other displays. That had been a factor in Maura and Maddie's offer to host, knowing their donkeys wouldn't panic at the sounds and flashing lights.

"No, I think I'll be ready to sit and put my feet up. How about you?"

He chuckled. "Same here. And thanks for the supper invite. Maddie mentioned it when Bill and I were stringing the fairy lights. He can't stay, but I'd love to."

The plan for a simple barbecue with a few friends at the end of the day had been concocted at breakfast that morning. She'd almost forgotten, though she knew she'd invited Theo and Luke. Maddie had said she'd like to ask Finn and Shawn because they'd have to stay longer to dismantle the first aid station, and Maura had given her a knowing grin that had her sister blushing.

Maura took a deep breath. She had to rally the energy to get through the rest of the day, help host a barbecue and then deal with this new, unwelcome situation with Theo. "That's great, Walter, and thanks for staying on to help. If you see Rita, pass on the invitation to her."

His smile shifted. "I would, but I think she's already left." He must have seen Maura's expression. "Likely she has another fair or some other small-town event to head for and figured she'd beat the inevitable traffic jam of folks leaving the parking area at Theo's."

"Oh, I'm sorry I didn't get a chance to say goodbye."

"I think she wanted it that way," Walter said. "Goodbyes aren't such a big deal when you're always making them. I guess that might be her philosophy, as a nomad."

Maura thought back to Walter's words throughout the rest of the day. The goodbyes in her life had been a mix of pain, relief and, occasionally, pleasure. They definitely had never been easy. The stark image of a goodbye to Theo and Luke hit her in the pit of her stomach. She knew that one wouldn't be the "see you later" kind of goodbye.

As the last stragglers trudged down the drive, Maura headed into the kitchen, where she'd seen Maddie disappear minutes ago. She let out a long and loud sigh of relief when the kitchen screen door closed behind her.

Maddie looked up from the salad she was preparing and smiled. "Same here. I think this will be enough with the burgers and hot dogs, won't it?"

"We have potato chips, too."

"That's a yes, then. By the way, Luke asked if Ashley could stay, too, and her parents said it was okay. Finn offered to drop her home on his way, afterward."

"Shawn staying?"

Maddie grabbed a tomato from the bowl on the table and began chopping it up.

"That's a yes, then?" Maura teased, mimicking her sister. She'd have pushed a bit more to see how far the color rising up into Maddie's neck would go, but this was the best time—maybe the only time—to tell her what Theo had revealed.

Maddie set the knife onto the cutting board and listened, the color draining out of her face. "I don't like the sound of that. I…well… It's difficult to process the impact on our business. I mean, the donkeys are skittish enough when that farmer from Wallingford who rents Theo's back acreage comes with his combine."

Another factor Maura hadn't considered—she'd been so focused on Theo keeping the information to himself. "Maybe *he* could buy the land." At her sister's frown, she added, "The farmer, I mean."

Maddie dismissed the glib suggestion with a shrug. "I'm sure other options will come up when we know for sure what's going to happen. In the meantime, let's end today on a positive note, okay? We've got good friends coming for supper and hopefully an early night for both of us."

Maura wanted to pursue those options, but Maddie was right. She needed to collect her thoughts and present as a calm, rational person when the others—especially Theo—came for supper. "Want help with prepping?" she finally asked.

"I think I can handle this. Luke and Ashley are setting up the veranda, where I thought we'd eat. Theo's getting the barbecue ready out by the barn. Shawn and Finn, as you may have seen, are packing up the first aid tent."

"Okay. Walter and Bill are collecting trash and anything perishable left behind on tables. And Bill can't stay, but Walter will."

"What about Rita? Did we invite her?" Maddie asked as she scooped the tomatoes into the salad bowl.

"She left early."

"Hmm. I suppose that makes sense. She probably has other places to travel to. I liked her, but there was something about her…" She thought for a minute, then shook her head. "Can't say what, exactly." She raised her eyes to Maura. "Did she read your cards?"

"Yep."

"And?"

Maura grinned. "I'll never tell." And she knew she definitely would not, especially now. "How about you?"

Maddie nodded and began slicing a cucumber. "C'mon. I asked first."

Maura chose the easy way out. "She hinted I'd be making a decision."

"Only *one*?" Maddie teased. "Given what we've been discussing, I imagine there'll be *many* decisions in your future, Maura Stuart."

If only it were a future I'd want, Maura thought. "I think any options informing my decision now will be seriously limited."

Maddie pursed her lips. "Let's not jump ahead, Maura. We don't know anything about Theo's plans, much less what's going through his mind."

Trust Mads to think of the other guy. She'd been the peacemaker as a kid and teen, the one who wanted to mend situations, whereas Maura always wanted to leave, walk out the door and forget everything. "I hope whatever Rita helped you to see involves happiness," she said in a low voice.

Maddie ducked her head, but finally replied, "I

drew this card called Strength, or Fortitude. My first thought was how ironic because I've never considered myself a strong person, you know? But then she put a spin on it, saying how we perceive ourselves isn't necessarily how others do. I mean, that's obvious, right? But later I began to think of another way of looking at it. What if my real strength was *giving* courage rather than having it?"

Maura could only nod around the swelling in her throat.

"So what I'm telling you right now, dear twin, is that I know you will find the way to tell Theo what's really on your mind. That you will focus on the long term and not the short. That you will search inside yourself for an answer to the question 'how much would I give up to have Theo?' And last, but this is the most important one, Maura, you will tell him exactly how much he means to you—without reservation."

Maura brushed a finger across her damp cheek. "I love you, Mads." She hugged her sister.

THEO MUTTERED AND cursed as he wrestled with the barbecue as if it were a living creature. It certainly had lots of life inside, as he discovered when he opened the lid and strands of cobwebs and scattering spiders made him jump back in alarm. He was glad Luke wasn't around at the moment. Tasks like this weren't really his thing, but Maura had asked and…well…he'd do anything for Maura.

That thought made him pause. Anything? Like turn down a mega offer on his land, should it arise? Days ago, he'd have laughed at the absurd idea. Now he was more confused than ever. What was it that Rita had said as he'd been about to leave? "Don't be afraid of the *M* word"? He realized he could add "magician" to the list of *M* words he'd already compiled, because he knew it would take some magic—or a lot of it—to get Maura to forgive his lapse in judgment about keeping the buyer's identity to himself. That was all it had been, really—a poor decision—and he knew her reaction hadn't been about that miscall, but the unthinkable impact a large building site would have on her riding program.

He found a broom inside the barn to sweep out the interior of the barbecue, and with each hard brushstroke, he cursed himself for all the missed chances to tell Maura exactly how he felt about her, the sale of his land, even Maple Glen itself.

"Dad?"

Startled, Theo looked up to see Luke standing in front of him, holding a large, clear plastic bag of recycling in one hand.

"What's happening?"

Theo pointed to the barbecue. "Just cleaning it up a bit. Why?"

Luke shrugged. "You had a funny look on your

face, that's all. But now that I see you, and we're alone, I've got something to tell you."

That sounded ominous. Theo set the broom across the top of the barbecue. "Okay. Go ahead."

"Today was so much fun and…well…I want to come back next year for it. Even if our farm and land are gone, we could stay at Mr. Watson's B and B or in Wallingford, but I will always want to be here on the Fourth of July."

Theo felt his heart constrict. Not only at the solemn earnestness in his son's expression, but his phrase "our farm and land." *Our.* A connection to his birthright, an inheritance, and the Danby family. He nodded, too overcome to speak.

"The other thing is, I've decided I want to stay with you in the fall. I can see Mom in the holidays, and since I'll have my own cell phone, I can keep in contact with you when you're working. Okay?"

Theo could only nod his answer. He drew his son close in a long, tight hug until Luke said, "I've got to finish helping tidy up. See you at supper." And he disappeared into the barn, towing the bag of recycling.

Thoughts and ideas were flitting across Theo's mind. Decisions were already being made without his input. He had to get moving and start making some of his own. When a voice broke through his mental confusion, he looked up to see Walter standing where Luke had been minutes ago.

"Want a hand with that?" His tone was amused, his eyes twinkling.

"Please," Theo murmured. He handed Walter the broom, and then he went to find a private place to make a phone call before looking for Maura.

She was in the kitchen chatting to Maddie, and they both raised surprised faces when he walked in.

"We have to talk," he said quickly, before he could be sidetracked. He held out his hand and was relieved when Maura reached for it, no questions asked. As he led her out the door, he caught Maddie's encouraging smile.

They walked silently together, Theo heading for the gap in the cedar hedge—their old escape route—and out onto his front lawn, now an empty expanse of churned-up dirt ruts and tire marks. He grasped her hand a bit tighter, giving himself courage, and told her what Luke had expressed moments ago. She didn't say anything, but he saw her eyes glistening.

"After he told me that," Theo went on, "I felt a bit guilty, that a twelve-year-old could make a life-changing decision quicker than I could."

Maura's mouth lifted in a light smile, so he pushed on. "This land—" he gestured in a broad arc "—is more than money in the bank. It's a legacy—the Danby legacy—from my loving aunt and uncle who nurtured me here all those summers. I...I'm sorry it's taken me so long to accept that importance. That my son and you, Maddie and even Walter saw what

I couldn't." He dropped his hand from hers and forked it through his hair, giving himself time to find the right words. "The irreparable damage to the very soul of Maple Glen that selling this to...to that outfit...would bring."

He inhaled. "That's one thing I have to say. And, for the record, I've just made a phone call to remove the property from the market." He ignored her gasp and went on. "The second thing is that Finn told me about the approval of a medical clinic in Wallingford. He's the community representative for the project, and they're looking for doctors. He said he'd support my application if I was interested." He paused, taking another deep breath. "The thing is, I *am* interested, Maura. And I'm more than ready to make a career change from emergency medicine. I liked the low-key approach with people and patients while I worked at the first aid tent and the connection I made with them. Finally, the most important thing I need to say is that I have decisions to make about the future, but I want you to be part of that. I want—with all my heart, Maura—for you to be in my future and Luke's."

She brought her hands up to the back of his neck and drew his face to hers. "Theo," she whispered, her voice husky, "I'm in your future right now and for always."

MAURA LEANED BACK in her chair, surveying the group sitting around the table they'd set up on the veranda. Walter, Finn, Shawn, Theo, Luke, Ashley and Maddie. Not exactly a family, she thought, but perhaps the closest she and her sister might come to have.

Walter left first, followed by Finn, who was driving Ashley home.

Theo took her aside. "Got a minute—or two?"

She caught the glint of a tease in his eyes and eagerly followed him onto the dark front lawn, lit by the sparkling fairy lights strung through the trees. He took her hand in his and led her past the barn to the pasture where they stood gazing up at the moon.

The silence and scents raised childhood memories of hot summer nights when she and her sister sat out on the veranda with their parents, absorbing the sounds of the country—crickets, owls, night-hawks, and frogs singing from some pond miles away. *How could I ever leave this?* she asked herself.

Yet right after Theo's news earlier, she'd blurted that if she had to sell the business and move to Augusta, she would. He'd smiled and held her closer. "I won't hold you to that, Maura," he'd assured her before kissing her again.

Now she leaned against the pasture fence, soaking up the balmy night air while Theo stood behind her, his warm arms compensating for the sweater she'd left on the veranda.

"Can we make it work, Theo? A future together?"

she asked, her voice wobbly at the seemingly impossible obstacles ahead. "There'd be some commuting while you organize the change in jobs, whenever that can happen. And at some point Luke would have to change schools if you move back to the Glen. How does he feel about that?"

"I discussed it with him briefly before supper, and he surprised me by interrupting to say he'd give up graduating from eighth grade in Augusta for the chance to live in Maple Glen."

"Wow! That's quite a concession for a twelve-year-old."

"I think he made that decision before our talk. Today's celebration was simply the icing on the cake, so to speak."

Maura's mind was already buzzing with plans. She smiled, thinking how Maddie would tease her later on, when she recounted all of this to her sister. They'd agreed to talk about the future of Jake & Friends, as well as the farm. Although Maddie hadn't revealed the reason for her smiles and glances Shawn's way during supper, Maura was guessing a future in Maple Glen for Maddie might be possible. She certainly hoped so. She was about to tell Theo how much she loved him when a loud explosion sounded from the west. They spun around to see bursts of color striking the dark sky. "The Wallingford fireworks," Theo said. "Luke will be watching with Shawn and Maddie from your veranda."

"Shall we join them?"

"In a minute," he murmured, tilting her chin ever so slightly and lowering his mouth to hers.

It was a long kiss, one that made up for all the missed kisses since they were teenagers, Maura figured. They broke apart only when another firework hit the sky, followed immediately by eruptions from the barn. Donkeys braying.

Theo laughed. "Good thing you left them inside for the night. What were you saying about this coming fall?"

"Can we make it all work?"

He brought her back into his arms. "I love you and you love me. We'll find a way to make it work, Maura."

And she knew they would.

* * * * *